AMERICAN MEDIEVAL

HOCK HOCHHEIM

WOLFPACK
PUBLISHING
— EST 2013 —

WOLFPACK
PUBLISHING
— EST 2013 —

Paperback Edition
Copyright © 2021 Hock Hochheim

Published in the United States by Wolfpack Publishing, Las Vegas

Wolfpack Publishing
6032 Wheat Penny Avenue
Las Vegas, NV 89122

wolfpackpublishing.com

Paperback ISBN 978-1-64734-245-6
eBook ISBN 978-1-64734-241-8

AMERICAN MEDIEVAL

A JOHANN GUNTHER WESTERN

PART I
CRUSADE 1

CHAPTER 1
THE DEVIL'S EGG BEHIND ALICE'S KNEE

Southeast Oklahoma
February 1896

The intense pain came in waves. Her whole leg burned like the summer sun and in waves that ate like an acid up to her lower back. Every slight turn and bump on the crude road to Egad City felt like a high-caliber bullet passing through her. Alice hung on. Just a mile to Egad. One more mile. She sat atop her stagecoach box like a frozen lighthouse in a Yankee coastline storm. The freezing February winds whipped down every hillside. If only that biting cold could reach down into that leg boil.

She knew she was in deep trouble when four hours earlier her Egad line driver's son ran into the office and told her the bad news.

"My omma said my daddy is too sick to run the coach tonight. He's got the flu. He's pukin' and shiverin' and shittin' all over the house, and Momma said he can't work."

That meant Alice was doomed to whip her own stage. Alice had been developing a tender boil behind her knee for two months now. The boil got bigger and redder with each passing week until she could barely walk. She had to run the stage lines herself once in a while, but tonight? The cold! The boil! It was worse. Sitting on any soft couch, much less a coach or stage box, would be torture. But it was her business. Just the feel of her boot on her upper calf was like a hot branding iron. Alice had an office full of passengers at thirty cents each, including a gaunt gentleman all the way from England. All bound for Egad City, Oklahoma. The run had to go, no two ways about it.

To make matters worse, she'd been thinking about her old co-worker Billy Trusty, a Stage-Charlie she knew in Tulsa, who had the same boil problem on his leg, and they had to cut his whole…leg…off!

But now the run was almost done. One more mile. Alice wanted to cry but she couldn't muster up the tears from the breath-taking wind chill. She entered the outskirts of Egad City.

"A few more streets," she thought, seeing the city lights bouncing off the ice patches on the road. She felt faint. A few more. A right turn felt like a cut to the leg bone, then a left. She cried out. Finally, there was her Egad City station. Paddy Jones ran out to catch the horses, as was his way.

"Alice! What in tarnation are you doing whippin'…"

He couldn't finish. Alice fell off the stage and hit the frozen ground.

"Alice!"

The passengers stumbled out, pulling up their collars and tugging down their hats. Paddy grabbed Alice by the shoulders and hauled her up on the sidewalk. The pain of scraping her leg on the wooden planks woke her. The passengers gathered around.

"Was it the cold?" one man asked.

"What is it?" the Englishman asked her, pointing at her leg.

"My leg. My...leg," she said.

"Is it broken, milady?"

"No. A boil. It's a devil's egg back there."

"I am a doctor, Miss Alice," the Englishman said.

"Fetch Dr. Well," Paddy said to a man nearby, wanting nothing to do with some strangedoctor.

"Inside," the Englishman said. He grabbed a teenager by the arm and pointed to a brown suitcase. "I need that bag, laddy."

The group lifted and hauled Alice into the station lobby.

"My...leg!" Alice said again. She explained the details of her dilemma as the Englishman took off his two jackets and hat. He rolled up his white shirt sleeves.

They got her on the station counter, which was quite high off the floor, and helped him examine her more closely. He rolled her over and removed her right boot, much to her cussing dismay. He took scissors he spotted from the counter and cut the rear pant leg all the way up to her butt.

The onlookers recoiled in horror at the sight of this devil's egg festering on her leg.

"You there," he said to a traveler in the lobby. "Take out your knife and stick the blade in that oven until it turns red."

"Red?"

"Maroon will do, sir."

The man did, unsheathing his knife from his belt. He opened the cookstove and partially inserted the knife.

"Hot water," he told Paddy.

"Miss Alice," the Englishman said, "I am a surgeon from England. I can see you have an aneurysm on your leg. I thought as much. It is very common to coach drivers in England and probably here in the United States also. Equestrians too. People die from this, or they die from the misguided treatment for it."

"What's going on here?" demanded Dr. Well, as he barged into the room.

The Englishman barely looked at Well.

"At times, the weakened blood vessel bursts, and patients bleed to death. This looks very much as if it is about to burst and could have happened to you tonight, my dear."

He saw the teenager standing by, holding the suitcase.

"My kit, boy. I have a brown bag inside. Get it out, please."

The boy did and even snapped open the top of the small kit. The Englishman pulled out some gear.

"Knife?"

"Maroon's the color I got me so far."

"I hope it's sharp, sir," he looked at the people around him.

"Hold her," he said calmly.

The Englishman made an incision about five inches behind her knee. Alice screamed out.

"My name is Dr. Well, what do you think you are doing?"

"Saving this hard-working lady's life."

"Go on ahead, you son of a bitch," Alice cried out. "Cut it out or cut it off. I need me some relief!"

The artery was exposed. The doctor grasped it in his fingertips and separated it from the membrane and the nerve. He worked on the swollen part with the knife and needles from his kit. Parts filled with blood. He squeezed some buildup loose and stitched off other parts.

"Miss Alice, how are you?" he asked.

"It all...hurts like...like I'm in a bear trap," she mumbled, as she had her mouth full of her jacket collar crushed between her teeth.

"It will soon be over."

Dr. Well leaned in really close to watch.

"Let's not breathe on the wound, shall we? And...we are done," the Englishman said with a smile. He looked at his audience. "A technique developed in my country by a Dr. John Hunter. You might be driving your stagecoach in one week, my lady. And with a perfect leg."

The onlookers actually clapped. Alice fainted.

"And Dr. Well, if you have any sort of a hospital here, I suggest you get Alice over there and clean her up. Go on. Go on. This is hardly an operating theater here." He sniffed the air and grimaced. Several men hoisted her off the counter.

The Englishman propped an arm on the counter and watched them all leave. He wore a broad smile.

"What's your name, sir?" Paddy Jones asked.

"Dr. Milton Trafalgar. Like the Square," he said.

"What...what brings you to Egad City, Oklahoma?"

"Oh...research, you might say. Human research."

CHAPTER 2
THE CHRISTMAS BALLAD OF GUSTAV AND SAW

Paris, France
December 24th, 1886—2:55 a.m.

The eight members of the Paris Gendarmes investigation team slipped down in front of the small businesses, hugging the windows and doors of the narrow Paris cobblestone side street, just off the Boulevard de Clichy. Four detectives on each side. Each man held a revolver and a leather sap impact weapon. Two had shotguns. Their goal, a skinny two-story building ahead. Fearing a lookout, they dressed in dark clothes, turtleneck sweaters, and black skull caps. They dashed past the few gaslit streetlamps and some window filled with Christmas lights and crept low and slow in the darker areas. Four other gendarmes approached the back door from a winding alleyway. The plan was to attack at 3 a.m.

Investigator Gustav Henri had forged the raid and led one of the teams on the street side. He hoped the gang and the goods were in the target building. To suggest that the leader of the

French Indochina gang, known only to the Sûreté as "Saw," had become another one of Gustav's many arrests was misleading. Saw was more. Saw was his obsession. Saw murdered. Saw prostituted. Saw intimidated. Saw brought Asian sex slaves, opium, and guns into France. Saw had killed several gendarmes. Finally, thanks to informants, Gustav Henri might bring the gang to its end.

And there the building stood—a tall, dark, thin, worn brick building as was the model for all the small shops on this *rue*. The windows were covered on the inside with thick cloth. A thin thread of light from inside bounced off the window frame. A shadow interrupted the slim beam every few seconds. There was movement inside.

Gustav and his men were hunkered down across the street. He scanned the rooftops and windows. The other team waited beside the storefront. He looked at his pocket watch. It said 3 a.m. Guns drawn, he and his men jogged across the street.

The front door was, of course, locked. An officer with a shotgun dashed up and blasted it three times. With one round he blew apart the doorknob area, then shot the two hinges. Two policemen bashed into the door, still having some stumbling trouble entering, but they made it through. An officer blew a whistle.

As if the whistle was a cue for a gunfight, firearms instantly erupted. A wave of sporadic gunfire hit near the officers as they ducked, dodged, and rolled inside, firing back. Gustav dove into the front room, firing his revolver. He could see pandemonium as at least a dozen or so gangsters were startled and confused at the raid. They seemed to have at hand only pistols to shoot back. They were surrounded by haphazard piles of wooden boxes.

Someone opened the backdoor to escape and was immediately shot by the alleyway squad. A police shotgun round tore into his stomach and the thug flew backward so fast, his cap popped off his head.

One man ran up the stairs. It was Saw. Gustav took to the wall and ran alongside it. Then to the stairwell and up the stairs. As he charged, he glimpsed Saw turn at the top and onto a hall. Gustav shot through the banisters along the hall. Once. Twice. Click! Empty! But he heard Saw call out in an agonized shriek. And, in the seconds of climbing the remaining stairs, he spotted Saw slide down the wall and collapse.

Gustav wanted to reload. He stopped at the top of the stairs. He saw a pistol on the floor. Saw's dropped gun. And Saw was reaching, digging inside his jacket. Another gun? Gustav dashed in, pulling his lead sap from a pants pocket, and dove onto Saw, sap first as it came crashing down on the gangster's head. He beat the head with the lead-ensconced leather tool.

Bullets from downstairs ripped through the floor around them, shooting splinters and light beams into the air. He beat the face and head with his sap until Saw was motionless. He reached into the man's jacket and pulled out Saw's back-up, a small revolver.

"*Connard*," Gustav whispered, calling him a bastard.

The shooting downstairs stopped. He heard his men yelling to each other. He rolled off of Saw's body and rested on the floor beside him, catching his breath. After a moment, he stood. He grabbed Saw's dropped pistol and shoved it into a pocket. He stood, grabbed Saw's legs and dragged him to the stairs. Then he pitched the limp body all the way down the stairs. Saw tumbled and rolled to the first floor in a heap. Gustav reloaded his pistol and followed.

Three gendarmes were wounded. An ambulance waiting down the street was summoned in with an outside police whistle. One of the detectives pried open a wooden box.

"Guns," he reported.

Gustav nodded.

"He dead?" a detective asked about Saw.

"No."

Medical personnel arrived.

"Gendarmes first. Then these scum," Gustav ordered.

A detective and Gustav searched Saw. Removing the gang leader's jacket, they looked Saw over. He was shot in the shoulder and leg. His face and head bled from the sap strikes. The search shook Saw awake.

"You shot me, you *merde*," Saw growled, calling Gustav a "fuck, or piece of shit."

"That I did," Gustav said.

They stared at each other, hate in their eyes. Gustav the quintessential, tough French detective, and Saw, who too closely resembled the ugly, anti-Asian, political cartoons published regularly in the newspapers.

"You should have killed me," Saw said. "You will regret not killing me. I will see to your slow, painful demise. Butchered by a knife!"

"I will keep you alive, so that you will die each and every day on Devil's Island."

"Merde!"

"Connard!"

CHAPTER 3
STINKY'S WAY

Fort Worth, Texas
Remedies Detective Agency
March 1916

Someone pounded on the front double doors. Johann Gunther, passing through the big lobby of his Remedy's private detective office, stopped short with the hammering, casting a quizzical look at the door. Clients just walked in. The business hours were posted on the door. No one knocked, or...pounded, and then waited. They just walked right in.

He stepped over to the heavy double doors and pulled the right door open.

"Stinky!" Gunther blurted at the six-foot-nine man. "Stinky Moses!" Gunther reached out and instinctively hugged the giant man. Stinky did not hug back. He froze in horror upon contact. It didn't matter to Gunther. Gunther noticed that Stinky had his pocket watch open in his hand, and how he closed it after noting the time. Stinky always noted the time on things.

"What…what are you doing here?" Gunther asked. Gunther was dumbfounded and grinned like a wild child. He looked at Stinky's clothes and saw a federal marshal's badge pinned on Stinky's vest under a brown tweed jacket.

Stinky Moses stood towering tall and erect, dressed the same as when Gunther knew him, almost twenty years earlier when they were both deputies together in Paris, Texas. A brown vest. White shirt. Brown pants and boots. Awful hat. Stinky still had that odd twist to his face and that curled lip. Those wide-set eyes. His head hung with a slight cant. He took off his awful hat and exposed those swirling cowlicks no hair wax could control. He almost smiled at Gunther.

People back in Paris, Texas always thought Stinky was somewhat "ill in the head."

"He ain't right," neighbors would say.

"Touched," and, "touched in the head," others said.

But to this day, Gunther hadn't found a better, smarter, more successful law enforcement officer than Stinky Moses. Stinky taught him how to be a deputy way back when. Stinky solved everyday people problems and people-Choctaw problems. He caught dangerous fugitives single-handed. He killed off more than a few. The Choctaw Nation thought he was a mighty friend and revered his solid honesty. They laughed at his quirky ways of talking and moving and welcomed him on sight with waves and hoots, though Stinky hardly ever laughed or even smiled. When he smiled, the Choctaw around him roared and clapped in laughter and sometimes jumped into the air to celebrate! This only confused Stinky even more. Stinky was a walking Ten Commandments and a Texas lawbook in custom-made, size-fifteen boots.

The two stared at each other. No doubt, Stinky was eyeing up his old partner Gunther, but he would not say a word about his assessment. Non-business words were not Stinky's way, unless he was solving a citizen's problem and needed to use them. Then he was a wordsmith.

Gunther was still a tall, "blond-headed, German feller" in the same physical shape as back in the late 1880s and 1890s when they walked and rode the streets of Paris together.

"There's eight men coming to kill Gustav," Stinky finally said.

"Huh? Eight...wha...come on in here. Come on," Gunther said solemnly, waving his hand toward his conference room.

Stinky picked up a suitcase and walked in with that same head bob he took with each step as he had as a teenager.

"Jefe!" Gunther shouted down the hall.

Jefe, Gunther's partner in the Remedies business, jogged down the hall to the meeting room.

"Jefe, this is my old deputy friend from Paris, Texas, Stinky Moses. Stink, this is Jefe. He owns half this business here with me. We met in the Philippines. Soldiering. I don't do much without him."

Jefe, five foot ten, looked way up and up to see Stinky's face. He raised his hand for a shake, and Stinky glared at it, then reluctantly shook it. Just one shake, in a dramatic, awkward manner. This just amused Gunther. Stinky was never much of a hand-shaker.

"I have heard quite a bit about you from Gunth," Jefe said.

"Stinky says my old Police Chief from Paris, Texas, Gustav Henri, is in big trouble. I think we need to hear this."

All three sat at the big table. Stinky loomed over the furniture, looking uncomfortable.

"The French police has wired Gustav that eight men from French Indochina are coming to kill him," Stinky said.

"Indo…China?" Jefe said.

"No doubt from the Chief's French days and Devil's Island days," Gunther said.

"Yup. Blood vendetta," Stinky said.

Jefe looked puzzled. Gunther explained.

"My old chief from Paris, Texas…you know…he was first a police detective in Paris, France."

"The first Paris," Jefe said.

"The first Paris. He…he got himself into trouble with the French government and was transferred to work on Devil's Island as a supervisor. Did two years there. Felt like a prisoner himself. Retired and moved to Texas. Paris, Texas."

"The second Paris. Yes, yes," Jefe recalled the old story he'd previously heard from Gunther.

Stinky stared at the top of the table and said, "Devil's Island. French Guiana. Horrible place. The worst of the worst criminals are sent there. No escape. Men in chains. Torture. Rats. Bats…"

"It's a hellhole. Like the Black Hole of Calcutta," Gunther said. "Gustav use to tell us stories about the Island. The worst criminals. The worst guards. The worst of everything."

"The Chief told some stories, alright," Stinky repeated. He rolled his hands together, a fist in a palm, so tightly that they could hear a few knuckles crack and the creaking, flesh-rubbing sound.

"Eight men coming to kill him? What happened?" Gunther said.

"Chief said he had a prisoner there on the Island named 'Saw' from Indochina. Saw was a gang leader and smuggled women, drugs, and guns into France. A dilly of a killer. Chief helped arrest him in a raid in France, and the Chief wounded Saw in a gunfight. They sent Saw to Devil's Island. Then, years later, the government sent the Chief to work on Devil's Island. They met again."

"That ain't good," Gunther said.

"T'was no good. The Chief had problems with Saw right away. He said Saw tried to organize gangs on the Island. The Chief said he stopped him. The Chief fired the corrupt guards helping Saw. You know how the Chief is."

Gunther nodded.

"The Chief's guards beat Saw nearly to death once; and Saw told the Chief he'd had enough of him! Saw said he would kill him. Kill him for everything. Shooting him in Paris. Kill him for the beatings. Kill him for…for thwarting his wicked ways on the Island."

"Why now?" Gunther asked.

"Don't know."

"After all these years."

"After all these years," Stinky repeated.

"Where is Gustav now?" Gunther asked.

"Chief's retired. He has him a little house outside of downtown Paris. It looks like a little French house inside."

"Of course. He married?"

"Finally."

Gunther smiled and Stinky almost smiled. The women in Paris, Texas, were all over this handsome, international, husky man from Paris, France. Add that gun and badge to the title Police Chief and he was a threat to all the married and unmarried men in the county.

"Who'd he marry?"

"You don't know her."

"He still a brawler?" Gunther asked. "With his 'Cowboy Savate?'"

"Can be. Could be," Stinky said. "But he can't make do against eight slick killers."

"He still mad at me?" Gunther asked.

"Yup. He still calls you the 'Goth.' Gother, not Gunther."

"Does he know you came here to see me?"

"Nope. He still thinks he helped make you into a killer."

"He didn't."

"I know."

"The Army did that."

"I know."

"Where are these Asian killers now?" Jefe asked.

Stinky didn't look at Jefe, or Gunther. Gunther realized that Stinky was looking at their reflections only, on the top of the glossy table. Such was Stinky's way.

"We hear tell they are about to come ashore somewhere between New Orleans and Galveston."

"That's...a mighty wide swath of territory. That doesn't help much."

Gunther raised a pointy finger off the table and pointed it in the direction of the badge on Stinky's vest. "Where you working?"

"Amarillo. Federal Deputy Marshal. I am Federal now."

"I see. And a damn fine one, I'll bet."

"Dry out there. Dry. Dry. Dry. Dry. Lakes are like brown

21

water, mud. You can't see the fish. You can't see the bottom. Not like our lakes in Paris. You just hope to see the bottom."

"What do you want to do, Stink?"

"Nothing can happen to that man," Stinky said, finally looking up at Gunther's face and then Jefe's face. "He raised me as though I was kin. Or...or as if I was his adopted. Sometimes adopted kids get treated better than blood kids. You know?"

"I agree. Nothing can happen to Gustav," Gunther said, "I always say that you taught me how to be a deputy, and Gustav taught me how to be detective. I'm in, Stink. You got a plan on this?"

"You always had good plans, Gunth," Stinky said, eyes back on the table.

Gunther shook his head on that. "Well, Gustav had all the plans. We just followed them. Maybe he's got a new plan? So, he did not send you here to get me?"

"Nope."

"Didn't think so. Where you staying?" Gunther asked.

"Don't know."

"We have a room here in the back. It's yours. We have Jefe's family here too, and I room upstairs."

"Maria!" Jefe called out for his wife.

A small monkey wearing red striped pants wandered into the room. Stinky looked at it and never said a word. It jumped up on Stinky's lap. He pretended it wasn't there.

"That's my monkey," Gunther said.

"Uh-huh."

"I got it in India."

"India. Uh-huh. This...this Maria?"

"No," Jefe said. "Maria is my wife. That's Gunther's pet

monkey."

Stinky finally looked down at it. The monkey looked back at him with a quizzical expression.

Maria stepped into the doorway.

"My wife," Jefe said with a raise of his hand, clearing up the name-calling. "Maria, this is Gunther's old amigo, Stinky Moses. We're letting him stay in the guest room. Can you show him the way?"

Maria nodded. "Senior...Stinky...follow me, *por favor.*"

The monkey jumped down and ran to Maria's right foot, sat on it and hugged her ankle. It smiled and Maria walked off with the monkey along for the ride. Stinky stood, grabbed his suitcase, and followed.

Gunther and Jefe looked at each other.

"Stinky...is a nickname?" Jefe asked.

"Ahhh, no. No, that is his real, first name."

"Stinky?"

"Stinky."

Gunther leaned back and threw his feet up on the table and crossed his boots. Mesha, his rescued slave from India and live-in helper and the true owner of the monkey, saw this from the lobby. She shuffled into the conference room with a disgusted expression, lifted his boots by the ankles and shoved a towel under them. Gunther never missed a beat with his answer.

"Story goes...back in Paris, as in Texas, that Stinky was born...in the run-down Moses family shack, and they never gave the boy an official first name for more than a year. Just, just never got around to it. His mother complained all the time about how stinky his diapers were, so she called him Stinky. It stuck. He was eventually recorded in Lamar County records as one Stinky Moses."

"Why is this French man that you admire so much so mad at you? Still mad after all this time?"

"Toward the end of my time in Paris...I killed some people in Oklahoma. I was hunting down a Paris murderer and looking for information on missing people. But, you know me, Jefe, they were KKK! Killers and they needed killing. And I shot them in legal gunfights. Gustav Henri was...is a consummate policeman. He taught me how to shoot a pistol and, more importantly, when to shoot a pistol. He taught me how to fight."

"The Savate," Jefe said. "The Cowboy Savate."

"Yes. Gustav follows the law. After Oklahoma, he started calling me 'The Goth,' after..."

"The northern Germans who raided the Roman Empire," Jefe said.

"Yeah. Them. He thought that I was too quick on the draw, as they say. He thinks I had, I have, what he calls, 'gun burn' on my...on my hands. My...nerves, my control in my gun hands are burned away from...from violence."

"You have many strange friends, Gunth. That Stinky is a very strange man."

"That's Stinky's way."

Gunther stood up. The towel remained on the table under where his boots had rested. He walked over to the front windows and stared outside, thinking about the day he left the Army, the first time, and the days when he met Police Chief Henri Gustav and Stinky Moses. It was 1889...

CHAPTER 4
CARCASSES BE DAMMED

Fort Sill, Oklahoma
May 1889

Gunther, in new civilian clothes, the reins of his own new horse in hand, lingered outside the cavalry headquarters for the final goodbye. He'd just said farewell to his fellow troopers in D Platoon of the 5th Cavalry.

Captain Latisimo, burst through the office door, his arms spread wide, and charged down the stairs to grab Gunther by the shoulders with his massive hands.

"Dutch! You are actually leaving us. I can't believe it," he said.

"Yes, sir, I am."

"Thank you for waiting a few moments to say goodbye. You were a damn fine corporal, and the United States Army will miss you."

"Thank you, sir."

"Whatcha gonna do now?" the big Italian asked.

"I don't know. I am going to travel around…"

"Travel around. *Paisano*, if you want to re-enlist? See me. Enlist back here at Sill and I will make sure you get your old rank and job back."

"Oh, thank you, sir."

"Whatcha packin', boy?" Latisimo said, eyeing the pistol on Gunther's hip and the rifle stock on his saddle.

"Colt. Model 1878. Double action," Gunther said of the pistol on his hip. "Marlin. Lever action. Barrel's been cut down," he said of the rifle in a scabbard on the saddle.

"Well provisioned. Well, good day to you, Dutch, and take care."

Gunther mounted up and led his new horse, Casey, to the east gates of Ft. Sill. He'd never had his own horse before, being from Germany, and then living in New York City before joining the Army at seventeen years old. He'd just bought Casey, the horse and tack, down in Lawton with his last Army payroll check. He'd grown to love horses from his stint in the 5th. Most do in the Cavalry. He loved his horse and the other horses in his troop, too. Now he had Casey, a fine bay with a deep chest and powerful hindquarters which, he felt, would eat up the miles. And he had a white blaze that accented his intelligent eyes. Those eyes were what sold Gunther on him. Casey seemed to have smarts. No one at the stables knew Casey's exact past, but they suspected he was prior Army. Maybe the cavalry? But the US government had a terrible habit now and again of killing their horses when they aged. And some of the animals grew quirks that made them undesirable as well. They did advise Gunther that Casey had a habit of lying down a lot to rest or sleep, especially in the sunshine. Sometimes on his side, sometimes down but with head and torso/barrel upright.

"Somebody, sometime, trained him to lay down, to lay down as a shield for a soldier," the handler at the stable told him. "And it appears he's grown quite fond of the position. He'll do it on command. To geet him down, you just have to declare "sleep," and the horse will geet itself down."

"Sleep," Gunther whispered, so as not to inspire the horse. "What do you say to get him up?"

"Geet up," the man said, "but he's purty smart and can figure out what's going on and geet up hisself."

Gunther had seen many tricks taught to horses at the barracks, and horses were trained to lay down for cover when under attack. Horses usually slept standing, but when they needed deep sleep, they would lie down on their side. Some liked to sun that way too.

The land east of Ft. Sill was well known to Gunther. He'd been on many a patrol and hunted the declared renegade Indians and outlaws after the Land Rush, all the way into Arkansas. The Oklahoma Territory lacked law enforcement and the Army was often ordered to hunt down outlaws too. For many Americans, Oklahoma seemed like a flat, dry land, almost a rocky desert, but the Indian Territory and Eastern Oklahoma was different. Lush, rolling hills, lakes and trees, an interesting landscape to discover. He'd been dry and uncomfortable in Western Oklahoma too many times to wander west. East it was.

Gunther's next few weeks were ones of aimless wandering. He stuck to the rutted roads, passed through small towns, and sporadic settlers' homes. The city and house lights in the evening, the smells in the morning, left him feeling lonely. There was some kind of "life" somewhere. Normal life, inside those buildings and on those sidewalks. Whatever that was. Something he couldn't quite relate to or even understand. Perhaps he thought, he missed the mission and comradery of the service? He'd never been alone much in the Army. And now he had the opposite. He was alone. Detached.

He shot some small game, ate in some small towns, and would soon run out of money if he didn't find work. He stayed at an inn here and there, but mostly set up small camps. With a lamp and a fire, he read before sleeping every night. In his pack were three books, *Men of Iron* by Howard Pyle, *On the Border with Crook* by John Burke, and *American Notes* by Rudyard Kipling. As he read each page, he tore it out and tossed it into the fire to lighten his load. Each night he tethered Casey with a long lead rope, and after grazing for a while, Casey would lie down next to Gunther. And Gunther would at times prop up against his warm body and look up at the stars. On rainy nights, Gunther rolled up in a canvas sheet to stay dry. Casey did not mind the rain.

Gunther knew he would soon have to do something—stop in one of these towns and get a job. But what job? He was essentially skill-less. And where? He could even go back to Germany, but it was already too foreign a land for him to fathom.

One night in the third month of travel, his books almost gone into smoke, his small campfire gave away his position to desperate strangers from the deep and rocky woods nearby.

"Hey there, you in the camp," came a whispered voice from the fringes of red and orange light.

Gunther sat up from his recline against his grounded saddle.

"You, there, we have to come in."

The voice had a strange accent, not Italian like his old Captain Latisimo. Different.

A large, black-haired man emerged, in roughed-up, dirty clothes, a rifle in one hand, hat in the other.

"Son, we need some help," the man said.

Gunther, surprised, did not answer. His pistol belt was nearby on the grass. He thought of snatching it up.

Then two more men emerged from the tree line, one a giant, gaunt, odd-looking teenager, maybe fifteen years old? The teen's arm wrapped through the arm of a second man, filthy and bearded. This man had his hands bound behind his back.

"My name is Gustav Henri. I am the Police Chief of Paris, Texas," the first man said. "This is my deputy Stinky Moses."

The teenager barely nodded.

"And this is…" Gustav pointed to the bound man, "…is Rooftop Hutash."

Stinky Moses threw Rooftop Hutash facedown on the ground. Stinky and Gustav turned back to the woods, knelt down, and took out their pistols.

"Can you put out that fire? That lantern?" Gustav said.

"Okay," Gunther said. He reached for his small shovel and used it to toss some turf on the fire.

"Rooftop is wanted in Paris for burglary and murder," Gustav said over his shoulder.

"I ain't killed nobody," the man said.

The fire out, Gunther put on his gun belt, and took out his pistol too.

"We caught him at the annual Hutash Family picnic, two days ago. And his cousins have been tracking us ever since. They shot all our horses this morning…" Gustav whispered.

"You two are dead meat," Rooftop growled. "And yer dead too, if you take up with them," he told Gunther.

"Speak again and die," Stinky whispered.

Rooftop glared at Stinky. He spoke no more.

"How many?" Gunther asked.

"Six, or seven," Gustav said.

"Five men and one woman," Stinky said.

Moments passed. Gunther was worried that Casey, tied off on a long lead behind them, might get shot too. The clouds passed under a three-quarter moon.

In this darkness, Gustav heard something. A rustle of leaves. He pointed to the northeast and Stinky moved away to the west. Gunther, no stranger to a military ambush, as both a giver and receiver, moved east. The Army taught him to try and stay at least one shotgun blast apart from each other. He knelt. The three positioned themselves in a half-circle.

"What's your name, son," Gustav asked.

"Johann. Johann Gunther."

"Sorry about this, Johann."

"Rooftop, hit the ground!" a gruff woman's voice, in a frightening pitch, called out from the darkness.

Hutash rubbed his right cheek to the ground.

Gunther, Gustav, and Stinky, already half-way down, went fully prone.

"Aunt Gretchen," Hutash mumbled, just as the gunfire erupted from the woods. All about waist high, meant to cut standing men down. The trees and bushes shredded before them. The sound. The flashes.

And the three men, flat, well below the level of ripping rounds, returned fire at the flashes. The two lawmen switched to a second pistol. Gunther fired five rounds, keeping only one. Gunther rolled a few more times to the right and started reloading.

The ballistics stopped. Silence followed.

Moaning. Then screaming. The screams died down. Gasps.

Stinky Moses got to a knee and leaped off to the left.

"You still with us, Mr. Rooftop?" Gustav whispered without looking.

"Fuck you."

Gustav smiled.

"Do...we...go?" Stinky asked.

"No," Gustav said.

A minute passed. More moaning and gasping from the darkness.

Then, like a banshee, like a gray, crazy, screaming ghost, a tall, gaunt woman appeared from the tree line at a full run, in a long gray dress. Screeching, her mouth wide open, with disgusting teeth and wild, wiry hair, she ran in, firing two pistols at random into the campsite.

The three men fired into her. She jolted as if hit by lightning. Her pistols went flying. Elbows jerked in unnatural positions. She landed face-first in the dirt with a grunt.

"Aunt...Gretchen?" Rooftop Hutash said.

"Who's hit the ground now, ladybug?" Gustav said.

Gunther and Stinky kept an eye on the darkness.

"Who needs help in there?" Gustav yelled out.

"I...do," came a gasping voice.

"Come out here, then."

"I can't."

"Then we can't come in. You'll die in there."

Gunther looked back at where his horse was. Casey was gone from sight in the darkness. Gunther inched backward.

"Casey? Casey?" His heart skipped a beat.

"Case?" He scrambled, stumbled a bit in the darkness, toward the trees behind them. The horse was down on its side, alive and seemingly unhurt behind a big elm tree.

"Casey." He hugged the big bay's neck. He holstered his pistol and ran his hands down the side of the horse. No blood. No wounds. His eyes filled.

Gustav and Stinky retreated back near Gunther, farther away from the invisibles wounded in the brush.

Rooftop Hutash, like a snake, slithered over to the woman.

"Aunt Gretchen? Aunt Gretchen?" He said, his face inches from her face. It seemed he was crying when he spoke.

"What'll we do now, Chief?" Stinky asked.

"Cover me," Gustav said.

Stinky and Gunther raised their weapons. Gustav holstered his, ran over to Rooftop and grabbed him by the boots and dragged him back by them.

"Noooo, no, you skunks! You killers of women," Rooftop cried out.

The Chief dropped the criminal's feet back by the horse. Stinky pushed his revolver barrel up against Rooftop's neck.

"You're through talking," Stinky warned him.

The moaning in the woods ceased.

"We wait until sunrise," the Chief said. "We won't risk walking in there and won't risk leaving them behind us again. I've had enough of this, looking over my shoulder."

"It's 11 minutes after 10," Stinky said, struggling to see the time on his pocket watch, via a fresh moonbeam.

Gunther eyed the rifle in its scabbard, on the saddle, on the ground where he was once calmly reading about ten minutes earlier.

"My rifle is over there."

"Get it," the Chief said.

Gunther dashed over and slipped the gun out, grabbed another satchel and then ran back.

"You see any houses or towns near here, Johann?" The Chief asked.

"About a mile that way, there's a little community."

"When morning comes, I am going to ask you to ride there. Tell them about us. We will start walking that way. We may need three horses. If the wounded and dead in the woods have any horses left, we'll use them. We'll see."

"Okay, sir. It's a clear highway. You can connect with it just over there," Gunther said.

"You did well, helping us. Wise positioning. Wise ammo control. And no fear."

"I am fresh out of the Army, sir."

"The Army?"

"Cavalry. This...all this, is not new to me."

"I see. I can see that. Yes. Well, *monsieur,* you will be repaid for this help. This man we have here is a rooftop burglar. He has worked all over Northeast Texas, and Southeast Oklahoma. Southwest Arkansas. In one of his burglaries, he killed a man. A very nice man in Paris, Texas, who chose to sleep in his store on occasion. I wish to kill Rooftop myself, you know? But it is not up to me. The law must decide these things."

Gunther nodded.

Both men stared at the danger zone. The crickets, other bugs, and frogs resumed their noisy announcements and activities.

"I am here from Paris, France. I was a policeman there for many years. I was, as you call them, a detective. I do not fully understand many things here in your country. The Army. The Indians. But we have our own crazy problems in Europe."

"I don't understand much of it either," Gunther said.

"But I understand murder. I understand justice."

Gunther nodded again.

"Do you have a map?"

"No, sir. I…wasn't going anywhere in particular."

"We lost my map. In my saddle. You do have a shovel?" the Chief asked.

"I have an old Army shovel. Yes, sir."

The Chief walked over to Rooftop.

"Tomorrow morning you can bury your aunt, before we leave."

"I'm starving," Rooftop said.

"You are not listening to me. You will bury your aunt. Then, we will leave. If we are lucky, thanks to our new friend, we will get some food and horses from a community nearby."

"What about my damn cousins?"

"You want to bury them too?"

"No. No, not my aunt either. Their spirits have flown on."

"Yes, they have."

"What's on the ground is carcasses. Empty bodies."

"This is true. Like the body of the shopkeeper you killed in Paris."

"I ain't killed nobody. Nobody! And I ain't no rooftop burglar. I am not ripe fer yer hangin'."

"Why then did your aunt just call you Rooftop?"

"I…I…like to, to…sit on rooftops."

"I see."

"When I was a kid."

"I see."

"I ain't shoveling no hole fer none of them."

"Such is your decision. Then we shall march on to the nearby village in the morning."

Gunther opened his satchel and pulled out two cans of beans and some bread wrapped in newspaper.

The lawmen opened the cans with their knives and poured some black and brown beans into their mouths. Stinky grabbed a handful of Rooftop's long hair, yanked it back, and poured some beans into his mouth. He coughed. But he swallowed.

The men stayed awake all night. The warm sun hit their faces at dawn, and they stood. They spread out and marched into the woods, guns at the ready. Not far in, they saw five dead men, sprawled out. Three of their horses were down and dead. Three were okay and grazing.

"It is good to see that all the horses are here and accounted for, yes, Johann?"

"Yes, sir."

"Because?" the Chief asked.

"Because no one left to get more help," Gunther said.

"Yes."

Stinky collected the horses' reins and walked them out. Gunther and the Chief collected some of the guns and ammo, then followed Stinky.

Stinky lifted Rooftop off the ground and helped him aboard one horse.

"This is my cousin Randy's horse, Marmalade," Rooftop noted.

Gunther saddled up Casey. The Chief closely watched Gunther at work.

"We shall only ask for some food," the Chief said, climbing a horse, "and for the best directions to Paris. I must confess, I am a little lost from being chased. Lead the way, *monsieur.*"

Gunther and Casey took the front, found the road, and they all headed for the little group of houses to their west.

"And so, *Monsieur* Gunther," the Chief said, "what is it you will do with yourself out of the Army?"

"I don't rightly know," Gunther said, not looking back.

"Paris always needs good deputies. We can pay you $275 a year."

Stinky curled up his lips, trying not to smile. "That sounds like a lot, Johann Gunther. Until they start shooting at you," Stinky said, with his head jerking from side to side.

"You shut up, Stinky," the Chief said.

Stinky struggled to hold back a smile.

"I will think about, sir," Gunther said.

CHAPTER 5
MEDIEVAL AMERICA

Paris, Texas
1899

The dream was marvelous but the terror was great; we must treasure the dream whatever the terror; for the dream has shown that misery comes at last...

— Anonymous, *The Epic of Gilgamesh*

Chief Gustav Henri, behind his police-chief desk, placed the police badge facedown, pin-up, on the desk blotter before him. Then he covered it with his right palm. Gunther stood in front of the desk.

"Johann, surely have you heard the word...*medieval?*"

"*Mittelalterlich,*" Gunther said back, in German.

"Yes. A word in Europe to describe a very barbaric time, a dark time in history, where we Europeans made many mistakes. It is like that here now. Here. All countries have their medieval times. America too. Only I think that it is now. We have murderers, robbers, death feuds, bushwhackers...," he drew a deep breath, "...rapists, thieves, strange religions, the KKK, people who torture other people. Some are educated and some are as dumb as a rock. I have seen vicious, sick criminals commit crimes in the big cities like Paris, France, but they are no worse than the horrors you can find in a little wooden shack in the woods or out on the plains. It is the hatred and slavery of the mind. All countries, Johann, all countries have their Medieval Period, where people do terrible things to each other. Our Medieval Period in America is now. We have disease, pestilence, religious wars, like all the plagues on humanity that Europe experienced. Poverty. Ignorance. It is all here."

Gustav spun the slightly-curved badge on his desk.

"It all seems...it seems to be part of the human evolution, you know? The Dark Ages. American...medieval. This piece of history will now be your problem. If you pick up the badge, our problem."

Gunther had to think about all that for a second.

"Our jurisdiction here in Paris covers all of this. The city and the countryside. The woods and plains. It is a medieval jurisdiction in a medieval time."

Gustav withdrew his hand from the badge and stared at Gunther. What was he getting himself into, Gunther thought? But, he reached for the badge and read the front.

"City of Paris, Texas Police Officer."

He pinned it to his black shirt. With his left hand, Gustav tapped on a piece of paper on the desk. He shoved it forward. Gunther signed his name.

The Chief pulled open a drawer and tossed a Bible onto

the desk. He pointed to Gunther's left hand. Gunther put his left hand upon the book. The Chief raised his right hand and Gunther raised his right hand accordingly.

"Johann Gunther, you swear to do the right thing?"

"I do."

"You are now a deputy, a police officer. You may be called both, because we are a new and a growing police department and some people around here are very used to calling us Marshal or Sheriff or Deputy. There are eight of you, now. You are the eighth man."

"Is there any training?"

"Training?" the Chief smiled. "No. That is why I just asked you to always do the right thing."

"Okay," Gunther said.

"As long as, in your heart, you will do the right thing. If you have a good heart—and it is important for a policeman to have a good heart—then, my son, you will be okay. But, you will learn as you go, my friend. You will work with Stinky Moses. He is my best man."

A teenager among eight deputies and Stinky the odd teen was his best man? Gunther wondered about this too.

"I built this building, you know. When I started out here, we first had a room in the land office. No jail. We locked people up in the Ascot Hotel. They had room service. They had better beds and better food than we had. But Paris is growing. It is a city of budding commerce. A center of transportation of people and goods. I finally got a budget and here we are. I planned it to look like a substation in Paris that I worked in. France that is."

"Yes, sir. France."

"And there will be no lynchings in Paris, Texas. Of any kind.

Law and order. Arrest and trial. It seems that while the North won the Civil War, the South did not completely lose. And they have still made an open and secret war upon the negro. That war will not happen in Paris, Texas."

Gunther nodded.

"That's it. And that is today's history lesson for you. Go to work. Stinky is waiting for you."

Gunther left the Chief's office for the lobby of the police station, looking around it and trying to imagine what the original French police substation looked like. Four deputies were there up front, doing various things, Stinky among them.

"Let's go," Stinky said. "We have a problem." He checked his pocket watch.

Gunther and Stinky left the police station, a one-story stone building, onto the main street of Paris, Texas. The city resembled any growing Western town, with pounded-down dirt roads, stores, bars, houses, eateries, hotels, and many side streets and avenues. It was a key trade center and roadway for the surrounding cities in Texas and Oklahoma.

Stinky had a very stiff, deliberate walk, with a bobbing head. He had to duck often under canopies and store signs. His big hat didn't help him.

"Elly Whitehouse has stolen books from her school," Stinky told Gunther. "The teacher came in and reported her, this morning." And that was all he said.

He led the way about six streets over to a new house on a road of new and old homes. Stinky knocked, and Mrs. Whitehouse answered. She was taken aback at their presence.

"Stinky?" she said, almost in question.

"Mrs. Whitehouse." Stinky's voice softened.

She let them in and both officers took off their hats. She eyed up Gunther as a stranger.

"This is our new officer, Johann Gunther. He is fresh from the Army. Is Elly here?"

"Well, yes."

"We need to talk to you and her. Please, ma'am."

She called the nine-year-old from the back rooms. They sat at the dining room table.

"Elly," Stinky said, "I…I know you really like to read. Readin' is a good thing. I am proud of you fer all the readin' you do. It makes me feel hopeful for the world."

He looked at the mom, then back at Elly's face.

"But Miss Elly, I can get you books from some of my neighbors, who are very smart folks. And there's talk we will soon have a library here, a whole building full of books. What kind of books do you like?"

"Ah…I like poetry and I like some history books."

"Uh-huh. Uh-huh. Miss Elly, I will get you some of these kinds of books. Okay?"

"Okay."

"But, Miss Elly, these schoolbooks. These books belong to the school. We can't take those special books from the schoolhouse. All the children need to read them, but in, inside the schoolhouse. They all want to be as smart and special as you are, too."

Elly stared into Stinky's eyes. He smiled at her.

"Can you get the books you took? I need to get them back to the school."

Elly got up, ran to the back rooms and returned with three books, placing them on the table. One was *Little Women*.

"Oh my, can you understand this book? I heard of this book. Lots of adults have read this book, and I should like it."

"I try. I haven't finished it."

Stinky reached out and held Elly's hand with one hand, and the mom's hand with the other. This from a teen who otherwise did not want to shake anyone's hand. But now, he was doing his job.

"I will get you some books. I want you to be the smartest girl in Texas. I will get you this book, *Little Women*. I will order it in the mail."

Stinky stood, grabbed the books, and he and Gunther walked to the front door. Stinky put on his hat, turned and said, "Goodbye, ladies." And he ducked way down to clear the doorway, hat and all.

"Goodbye," Gunther said.

"To the Arbor School House," Stinky said sternly. "It's this way."

"Are you gonna get that girl that book?" Gunther asked.

"Why of course," Stinky said, with an air of astonishment in his voice. "I...I told her I would get her that book."

Off they went with Stinky in the lead. Gunther thought about his first assignment on the Paris, Texas Police Department—hardly a medieval crime lesson, or a bank robbery, but a lesson of another kind. And he started to realize, from the gunfight in Oklahoma to this little session at the dinner table with a child, why this odd, giant teenager named Stinky was indeed the Chief's best man.

CHAPTER 6
ARMES À FEU COMPETENCE

Shooting range, Lamar County
1888

In the days that followed, Siegfried was a most welcome guest among the Burgundians, and, believe me, he was honoured by them for his manly courage a thousand times more than I can tell you, so that none could see him and harbour any grudge against him.

—Anonymous, *Nibelungenlied*

As he did in Paris, France, twice a year, Gustav took his patrolmen, or later, his detectives, or later still, his Devil's Island guards out to train. In Paris, Texas, he ordered his employees to an open spot south of town to shoot and qualify. He had arrived early in the department wagon and nailed up paper targets on wooden fence posts. He stuck several wooden sticks with red flags into the ground. He hummed several French songs as he worked.

The eight policemen rode up thirty minutes later. This was Gunther's first trip to a Chief Henri's "*armes à feu competence.*" The competence of arms.

Upon Gustav's commands, standing by little red flags, the men took up positions five yards, ten yards, and twenty yards out from the targets, drew and fired. Then they shot lever-action rifles at twenty-five, fifty, and one hundred yards. Gunther did exceptionally well with the rifle but was only adequate with the pistol.

During a break, the men drank ice tea and ate sandwiches and apples.

"Did the Army teach you to shoot pistols, Johann?" Gustav asked, chowing down on a thick, dripping brisket sandwich.

"Not much, sir. Mostly rifles. But we all had pistols too."

"I see. I see. Flap holsters?"

"Yes."

"I see. This flap is good to keep your gun clean, but not very good for a fast draw. We also have such holsters in Europe."

"Yes, sir."

"I learned to shoot a rifle in the French Army. No pistols. Then I learned pistol shooting in the National Gendarmerie. On Devil's Island, we also had rifles. There I learned more. The purpose of rifles there on the island of exiles was to shoot *Condamnés* from a watchtower. With the *pistolet*, it is important, especially here in Texas, that you draw very fast; and the flap holster slows you down."

"They do."

"No one in *Paree* really taught us how to fight, hand to hand. Just some tricks. Some of the men boxed. I studied Savate. It comes from various street-fighting systems used in France in the late 17th Century. *Boxe Francaise* is another name for Savate. It was started in 1838 by Charles Lecour."

"Savate," Gunther repeated.

"It is always important for police to know how to fight. This way, you do not have to shoot someone. We will do some of this, this afternoon. I call it now 'Cowboy Savate,' HA! because you and me? We are the cowboys."

When they finished eating, yet still during the lunch hour, Gustav motioned for Gunther to step away from the wagon and out toward the shooting range. Stinky followed out of curiosity.

"Let me see you empty your pistol."

Gunther did and re-holstered. Gustav did the same.

"Now look at me. Elbow up. Grab the pistol. Elbow down. Elbow up. Elbow down," Gustav said, pulling his pistol from his gun belt in what seemed to be but a second each time. His gun side hip dropped a little each time too, to help with the holster clearance.

Gunther practiced these moves.

"Your gun barrel is too long. It is the pistol of the cowboy, the cowhand. It should be shorter. It must get out of the holster fast. Look at my barrel, huh? Shorter. In the *Paree* police, we had some heavy caliber pistols, but the barrels were not as long, as long as these…these cowboy guns you see everywhere here. Many of your shootings will be close. For far away? That is why God made the *fusil*…the rifle. The hip goes down a bit so the holster goes down too, and the barrel is clear of it faster, so it can turn up. Fast."

Gustav motioned his head down range.

"Come on."

They walked all the way up to a paper target and stopped

right in front of one.

"Now, stand right in front of the target. Closer. Even closer. Now pull out your pistol. Elbow up. Elbow down and touch the bullseye with the tip of the barrel. Touch it."

Gunther did. Stinky, having been through this years ago, watched.

"Yes. Slower. Slowly. Again. Again."

Gunther did.

"Now a little bit faster. There you see?"

Gunther pulled and put the gun barrel right on the target. Pulled and put. Pulled and put. Pulled and put.

"Am I looking at the bullseye?" Gunther asked.

"In the beginning, yes, but after much practice you will find the general spot of the center without looking. Because of your practice, in *réalité*, you are just shooting a criminal in the chest or stomach. It will be bigger than a little dot."

"You have a left-handed pistol, too. So, you see, you must do this with your left hand, too. Over and over. Listen to me. I want you to do this. You come out here, with the targets. Listen, you do this...oh...fifty times right hand. Fifty times left. No bullets! You pull the trigger. Click. Then you use bullets. A hole will be made and there will be nothing for the barrel to touch, so you put the barrel almost in the hole." Gustav touched the center of the bullseye with his finger. "Then, then...you take one step back. Just one step! You do it all over again. Fifty right. Fifty left. Then two steps back and you do it all over again. Then three steps. Do you understand?"

Gunther nodded.

"Soon, the distance is greater and you want to raise the pistol higher up to your eyes. With practice you will learn how far away that need is. At some point, you may even have to shoot with two hands. But you must start your practice close. Close up. You promise me you will do this?"

"Yes, sir."

"Good."

They started walking back to the wagon.

A one-horse coach trotted up on the dirt road. A woman stopped the coach on the roadway. She was beautifully dressed in a ruffled white top and pink skirt and on her head she wore a large, frilly, white hat. She stood and shouted, "Hellllo Gustav!" she sang out, waving her gloved hand.

"*Bonjour! Bonjour*, Louise!" he shouted back to her with a big smile.

She sat back down, rolled a rein over the horse's rump, and the coach continued down the road.

"Oh, she is luscious," Gustav said, shaking his head. "You know…women like to know the men that they are with will make them safe. Keep them safe. Some women? No babies. They do not want to have babies with you. And no diseases. They… they must trust you. And…" his eyebrows went way up, "you can keep a secret. Ahhaaa, many secrets."

Stinky shook his head side to side.

Louise barely waved at the men back at the wagon, as she passed them. They contained themselves from chuckling at the situation.

"The stories of the Western novels, the Western "blood and thunder" stories written in New York and Boston," Gustav continued back with his shooting advice, "they…they make the cowboy shoot-outs, like, like a fencing duel of Europe." He stopped, put his hands down by his side, and his head shifted left to right, mimicking the classic gun duel pose. "And you know, we have seen it, yes, but this is not what mostly happens. Once in a while, maybe, but they are not dueling shoot-outs. Every shooting is crazy. A crazy story. Many very close up. That is why it is very important for you to learn this way that I showed you, huh?"

"Yes."

After lunch, Gustav always showed at least one "Cowboy Savate" trick to his men. He gathered them around.

"Look, the man stands near you and he means to start trouble." He pulled Stinky, the biggest fellow on the force, out, to stand close to him.

"You make a very still face. If you smile, it will make him mad. If you look scared, it will make him feel bigger. If you look angry, it will make him more angry. Stonefaced. You say—poker face. If you are right-handed, put your left hand like this."

He put his left hand on the buckle of his belt.

"Here. This looks innocent, you know, but your hand is now in the center. In the middle. Then you take this nice hand, make a fist, take this hand and hit him in the neck, or jaw. Use the bottom of your fist. It is a 'hammer fist,' they call it."

He slowly showed the path—Left hand to the left side of Stinky's jaw, or left side neck.

"Just as your hand gets high enough, your right hand makes a fist and punches him straight in the gut."

He showed that.

"You see? Two punches almost at the same time. And look, see, the gut punch is very much like your pistol draw! You see? Elbow up, elbow down, but you are punching not drawing your pistol. Later, you can hit this man with your left hand and draw your handgun with your right. Lester, the opposite for you, huh?" he said to the lefty in the group, Lester.

Everyone made these moves in the air by themselves, as Gustav and Stinky pulled flour sacks from the bed of the wagon, tossing them on the ground. Gustav had rags stuffed in them and had them sewed up. An old Savate training tool. Half the men picked up the bags, held them in front of themselves, and the other half punched them, high hammer-fist to the neck, low thrust to the gut. Then they switched taking turns holding the sacks.

"That is all we shall do today, my knights in shining armor," Gustav said.

The men started packing the wagon back up. When done, they walked to their tied-off horses.

"Gunth, looks like your horse is napping again," Lester said.

Casey was indeed the only horse down on his side.

"He's sunbathing. He lays down all the time. The man I bought him from in Oklahoma said that he was trained to lie down. Like for cover for a soldier, and that when I say 'Casey. Sleep,' he'll lie right down."

"You tried that?"

"Oh yeah. He does. Let's go, Case!" Gunther said as he got closer to the horse.

Casey rolled up and shook first his head, then his body. Gunther slapped as much dirt as he could from the side of the saddle.

Stinky almost laughed. Almost.

CHAPTER 7
DEAD MAN GEPPARD

Paris, Texas
1888

How many valiant men, how many fair ladies, breakfast with their kinfolk and the same night supped with their ancestors in the next world!

—Giovanni Boccaccio, *The Black Death*

"Chief Henri! Chief Henri!" the boy called out, riding his bicycle right through the open doors of the police station. Gustav appeared in his office door with a cup of coffee in his hand.

"What is it, lad?"

"Old man Geppard has been murdered in his bed. Old lady Geppard sent me to get you."

"Okay. Okay, tell her I will be right there."

The boy hefted the bike into a turnaround, and zipped back out the door.

"Jerry, follow us down on horseback," the chief told a deputy. "Johann, come with me."

They walked out the back to a lot and stables. They hitched a horse to a buggy marked "police," with a sign and climbed in. The chief steered the horse off the back lot.

"Old man Geppard has no enemies," the chief said, talking more to himself, as they went.

They turned down a long residential street of homes, each with a well-established oak tree in front. There was a crowd of men and women standing in the shade of one.

"Here he comes," a man said.

They stopped the buggy a house away, jumped out, and the chief opened a trunk in the back. He pulled out a white butcher's coat, like a laboratory jacket and wrapped a tool belt around his waist. All of this intrigued Gunther. Gustav looked like an Army doctor.

"Hello, everyone," the Chief said. "Hello. Hello."

"What happened?"

"We shall see," he said with a smile. "Please do not crowd the grounds, or step on the lawn, please. Please. Please, step back."

"Many relatives were in the house when they entered, and the elderly Mrs. Geppard was sitting in a wing-back chair in the den, sobbing. Her son Wilhelm guided the two officers to the rear of the house, back to the bedroom, where more people were standing.

"Please, oh please," the Chief said, "please, everyone please leave the room. And leave the house. Please." He swept his hands in a circle and stepped toward them to pressure them out.

"Wilhelm, you...please stay, but in the doorway," he told the son.

51

The Chief stepped to the bed. It was covered in blood.

"How old was your father?"

"Eighty-five."

"Hmmm."

Gunther stepped to the far side of the bed.

"Does your mother sleep in here too?"

"No."

"Hmmm."

"She came in to wake him up for breakfast. He was like this."

"Hmmm. And nothing is missing? Stolen?"

"Nothing is missing."

The Chief felt the arm and the neck of the dead man.

"Cold," he told Gunther.

He pulled a Goodyear Rubber Company package from his tool belt, opened the package to reveal two rubber gloves. He tossed Gunther the empty box which the deputy caught.

"You never know what you are touching, Johann," he said, putting the gloves on. "These are now being used by doctors and nurses in operating rooms. Or, you never know what you might find that you do not want to mix with something else."

The Chief examined the bloody bedsheet and tossed it aside. He investigated the pajamas in view and then turned the stiff body over. Gunther moved in to help him, but Gustav threw up a wagging finger.

"No, no. You have no gloves."

He examined that side of the corpse. The body was stiff. Then he pulled a magnifying glass from the belt and looked over the face, his one hand turning the head back and forth by the chin.

"Wilhelm, can you ask your mother to come in?"

"Yes."

In a moment he reappeared, assisting his mother into the room. The Chief motioned for Gunther to pull a chair by the door over to the bed. He did and she sat. He sat in another creaky chair already by the bed, with a sad expression and peeled off the gloves.

"Did...did *monsieur* Geppard fall a lot? Did he, did he fall last night?"

"Yes, he did, Chief."

Gustav nodded. His bottom lip protruded. His expression got even sadder.

"Where did he fall?"

"On the front steps."

"Did he hit his head? Did he fall all the way down?"

"Yes, he did."

"How soon did he get to bed after this fall?"

"Very soon. He said he felt dizzy after the fall."

"Madame, there is a deep cut on his left eyebrow. It is the origin spot for all this blood. All of it. It started at the pillow by his eyebrow."

He motioned for Wilhelm to come over; he handed him the glass and pointed to his grandfather's eyebrow.

"As you can see, it is a rough opening."

Wilhelm nodded. "A cut."

"Yeees. I have worked many deaths in France. Accidental deaths. Suicides. Murders. Many." He seemed as though he was exhausted as he spoke. "I have learned, that when some people become very old, their...their blood cannot stop itself from bleeding. We called it in French *caillot*, or...clot...clotting, and without a clot, a person will just bleed and bleed, eventually to death. Madame, your husband was not murdered. I am sure he died of this cut. From this fall."

"Oh, oh…" she muttered.

"Of course, we will let our resident surgeon look him over. But I think this is what happened. You should not blame yourself, madame. As who could have known this would happen from such a cut inside his eyebrow."

Gustav stood.

"Johann will go outside and tell Jerry if he is here by now, to contact Dr Sadler and have him come to inspect the body?"

Gunther left the house to look for Jerry.

"My officer and I will inspect the house, of course. To see if there are any break-ins and so forth. Just to be thorough."

As the son comforted the mother, Gunther returned and nodded to the Chief. Then Chief and Gunther left the room. They looked around.

"May I assume, madame, that you do not lock your doors or windows at night?" Gustav asked.

"I don't. Ever."

"I wish that you would, because…because Paris and Texarkana are train stations and center points for travelers passing through for Arkansas, Oklahoma, and Texas. Many strangers come through here. We will look at the windows and doors," he said softly, "for any signs of anything unusual.

"Do you see the order of these plants and nicknacks on the windowsills, Johann? Nothing is messy. Placed with an art for… for placing things neatly. Nicely. Art. Not too close. Not too far apart. The tables by the windows? The items on the tables? Nothing messy or knocked over."

There was nothing of note.

They stepped outside the front door.

"Well, what happened, Chief Henri?" someone asked.

The Chief stood on the front porch.

"Ladies and gentlemen, it would appear, that *monsieur* Geppard has died of an accident. He hit his head in a fall last night… right here…right out here…and he could not stop bleeding through the night. A sickness of the blood, which occurs as we age, caused his death. We are, of course, continuing our investigation, but this is what appears to have happened."

Some of the people gasped.

"There is no crime, but since we are gathered here, might I remind you that you must lock your doors and windows at night. Paris is becoming a highly traveled city, and there are many strangers about. That is not what happened here, I assure you, but I would like to remind you to lock your house at night. Now, if you will excuse us, Officer Gunther and I must continue."

The two began looking at the steps and bannister of the front porch, where the fall occurred.

"There will be no blood here unless he laid here long enough to bleed," he told Gunther.

Then they examined the outsides of the windows.

"The windows are high. An intruder would need something to climb up on."

"It is no good to have all these people at the location of a crime. They will make a mess of things," Gustav said.

"Like tracks on top of tracks," Gunther said.

"Exactly, *mon ami*. And a human body, once dead, will become hard and then soft, depending upon the time and temperature of the surroundings," he added. You cannot be sure about the time of death. Only a witness can testify to this. Or, the murderer, or something like a smashed watch. Without these, only God knows the exact time of death."

"I have seen the leftover dead," Gunther said.

"Yes."

Nothing odd was found. Back at the buggy, Gustav unhooked the work belt, laid it down, and took off the white coat in the back. Just then Dr Sadler drove up in his coach.

"We'll let the good doctor draw his own conclusions free of my opinion, eh?"

Gunther studied the tools on the belt. He found the typical carpenter tools. There was a hammer and screwdrivers, and measuring tapes, along with a batch of very small picks, tweezers, and pliers. Small jars and sponges. Matches. And some things he'd never seen before. Gustav smiled and stalled, as Gunther leaned in.

"And now, you have seen your first police murder investigation. A murder that was not a murder. Never prejudge. Never jump to conclusions. Investigate. Think."

They sat in the buggy and waited. The doctor emerged from the house and came over to them.

"I think he hurt his head and bled to death," Sadler said.

"As do we," Gustav said.

"I'll finish up here and contact the caretakers for a coffin."

"Thank you, *monsieur.*"

Gustav touched off the buggy with a rein wiggle, and down the street they rolled, under the boughs of the thick trees.

"I like this street," Gustav said. "Very much. It reminds me of the outskirts of *Paree.*"

Gunther tried to picture the outskirts of Paris.

CHAPTER 8
SOME PEOPLE HAVE DISAPPEARED

Paris, Texas
1990

When fatigue finally forced him to pause, he ordered the men who were left to have their hearts torn out and their carcasses burned.

—Geoffrey of Monmouth, *The History of the Kings of Britain*

In Gunther's first twelve months in Paris, he and Stinky Moses walked the streets, rode out on assignments, made arrests, and quelled arguments between citizens and between Indians and citizens, tipped their hats many a time to the friendly folks of the small, country city. Gunther found the work challenging and at times thrilling; he found Stinky to be quite the quirky character, and the police chief from France a man much, much bigger than his small city job.

When people saw Gustav and Gunther walking or riding

together, they nicknamed them "Frenchie and Dutch," with a smile. The seven other city officers did their duties and became Gunther's friends, in relationships not unlike the soldiers in his Army platoon, where they too called him "Dutch." Everyone from Germany was a "Dutch," and German immigration into Texas was extensive.

Gunther settled into a boarding house and began to visit a girl from Clarksville named Ida, in Paris to take care of her elderly grandmother.

One afternoon, a deputy from the Lamar County Sheriff's Office walked into the police station with a handbill for the Chief to post. The Chief thumbtacked the announcement on the lobby bulletin board, and Gunther and Stinky read it.

ANNOUNCEMENT FROM THE SHERIFF OF LAMAR COUNTY

Attention all Lamar County Law Enforcement and North Texas Anti-Horse Thief Association Meeting, Tuesday night at 7 p.m. at the County Courthouse.

Special Presentation by the Oklahoma Anti-Horse Thief Association on the continual problems with horse theft, cattle theft, and other problems of a criminal nature.

"I've heard of the Anti-Horse Thief Association," Gunther said. "Are they well respected?"

"Yes," Stinky said. "They started up in Oklahoma, before the Civil War. And now there's hunnerds of them all over. Maybe a thousand. Good people. Landowners. Lawyers. Bankers. Ranchers. They ain't deputized, but they ain't vigilante neither. They track down horse thieves and take them to jail. Sometimes they get cattle thieves and other criminals too, as befalls them when chasin' after horse thieves. Get them to jail. Get them to court. No illegal hangin's. Chief works with them, especially because the Chief can't stand a vigilante, lynching."

That Tuesday night thirty-three men and six women showed up in the courtroom. The whole Paris Police Department, the county sheriff's officer, a Texas Ranger, the local judge (who chose to sit with the others in the pews and not up in his elevated chair), and some Paris citizens in the Association. The smell from cigars, corn cob, and elegantly carved pipes covered the room like a light bay fog, causing Stinky to squint and cough.

"Hello, everyone! My name is Hardigan Wilson. I am a civil attorney in Tulsa, Oklahoma, and an executive in the Anti-Horse Thief Association. I thank you all for being here tonight." The barrel-chested, bearded man in his fifties stood in front of the judge's bench, with some notes in hand.

"First, I would like to give a progress report from members of our state association. As you well know, horse theft is still a most pressing problem. Horses and teams of horses disappear all the time from our inner cities and from our rural farms. This is a problem in our border areas with Missouri, Arkansas, and Texas, as the horses are taken across the border for sales and trade..."

Hardigan Wilson ran the sad numbers of thefts, then the number of arrests and convictions. Near the close of the meeting, Wilson laid his notes down on a table and added, "I would like to say too, since we are all here, there's been another pressing problem." He looked perplexed and shook his head. "In Eastern Oklahoma and West Arkansas, we are...we are losing...people, not just horses. It seems, there is an unusual number of people...just vanishing. All kinds of people. Old people. Children. White. Black. Indian. Here and there. Always when they are alone."

"Injuns?" one attendee asked? "They's always been takin' people."

"No. It doesn't seem to be. In fact, we have heard that some Indians have disappeared too, right from our Indian Territory. We are working with the Indian police and they are just as perplexed. There's been no other lootin', burnin' or other signs of such activity associated with it."

Gustav, seated in the front row, seemed to get a little nervous. His head twitched a bit with each word.

"We had a grandma disappear in Sun Valley," a deputy declared from the back row, and everyone's head turned his way. "Seventy years old. She was home alone all day as her kinfolk were out working their acres. Looks like she got about half a way through making dinner and she...she was a gone." He snapped his fingers in the air. "Nothin' else missin'. Nothin' broken."

"I say Injuns," another said.

Wilson grimaced at that. "Well, I just thought I'd mention it. We always lose hunters and settlers and so forth, especially in bad weather, but usually we find out why. People of all races and ages from homes and churches and well...the circumstances are odd. Anyway, thank you all for coming. If I could meet with Chief Henri and the Sheriff for a moment before they leave, please? Thank you all for coming and thank you for your support."

There was clapping. Gustav and the Lamar Sheriff stepped up to meet with Wilson. The courtroom cleared out. Gunther made a move to leave too, but Stinky stayed seated and touched Gunther's arm. He jutted his pointy chin at the pow-wow up front, and Gunther sat back down.

After some talk, Wilson handed the two top lawmen some papers and they left. Gunther and Stinky followed behind them.

Gustav shoved the papers into his armpit and lit a cigarette on the front porch of the courthouse. Stinky stepped back from the smoke. They watched the Sheriff and the investigator walk off.

"I don't like this," Gustav said. "I don't like the story of the missing people. Something is not right about it. And…no one is doing anything about it because it covers so many jurisdictions. They worry about the horses, but not these people."

Gunther and Stinky remained quiet, watching his stern expressions.

"In France, we would have a team on this. Because, in each instance, there would be clues related to each disappearance that the other disappearances would not have. Together, the clues add up and could lead us somewhere."

Gustav took a big draw from his cigarette.

"Ahh, but what can I do? I am but small-town police chief, and no one is missing here."

"Yet," Stinky said.

"Yes, yes, Stinky. Not yet," Gustav said. "Yet. This is what concerns me."

He pulled the papers from his armpit and waved them about.

"Tomorrow, Johann, you will meet here…some deputies from the Sheriff's Office, some Association men, at 9 a.m. You will help in a…in a raid of the Sarasota Ranch."

Stinky's eyebrows shot up. "Sarasota? You know, those boys

of his, and those two new fellers from Hugo, they ain't right."

"You are correct, Stinky. *Monsieur* Wilson has given us federal papers on them. Most of the ranch is in the county, but the southeast portion is within the city limits. We need to be represented in the raid because of this. They are stealing horses and cattle in Oklahoma and running them through here, and then off somewhere into the Piney Woods."

"East Texas," Stinky whispered to Gunther.

"The agents of the Association have a spy, and he said that the new horses have arrived today and one agent will go with you and identify the horses."

Gunther nodded.

"Be careful out there. Something is going on at the Sarasota Ranch, I think. They say this is the biggest horse theft they have seen in years."

"My goin'?" Stinky asked.

"No, just Johann. You stay here and watch the bank, Stink. Perhaps some members of the Sarasota family may show up to draw money out. We need to know this."

"I'll sit inside the A and B Market across the street and keep a watch."

"Good idea."

"Plenty of soda pop available," Stinky said, almost but not quite smiling.

"And you will pay for every bottle," Gustav did smile then.

"Well, of course!" Stinky said, insulted at the remark.

CHAPTER 9
MORE MEN WITH MORE GUNS

The splendid armor of the combatants was now defaced with dust and blood, and gave way at every stroke of the sword and battle-axe. The gay plumage, shorn from the crests, drifted upon the breeze like snowflakes.

—Anonymous, *The Epic of Gilgamesh*

Gunther was the first at the courthouse the next morning. He sat on his horse drinking coffee he had in a canteen, an old habit from the Army. The canteen was wrapped in a furry canvas that kept the brew warm. Soon two Association members showed up. They too remained on horseback and leaned over to shake his hand.

"Marion Anderson, from Hugo, Oklahoma."

"Johann Gunther."

"Zip Hollar. Hugo."

"Johann Gunther."

"Where you from, Johann?" Zip asked.

"Most recent? Fort Sill, Oklahoma. Army. Before that, New York City. Before that, Germany."

"Can't say I detect an accent. Yankee or German," Marion said.

"Don't know why," Gunther said.

"Most be from the Army. All kinds of people talking to you from every-which-where. Well, Johann, we've been watching these boys for a while now," Zip said. "They've been gettin' horses and cattle from all around Hugo, and we trailed them down here. Lately, this is the biggest run they've made."

"Another deputy here said that the Sarasotas have affiliated themselves with some fellers from Hugo," Gunther said.

Two riders approached. One was a Texas Ranger that Gunther recognized from the night before.

"Hey!"

"Hey."

He introduced himself to Johann as Randy Richmond and his friend was Elijah Debonniorre. Just a friend, no lawman, or legal representative, and just along for the ride.

"Okay, we're all here," Zip said. "Mister Johann, sir, can you kindly lead us to the Sarasota front gate?"

"Yes, sir, I can."

And off they went. It took a little less than an hour to get near the front gates of the ranch. The talk was small, except for the thievery details Ranger Richmond asked Zip for.

In the distance, through the trees and rolling hills, they could see the Sarasota spread. Some houses, one big one, some barns, corrals and quite a lot of fenced-off acres. Horses and cattle roamed the area. Very serene. It was a bit before 10 o'clock and almost no human activity to be seen.

"Officer Gunther," Ranger Richmond said, "why don't you get around south of the main house, along the fence. Out there." He pointed. "Keep a watch, and make sure that nobody sneaks out the back door of this outfit when we ride up. Shoot twice in the air if they look dangerous."

Gunther, the youngest there, expected to be a second fiddle to the events anyway. He nodded and touched his horse Casey off to the south.

"We'll give ya a goodly head start," the Ranger said.

Gunther arrived at a good lookout spot within a grove of elm trees, pulled his lever-action rifle from the saddle and dismounted. He tied Casey's reins to a branch. Then he grabbed a small telescope from a saddlebag. He low-walked up to the barbwire fence and sat in some deep weeds and bushes, resting his back against an elm. He still saw no activity on the ranch, just a few dogs wandering around. He opened the telescope to take a deeper look around.

He saw the four men walk their horses through the open main gate. He could see that Marion, Zip, and Elijah had their rifles out, barrels down. Gunther felt odd about this. Everybody at the ranch was gone, or everybody was…hiding?

The Ranger led the way, and through his scope, Gunther could see Richmond yelling out for someone, anyone to respond as he got close to the main house. The dogs' tails wagging as they walked up to the men.

Then, something horrible happened. Gunther stood and lifted his rifle. Could he shoot that far?

Stinky Moses studied the legal papers on the Hugo, Oklahoma boys and the Sarasota boys. There were arrest warrants on Billy Blanchard and a Dee Weston with an alias of "Devastating." Stinky had to say that out loud.

"Devastating Dee Weston."

There were also warrants out for the father, James David Sarasota, his three sons, and four ranch hands.

"That's a...a lot a..." Stinky said.

"What, *ami*?" Gustav said.

"Just talking to myself, Chief. Just sayin', but that's a lot of warrants. That's ten warrants fer Gunth and them to serve up there."

"One riot. One Ranger," Gustav said, looking over his own stack of papers.

"Well, I best get over to the market. If I see any of these scoundrels at the bank, I'll put em in custody."

"Hmmm," Gustav murmured, not looking up.

Rifle in hand, Stinky walked down to the market, ducking under the signs and support beams, as usual. Folks said hello to him, and he replied in kind, but barely looked at each greeter's face.

The bell above the market door clanged loudly, and Stinky hunched again under the door frame, but he was so tall that the top of his hat hit the bell again.

"Mister Aransas," he shouted out to the owner. He grabbed a rolling chair from behind the counter and pulled it over to the front windows. He looked at his watch to mark the time.

"Stink?" Aransas said, appearing from the back.

"Sir, I gotta sit here fer awhile and watch the street this morning. Chief's orders."

"Oh no, any particular trouble? Bank robbery worries again? Need I put on a gun?"

"Oh, no, no, nothing like that, sir."

"Okay. Stink, you're always welcome company."

Stinky settled in and cradled the Winchester in his arms, looking over the morning activities on the street.

"I'll be gettin' me some soda pops and licorice," he shouted out. "I'll keep up."

Aransas walked up to him cradling a cup of coffee within his giant hands.

"Start with this. Here ya go, son."

"Arbuckle?" Stinky asked, sitting up, collecting the ceramic cup with two enormous hands.

"Arbuckle coffee."

"Barefoot?"

"Barefoot. I know you don't like no kinda milk or sugar."

"Thank you, Mister Aransas." He sniffed the barefoot, Arbuckle coffee.

He sat back and sipped the brew. He mostly looked west, as that was the direction of the Sarasota ranch. Not bad duty, he thought, all from a long-shot hunch of the Chief's. He wondered how and what Gunther was doing.

"That's a whole lot of warrants," he said out loud. "I don't know..."

Gunther couldn't believe his eyes. Suddenly more than ten men and two women, all wearing neckerchiefs as masks, poured out of the main house and barn, all with guns drawn and pointed at the lawmen. There was shouting but he could not hear. Roused by the men, the dogs started barking. Before Gunther could think straight, the four lawmen were tossing down their pistols and rifles to the ground. Their hands went up.

A wave of fear raced through Gunther's heart. What could he do? He couldn't just start shooting at them! Or could he? He knelt down and through his telescope counted thirteen masked people. THIRTEEN! They shoved and poked on the lawmen and the Ranger's friend until they got them down on their knees on the front porch of the main house. Two women were tying them up, tying their hands back behind them. If Gunther started shooting into them, a bloody gunfight would start. They'd start shooting back and charging him. One against thirteen.

Then he saw a man without a mask step out of the house. He was dressed in black with a black hat. Old man Sarasota. He talked with the captured lawmen. One tumbled over and laid on his side, probably unable to remain on his knees on the hard wood that long. The rope must have been attached to his ankles too because the downed lawman couldn't stretch out his legs.

Someone brought up a horse and Sarasota walked over to it and mounted. Then the old man spurred the horse and it trotted through the gate and off the ranch. Was he headed toward Gunther? Had they seen five riders approach?

No. Mr. Sarasota left the gates and stayed on the main trail. Gunther stepped back to Casey, got the reins, and walked directly south a bit, so as not to be seen. Then he got on his horse in the denser woods and took off for Paris. Believing Sarasota was off for Paris too, Gunther followed a different path. It would take just a bit longer but it was his only option. The only solution here at the ranch was to come back with more men with more guns.

CHAPTER 10
ONE FOOT IN

...parrying like a man who had the greatest respect for his own epidermis.

—Alexandre Dumas, *The Three Musketeers*

You couldn't say Stinky was daydreaming exactly, but he was tapping the toes of his boots on the worn, wooden floor and slowly eating a long strand of cherry licorice as he looked out the window. He started singing.

> *"But the cat came back, he couldn't stay no longer,*
> *yes, the cat came back de very next day,*
> *the cat came back, thought she were a goner,*
> *but the cat came back for it wouldn't stay away.*
> *But the cat...."*

Then he spotted old man Sarasota riding his horse in from the west.

"Mister Aransas!" Stinky shouted out to the shopkeeper.

"Yeees, Stinky?"

"Can you...er... or you get somebody to get word to the police station that Mister Sarasota is in town, and, yup, he is, going to the bank."

"I will get word myself."

"Don't look suspicious or anything. Don't look at em. Just walk on by him like nothin'."

"I will be careful," Aransas said. He took off his apron and left the store.

Stinky stood and watched Sarasota dismount and walk into the bank. Stinky looked around the street. Where was the best place to confront him? Where would no one else get hurt?

He left the market, rifle in hand, and walked across the street. He looked right and left, to make sure his man was traveling alone. He worked a round into the chamber. Then he entered the bank, with the rifle cradled in his crossed arms.

Sarasota was sitting with the bank manager at his desk with his back to the lobby. One female customer stood at the counter.

"Mrs. Swanson," Stinky said quietly to her.

"Ah, ah yes, Stinky?"

"I beg you for a moment, could you please leave the bank? For a moment? It might get a little rodeo in here in the next minute or two."

Her eyes scanned the lobby. She picked up some papers and left. The male clerk helping her stepped back. Stinky nodded his approval at the move.

Stink walked to the tall, wooden table in the center of the lobby, a paperwork station, where he could see the manager's workspace. He laid the rifle on the table, pointed it straight at

Sarasota though, with a finger on the trigger. The wanted man was sitting at the bank manager's guest chair.

"Mister Sarasota?" Stinky said.

The man stopped talking to his clerk, but did not turn around.

"Mister Wolfawitz? I beg you to move away," Stinky warned the manager.

The manager did by shoving himself by way of the wheeled chair away from the desk, with a quizzed look on his face. The chair rolled fairly far from the desk then hit a wall.

"Mister Sarasota? Mister Sarasota!"

He swiveled his chair to glare at Stinky. His face looked stern. From his seated height, giant Stinky loomed even taller.

"What do *you* want, boy?" he growled.

"I've got a paper on you from Oklahoma."

"Okla..., fer what?"

"Stealin' horses. Stealin' cattle. A lot of em."

"Yer just a boy! Why should I..."

"A boy with a man's gun aimed right at yer guts."

Sarasota's eyes cut across the lobby. Stinky had seen that *escape look* before.

"Ain't nowheres to go, Mister Sarasota, except to give up the goat."

Sarasota stood, but not with a normal motion, not like a normal person would stand from a chair. Stinky watched him real close and sure enough, the man's hand moved his jacket aside and touched his revolver.

Stinky pulled the trigger and the bullet smacked into Sarasota's chest, cracking a bone, and ripping a lung. Stinky lifted the weapon to shoulder height, while working the lever action and made ready for the next shot.

Sarasota forgot about his holstered weapon and fell back against the manager's desk, the fingers of his hands extended, his mouth open wide. Then he slid down the desk to the floor, shoving his chair away in a spastic kick.

Manager Wolfawitz fell out of his chair in a dodging shock.

"Get a doc," Stinky said out of the corner of his mouth to the clerk. He never took his eyes off Sarasota.

"Mister Wolfawitz, I beg you, get aside even farther."

He did, at a fast crawl.

"Next one's in yer stubborn head," Stinky said. "Don't even rub or scratch on that pistol."

He walked up to the wounded man and removed the revolver from his holster. He patted all the other places a weapon might be. Sarasota just gurgled.

"What's his bidness, here today?" Stinky asked the manager.

"He was about to withdraw all his money. Said he was moving...leaving. Movin' away."

The bank door swung open and Chief Gustav Henri burst in, along with Deputy Broomhauser. Wide-eyed, pistols in hand, as they heard the gunshot as they approached. They surveyed the mess.

"Going for his gun, Chief. Doc summoned. He was here takin' out all his money. Movin' away. I fear for Gunther out there. I fear for him. It's a bad day."

Gustav walked up to Sarasota and looked at his bleeding chest.

"You want help?"

"Of...course. Of...course...I..."

"Lock the door, Broomhauser," he told the deputy, then he turned back to Sarasota. "You want help? You tell me what's going on."

"I've been shot by a damn boy!"

Gustav knelt down and leaned in, "And I am going to stick a finger deep in that hole in your chest and pick around in there until you tell me what in hell is going on?"

"You can't do that?"

"I can't? It's just you, me and my finger right now. I think I can."

"We…we got some horses and cattle from Oklahoma, and…and…it's time to move to East Texas. I didn't know anything about…"

There was banging on the locked front door.

"There's the doctor," Gustav said, "tell me some truth or I'll go fishing." He wiggled his finger in the air.

"The Hugo boys brought the stock in, but on the way, they found out the Thief Association knew about them and were coming to get us."

"How did they find out?"

"I don't know. A…a…spy? A spy, I guess."

"A spy. Let Doc Checkers in," Gustav said over his shoulder.

"God almighty, not Doc Checkers! He's the town butcher!" Sarasota cried out.

"Just part time," Gustav said calmly.

"I've got one foot in the grave here, get a real doctor in here!" Sarasota gasped.

Gustav stood.

"Yes, Gunther is in trouble," Gustav said to Stinky.

The door was unlocked and in ran the part-time doctor, also the part-time butcher.

Then…right behind Dr Checkers, Johann Gunther ran in.

Chapter 11
BOTH FEET IN

"Once metal hits metal and battle begins, no one wishes they had practiced less!"

—Alpha Four, *Far Forest Scrolls Na Cearcaill*

"What...hap-" Gustav started.

"The Ranger posted me on the south side of the ranch as a lookout. When the four of them rode in, they were all jumped by thirteen masked men and two women, and tied up. Then Sarasota rode out."

"He came here. He's on the floor over there," Gustav said.

"I shot em. Had to," Stinky said.

"I came back here for reinforcements," Gunther said.

Gustav turned to Sarasota and the doctor, "What will they do with those lawmen?"

No answer. Gustav stepped in closer, leaned in. "What will..."

"He can't answer, Chief. He's dead," Doc Checkers said.

"Now he has both feet in," Gustav muttered. He stood and

ordered, "Get some riders," to Stinky and Broomhauser.

"Yes, Chief."

"Sarasota was pulling out all his money. They were going to run the stock to East Texas," Gustav told Gunther.

They walked out of the bank.

"Thirteen men. Two women..." Gustav wondered out loud, "...how are we..."

"I have a plan," Gunther said. "But we're gonna need some wire cutters..."

Three hours later, Paris Police Chief Gustav Henri and his deputy Johann Gunther appeared on horseback at the Sarasota ranch gate. As soon as they were spotted, armed, masked figures filed out on the grounds between the big house and the barn.

Gunther and the Chief, exchanged glances, took some deep breaths, and tapped their horses into a slow walk into this valley of, seemingly, sure death.

The waiting men and women couldn't believe their eyes and gathered to meet them. Some even laughed. When they got up close to the house, they separated a bit, about a shotgun blast apart, with not much hope against that safety since several of the men held shotguns and there would not be a single blast. They looked over to the right, to the front porch and the lawmen were still there, tied up, and now all four were laying down on their sides.

"Chief Henri," one man said wearing a red flannel shirt and red neckerchief mask. "What in hell are you doing here? This is the county, not the city."

"Well, you're right, Louis," Gustav said, easily recognizing the man under the partial mask, by his voice, hair, clothes, and body shape. "But, we're still here to get those four men you have on the porch."

Gunther added very calmly, "And...to make matters worse? We're here to arrest all you sons-o-bitches."

"Whaaaat?" Red flannel Louis laughed, and then all fourteen laughed and cat-called. One man danced a little jig.

"You and what Army?" The red flannel man said.

"All the men I've got surrounding the fence line," Gunther said.

"AH-HA! HA! You think that idiot's trick is gonna work? How many secret men you got?"

"Sixteen."

"Sixteen."

"Sixteen men with repeating rifles, all good enough to shoot a mite off a donkey's ass," Gunther said.

"HA!"

"Good enough to puncture your skull," he continued.

"HA!"

Gunther put his left hand up and palm out. He smiled, and he ever so slowly pulled his pistol from his holster. This caused the people to raise their level of concentration and their weapons, too. Right at the lawman. Gunther aimed the barrel skyward, with a smile, and he pulled the trigger once.

The signal given, within a few seconds, there was a barrage of single shots that rang a three-quarter ring of rifle gunfire, south, east, and north of them. It was loud, it was long, and it was impressive.

"Sixteen," Gunther repeated. "Next volley? Right into y'all. Boys and girls, it'll be a massacre."

"You...they can't hit us all from the fence line," one man

cried out.

"Oh, they've cut the fence line," Gunther said. "They're closer than that."

"Look…," Gunther expected to lay out some surrender terms next, but instead, in a split second, all fourteen cowboys and cowgirls scattered in every direction! Even the dogs scattered. Some men were hollering and the women were screaming. Gunther and the Chief jumped from their horses expecting them all to run for cover and start shooting, but none of them did, none of them stopped. Some ran afoot west. Some mounted horses in the barn and also galloped west. One man turned the corner of the barn doors so fast, he flew off his horse. He rolled, stood, and ran on foot, his steed far out ahead of him. Four of them started to run, then stopped and dropped to their knees with their hands up.

"Like rats on a merchant ship," Gustav said.

Gustav ran to the four captured men on the front porch, knife out, and cut their bonds. They moaned and groaned as they tried to stretch their limbs and rub their wrists. Gunther, rifle now in hand, stood guard over the rescue. Gustav helped them to their feet. The Ranger and his friend seemed to recover quickly, but the two older Association men collapsed into porch chairs. The Ranger and Gunther shackled the four surrendered men and took their guns. The Ranger stuck one of their pistols in his empty holster.

"I guess I'll never see my guns again. And the quartermaster will never pay to replace them. That was quite a speech," the Ranger said to Gustav. "A humdinger of a plan."

Gustav smiled and his eyebrows lifted. He pointed to Gunther. The Ranger looked to the young man.

"We did that once in the Army, sir," Gunther said. "Some Apaches held some settlers. We set up a meeting. Two officers were allowed into their camp, to strike a deal, but we snuck up and surrounded the meeting. The captain fired a shot in the air, a signal to the surrounding troops to fire. About forty of us fired in the air. The Apaches let the settlers go. The captain let the Apaches go too. It was a good day."

"Well, we ain't lettin' these sons of bitches go," Ranger Richmond said.

They hauled the four men over to the porch. Gunfire of many calibers erupted to the west.

"Weeell, well, my friends," Gustav said to the four men, now facedown on the porch. "Quite a day it has been."

"We don't know what's going on here! We just thought we were gonna move some cattle to East Texas."

"Yes. Yes. Thus, the masks, huh. Yes, innocent, masked cowboys. Just pokin' along. Get along, you little doggies."

Within minutes, Stinky Moses and Broomhauser rode up and dismounted.

"Five of them dead. Three of them wounded. Some got plum away," Broomhauser reported.

"Us?" Gustav asked.

"We is all okay." Broomhauser said.

"Then, we is happy," Gustav said. He turned to the Association men.

"All our deputies, and we had some workers from town come up too. Some Sheriff's men on day shift, too."

"Praise be to the Lord," Zip Hollar said, rubbing his knees. "I was about to cry for my dead momma if I couldn't stretch my legs out."

Gunther left the porch and walked inside the house.

"When I saw young Dutch and ol' Frenchie ride up," the Ranger said, "I thought for sure they'd soon be roped up next to us one minute, and we'd all be dead by sundown."

"Mr. Sarasota is dead," Gustav told them. "Stinky here shot him at the bank when Sarasota tried to pull a gun on him. He was there trying to withdraw all his money. He told me before he died that they were tipped off that you were coming, by a spy."

"Oh no," Zip said.

"That's disconcerting," the Ranger said.

"Chief?" Gunther said solemnly, half stepping out onto the porch. He nodded his head to go with him back inside.

Gustav walked into the house behind Gunther as he led the way through a parlor, and a dining room. The insides looked like a normal house, of a normal family, the items worn well down from life. Then into the kitchen...

"Oh, my God," Gustav said. "Oh, dear God."

There on the floor, in a pool of blood, lay an elderly woman.

"Mrs. Sarasota?" Gunther asked.

"Yeeeees!" Gustav growled. He knelt beside her. He saw the bullet wound to the right side of her head. A pistol was on the floor near her right hand. The left top of her head was blasted open. Gustav looked up and saw the bits of brain and skull plastered high on the wallpaper. Gunther looked up too. Gustav considered the "math." The angles. The positioning. The body. The gun.

Gunther tapped a finger on the table. Gustav stepped over and saw the handwritten note and leaned in for a read. The handwriting was impeccable.

"You want me to leave my house. This is our house
of 34 years. We raised our children here. Now you
want me to leave, and we will become fugitives
of the law. I will not leave my house. Goodbye."

Gustav stared at the letter. Gunther saw one giant tear from Gustav's eye drop and hit the dry, old wooden floor. He rubbed his eyes and snorted.

"It has been my experience that women do not usually shoot themselves in the head," he said. "but it is a fast way to go."

Gunther nodded.

"This poor lady. It has been a very long day already, hasn't it? Hasn't it been, Johann?" he said, sounding out of breath.

"Yes, sir. Yes, it has."

Gustav pointed to a spot a foot higher in the air than the table. He drew an imaginary line sideways to a spot above the pulled-out, dining room chair, then he pointed to the mess on the wall. Then with two hands up, he shifted them downward to the body. He looked at Gunther with wet eyes and sad grimace.

Gunther nodded. No need to speak. He got the math lesson of the shooting. Gustav nodded back, then left the room, saying on the way, "We walk around every day with somebody near... with one foot in the grave. Or sometimes, both feet, in the grave. Don't we, son."

"Yes sir, we do."

Chapter 12
GUN BURNS BURN DEEP

"It's well to be upon one's guard, I mean, since all day long we meet the unforeseen."

— Geoffrey Chaucer, *The Canterbury Tales: The Knight's Tale*

The "Sarasota Shoot-out" became big news in Northeast Texas, Oklahoma, and Arkansas. Everyone who'd shot at the posse were, in turn, shot and killed that day. Two short weeks later the survivors were put on trial in the Lamar County Courthouse for cattle rustling, horse theft, and kidnapping. With Texas Ranger Richmond as the star witness, all received sentences of six years. And a reward was posted for the few that escaped. One who successfully fled? This "Devastating" Dee Weston was also wanted in Oklahoma. The Anti-Horse Thief Association was quoted in the newspapers "that Weston was very active since his flight. Robbery. Theft. Revenge. Beware of him."

Three months later, three days before Christmas...

Gustav was happily entertaining a lady friend, in from Texarkana for the coming holiday, in the Hotel Ascot's lobby restaurant, in its rather elegant-for-Paris Pyramid Dining Room. The room was resplendent in Christmas decorations with no less than three giant Christmas trees. All three pine trees were covered in small, burning candles.

"How many homes in Paris…in…in Europe…burned to the ground from candles on such trees," Gustav mentioned to his lady friend. She commiserated.

It was a Wednesday night, church night, and therefore not very crowded at that hour. A piano player mindlessly ran through some carols. By coincidence, Gunther and his girl-friend Ida walked in to have a bite to eat, but they chose not to sit with their friends, each pair wishing to be alone. They did, however, wave to each other. Gustav was dressed in a suit with a ruffled shirt, a pistol, no doubt, concealed under that velvet jacket. Gunther, Stetson-crowned, was reasonably well-dressed, having come directly where he'd just finished his day shift. He still wore a badge on his jacket, and his gun belt. His armed outfit was somewhat acceptable for the eatery, certainly for visiting law enforcement, though with each subsequent year, one would see fewer visible guns in such a high-brow place as The Pyramid Room.

"What's fer dinner," the *octogenarian* waiter asked, scratching his hairy ear. Although he was dressed well, he could never act the high-brow part.

"You tell me," Gunther replied.

"Huh?"

"What's for dinner here?"

"Well, Dutch, we have the same damn thing every damn night."

"Then I'll have the same damn thing. What about you, Ida?"

Suddenly, two men, not well-dressed at all, dusty and dirty, with sneers on their faces, walked in, wearing old worn hats, jackets, gun belts, and spurs which spun over the carpet. They made their way over to Gustav.

"You Chief Henri?" one of the two said. The second stood back a bit and off to the right.

Gustav first having heard the spurs, looked up at them, then looked down. But now he slowly raised his eyes again once his name was called out.

"Are you the Chief of Police, I said!"

"Yeees," Gustav said musically.

"Well, I am Devastating Dee Weston. And you killed my best friend."

"Actually, Mister Devastation..."

"Devastating..."

"Devastat-ing, I myself did not kill anyone that day. But I was around there," Gustav said calmly.

Gunther saw all this and was already sliding his chair out a bit to face them. He lifted a coffee cup to hide his badge.

"Then I will start with you," Devastating said.

"Start with me? Starting up what? Devastating. Listen, since you are far from devastatingly handsome, why do you call yourself Devastating?"

"I'll show you..."

From Gunther's perspective, the man, right-handed (Gunther was to his left), reached for his pistol. Gunther saw Devastating Dee lower his right hip and bend at the right knee.

Holster clearance. Gunther saw the tip of the man's right elbow appear behind his back. Holster draw. All physical tip-offs. Gunther dropped the cup, stood and drew, and blew a hole in Devastating's neck from nine feet away. Devastating was quite devastated and crumbled to the floor. The man's pistol was completely pulled as it dropped to the floor.

Gustav stood and drew a two-inch revolver from a shoulder holster as Devastating fell, and he shot the second man. Elbow up, elbow down, the first two shots, then shoved his gun straight forward and on eye level and pulled off the last three. Five times in the chest. The man shook and gasped with each hit.

The few customers screamed and scrambled toward the walls, falling out of chairs and crashing into tables as they fled. No need, the shooting was over in two seconds. But the man stumbled back and stumbled back...

"Oh, no!" Gustav said.

The man stumbled right back into the candle-lit Christmas tree. He and the tree by the front door fell over together. The tree, bone dry, and on display since December 10th, exploded into a fireball as the strategically placed candles hit the branches, and set them alight.

Gunther dashed to the tree. Three waiters followed. Gunther grabbed the very top, wrestled it to the doorway, pushed open the double doors with his back, and out to the street he went. The two waiters helped by pulling the dead man free and lifting the wooden, x-shaped tree stand and shoving it after Gunther. The curtains behind the tree were alight, and William Serani, the owner, yanked them down and ran outside waving them and cursing. Some customers charged over to the streaks of fire on the carpeted floor and stomped them out.

"Very, very sorry you had to see that, my dear," Gustav said to his lady friend, who had not had time to move an inch. He holstered his weapon and turned to the man on the floor

Gustav kicked Devastating's pistol away and took a close look at him. Blood was still pumping from his neck. Gustav pulled a white tablecloth from an empty table, lifted the man's head and shoved the cloth under the wound, spreading it out enough to save the expensive carpet. Devastating's eyes looked back at him.

"Tha...tha...thanks," Devastating mumbled.

"Ohhhh, nooo, not for you, you dolt. You are ruining the carpet."

"Ah...I..."

"Your sun has set, son, according to your own foolish actions," Gustav said.

And with that, Devastating devasted away.

The manager and employees ran back inside and surrounded them.

"I'm so sorry, William, but the men came here to kill me. 'Settle a score,' as you Westerners say."

"Ohhh, my carpet," William moaned.

"I know, I know. Let's get these tramps outside."

Back on the street, Gunther stood in the cold wind and watched the tree burn to cinders. Gustav and William hauled Devastating's devastated body outside and lay it beside the burning tree. Others pulled the second gangster out.

"You were very quick to shoot him, Johann," Gustav said.

"It looked to me that he was drawing his gun."

"From your side."

"From my side. From anybody's side."

"Good thing he was. He dropped the pistol when you shot him."

"Yeah," Gunther said, trying to understand his Chief's point.

"You have saved my life, Johann. Tonight. Tonight. But you were very, very quick to draw and shoot. What if he was producing some papers from his pocket to show me?" Gustav said.

Gunther did not know what to say.

"Be careful of that gun burn," he said. "In your hands. It burns deep," He wagged a finger at Gunther's gun hand. Then, he turned and returned inside.

Gunther was confused, surprised, and disappointed all at once. He knew he did the right thing. Yet, what? Maybe the Chief had a little too much to drink already?

Chapter 13
FRENCHIE AND DUTCH

Paris, Texas
1893

"And if you take a wife into your bed, you're very likely to be cuckolded."

—Geoffrey Chaucer, *The Canterbury Tales: The Merchant's Tale.*

"Thanks for coming over, Johann," Gustav said as Gunther walked up to the Chief's front porch. It was a brisk, April early evening that drew everyone out of their houses and onto their porches and streets for chores, walking, chatting, and cavorting about with the children.

Gustav's house was a single-story, wood-frame structure on the corner of 4th and Rekindle Street. The front lawn was small, the fencing short. Gunther took all the steps to the front porch at once and sat in a chair near his Chief. Gustav poured him a small glass of whiskey from a bottle on the table between them. Gunther removed his hat and tossed it on a small wicker table.

"Beautiful evening," Gustav said.

Gunther noticed that resting on Gustav's lap lay a large revolver, partially under a small knit blanket. Gustav knew he spotted it, but Gustav offered no explanation.

"I asked you here tonight, because...I have once again put myself into a bad social position. It seems...it seems there is an angry husband here in Paris, that has accused his wife of becoming too, too interested in me."

"Oh," Gunther said. "Is she?"

"Oh, we have gone beyond the interested stage."

Gunther looked the street over.

"Hmmm, Yes. Sally Turray," Gustav said.

"Of Turray Construction?"

"*That* Sally Turray. Beautiful woman. I still...I still get butterflies in my chest thinking of her! Yes. And...I have been informed that Mr. Turray is very, very mad, and that Mr. Turray is planning on visiting me tonight, here at my *la maison*,"

"Butterflies. Thus, the gun," Gunther said.

"Thus, the gun. And I believe that your presence here, that you sitting here with me, two against one, might perhaps, just might deter such a visit. And prevent a scene of violence."

Gustav raised his glass, "Ahhh...*à la vôtre.*"

"*A la...*"

"It's French for 'cheers,' Johann, which is what the Brits would say—cheers. You know '*Salute!*' Or, here in Texas, 'toss down your gullet a powerful drink and a great night to all!'... haha-hah!"

"*Prost,*" Gunther raised his glass and touched Gustav's glass, as his parents would say and do.

"*Prost*," Gustav repeated. "You, sitting here, will help, because you know, you have a growing reputation."

"I do?"

"You do. You are smart. Tough. And they know from gossip that you're an ex-Army rider. You are General George Custer *BEFORE*...Little Big Horn. And you have shot a lot of people."

"I've never shot anyone that..."

"I know, I know, that 'didn't...need...killing,' as they like to say here in the mysterious West."

They watched the neighbors walk by, either on a stroll or running errands, and others tend to their gardens and lawns.

"Did I ever tell you how I wound up here in Paris, Texas, from Paris, France?"

"No, sir."

"I was an investigator. A *commander* of detectives. I was very interested in science. I studied many things which I could use. A Frenchman, Jean Michon, back in the 1870s began a whole new police science on handwriting analysis. He wrote a book, published in 1872. *Graphology*. I know him, I met him. People write very, very differently, son, and in very unique ways. Yes. This interest of mine got me into big trouble. *Big* trouble.

Not that long ago really, a French Captain named Alfred Dreyfus...Jewish...was accused of sending military secrets to... to Germany." He waved his hand at Gunther as if to suggest, Germany—your country. "This was under investigation for years. A very big French scandal. It was as if a planned vigilante lynching of a Jew was underway. I was to testify one week in court on a robbery. I was waiting and waiting to testify.

I often waited in some offices, and this time I happened to wait in the court evidence rooms and speak to a pretty lady that worked there. In the room were the captured letters of the traitor Dreyfus. Next to them were court papers and a statement of innocence that he signed. I could not help myself and immediately I began looking back and forth at them. A…a Michon handwriting analysis. I saw that Captain Dreyfus did not write the treasonous letters. And I could prove it. Dreyfus was, as they say, set up."

He sipped his whiskey.

"Why?"

"He was Jewish! That is what I think. What many, many people think. The government, the military did not want Jews in command positions."

"Why?"

"Centuries of distrust, I presume. But think about the negroes here, Johann. Do you ever think of the negroes?"

"Not much…I…."

"We can never be this way. You are a police officer. You see, France and America, we once had such beautiful dreams, eh? We are brothers and sisters in the revolution of ideas! Yes? We worked together in your American Revolution. Thomas Jefferson! Franklin, eh? An ideal. We must still work through all of it. But it will take time."

Gustav was lost in his thoughts for a moment, then continued.

"I reported my discoveries to my superiors. The charges were fake! I demanded. I explained my conclusions. I…well…I was *immediately*, Johann, in *two* days…I received my transfer papers to, my God, Devil's Island. The end of the world. It ruined my pending marriage. My visits to my…my sister and her new family. My parents. They died while I was gone. Devil's Island! I was to take a supervisory position to help run the worst prison, exile, island…in…the…world. They hid me, Johann, hid me away, so they could falsely persecute this man. I think, yes, I think it was because he was Jewish. Yes."

He sipped his whiskey again, as Gunther tried to absorb these larger-than-his-life, international happenings.

"So, I spent years on Devil's Island. In some situations, in charge of the very dangerous men I put there. Men with no hope, in a hopeless place. One of the prisoners taught me English. His name was Rodolfo. From Mexico. He was a very bad man too, but men from French Indochina, scum I had arrested in France… a gang leader, a killer named Saw, killed Rudolfo when they found out I was his friend. They tried to kill me there, once, also. But I killed the killers with … with my own bare hands!" He shook one fist in the air. "It was as though, you know, I too was in prison there. So, I quit. I retired."

"How did you come to Paris, Texas?"

"The man Rodolfo, who taught me English, knew about our little burg here. He told me once, he said, 'You know there is a Paris, *Texas*! I've been there,' he said. He…told me all about this place. Ha! Where else was I to go next? I was sick of the big city and the big country politics. I…I…was…I am sad to say…sick of my France. A bad, you know, taste… *le* goût, in my mouth. I have served my time in hell, Johann."

"Does this Dreyfus feller know about this handwriting?"

"Yes, yes he does…his lawyers…I wrote them many times…" Gustav suddenly sat up. He pointed at a small, open wagon heading their way.

"Oh! There he is."

91

It was Mr. Turray in a single-horse-drawn, company wagon. His face was scowled in anger, and when spotting Gustav's house, he glared. The wagon slowed down.

"Evening!" Gustav shouted with a big smile. "*Evening*, Mr. Turray." Instead of waving with an empty hand, Gustav waved the big pistol from side to side, barrel up. This open display even surprised Gunther.

Then, at the sight of the gun and of Gunther, Turray did not slow down. He snarled and continued down Rekindle Street.

"I think he is through. I think you scared him," Gustav said.

"*I* scared him?"

"Yeees."

They sat quiet for a moment. Gustav leaned forward and watched the wagon disappear.

"Do you know Alaska Noot? The Eskimo?" Gustav asked.

"Yeah, yeah. Works for Frisco railroad. A watchman for their property."

"Tomorrow, I want you to ride out to the Frisco storage yards. Someone told me yesterday that they rode by the yards coming back from Clarksville and Eskimo Noot was not there. His horse and the wagon were in the stable by the cabin, but there was no sign of him anywhere."

"Isn't that out in the county, Chief?"

"Yes, yes, it is. But I want you to go and look around. Noot is a very interesting man, a graduate of the University of Oklahoma, and a long, long way from Nome, Alaska."

"Are you still worried about these missing people reports?"

"Yes, I am, Johann. There is something strange about them. Go out there and see if he is okay."

"First thing."

"Good. Let's go inside. Penelope brought me a peach cobbler today." He stood, stretched, pistol in hand, and headed for the front screen door.

"Are we expecting Mr. Penelope tonight too?" Gunther asked, following him.

Gustav turned, eyebrows up, lips pursed, "*Ohhh*, oh, I hope not!"

Chapter 14
THE SAD TULUGOT OF ALASKA NOOT

Gunther took a slow ride up a long grade, in a woodsy trail, in the April rain, to the Frisco Railroad storage yards, northeast of Paris. The raindrops popped on his hat brim and coat, and every few minutes when he happened to lean over, the collected water would drain off. Casey seemed oblivious to the rain. They slowly approached the main gate. It was closed but not locked. Gunther could see the piles of timber and iron and mechanical gear, used freight cars, and full engine on a wooden platform.

Gunther had met Noot several times in town. He was unforgettable because he was an Eskimo, one, like so many American Inuits, that attended college, got degrees, and spread out over Canada and the United States. For some, despite his Alaska origins, he was considered "just another Indian," but he wasn't. And, for some unknown reason, he wound up living alone in this storage area, like a caretaker-guard, an employee of Frisco.

"Nooooot!" Gunther yelled out.

Nothing.

He sidled Casey up beside the gate, lifted the rope hoop

holding it closed and gave the gate a shove.

"Noot!"

Gunther scanned everything as he nudged Casey toward the cabin. There he dismounted. He found the cabin door shut.

"Noot!"

He knocked, waited, then, shoved open the door. There was no smell, except for a little musty odor. A chill in the air, from a lack of long-term heat, was a point he was sure Gustav would notice. A red lantern sat on a big table in the middle of the single room. He touched it, and it too was cold. Gunther struck a match from his pocket on the table and lit it. There were a lot of engineering papers on the table, but the table was oddly askew from the center of the very neat and orderly room. Gunther looked around and couldn't see why it was unaligned with the rest of the place.

Everything else seemed in a proper position. A bed in the corner was made, the sink and cooking area looked very organized. He shook the metal coffee pot. There was liquid in it. He poured the black and green goop into the hand-pump sink. Rotten. He pumped some water in the sink, and the first few pumps produced brown water, then clear. Then he noticed one coffee cup on the floor, tipped over next to a dried brown stain on the wood. He got down on his knees and looked at it closely. He examined the cup without touching it. Dried coffee stained the inside bottom of the tipped cup. He even smelled it. Bad. Two chairs were pushed up to the table, but two more chairs were not pulled under it, but were angled outward.

Gunther walked outside and took some deep breaths. Still drizzling. He grabbed Casey's reins.

"Come on, handsome," he said to the horse.

He led his equine partner into the stable next door just as the rain picked up. When he turned toward the open doorway, he saw a skinny horse standing in the stall. It barely reacted to him, but only whinnied in a pathetic, weak way.

"Oh my God," Gunther said.

He opened the stall door, grabbed the halter and led the neglected horse out.

"Come on, baby, come on."

There were bags of feed piled up by a wall, and with his knife, Gunther ripped the top bag open. The horse immediately ate, which the veteran cavalryman liked to see.

"You poor thing," he said.

He grabbed a bucket and ran out to a water pump and pumped it full, then jogged back inside. He set the bucket down beside the horse. It drank and drank.

The official Frisco company buggy coach that Noot always used was still there in the barn.

The horse didn't look like it could make it back to town, but with some food and water it might manage in a day or two.

"I will leave you loose in the field. I saw a stream off a little way. You can eat and drink. Okay? Okay? I, or someone, will come back for you. Okay?" he said as he ran his palm up and down the horse's neck.

It started to pour outside. There was lightning too, and thunder.

Gunther leaned against the doorway.

"Noot," he said again, this time very quietly.

Noot was gone. Something terribly wrong had happened to Noot, and right there in the cabin he was staring at.

In the Chief's office that afternoon, Gunther explained what he had seen to Gustav, Stinky, and some of the other officers. Gustav rocked back and forth in his chair.

"This does not sound good," Gustav said.

"No," Gunther responded.

"Alright. I will go tell the sheriff. I will say you were just passing through and you stopped by to say hello, and you noticed this because we have no business out in the county. I will go to the Frisco office too. I need to stop in and see the manager and say hello anyway. They will have to see if anything has been stolen, because thieves may have killed him. You know?"

"What about Noot's horse?" Gunther asked.

"I will tell the sheriff about the horse. The horse will be okay."

The next afternoon, Jerry Malone, one of the Frisco rail supervisors stopped in the police station to see Gustav and Gunther after their inspection. He reported that deputies from the sheriff's office, along with Texas Ranger Richmond, rode out to storage yard, joined by supervisors of the Frisco line. They determined nothing was missing, other than Noot.

"Nothing was a missin' out there but ol' Noot hisself. We seen what Gunther saw, the table upset and all, the coffee cup on the floor. Reckon we have to tell Noot's next of kin up in Alaska he's a gone. Maybe he just left for home? Sudden? But if'n he did, why'd he left all his clothes and that poor horse of his. Nor took his pistol or rifle. He ain't took no train outta here, neither. We show no such record. The boys are walking the acreage, in case he was a huntin' with another rifle and had an accident. The deputies will be askin' folks in town if'n there was a grudge on him."

"Thanks for stopping by, Jerry," Gustav said.

Jerry left.

"There have been four more people in Northeast Texas just disappear, Johann. Just…just vanished. I tell you there are little clues in each case, and they need to be collected."

They sat in silence for a moment.

"I want you to…" Gustav rubbed his face with a hand and thought for a few seconds, "I want you to ride to each city, stop in the sheriff's offices, city marshals' office…social visit…be, be sociable…and find out what they know about this problem. We'll be all in their local business, and they don't want to look bad, so be casual."

"We've still got a warrant on Scott Freed, right?" Gunther said. "He's a killer. I'll just go around with the posters and have a coffee or a beer with them. Drop off the wanted posters. Freed's been spotted all over the region."

"YES! That's it! And…and the newspapers too. Stop in to see the editors of the newspapers too. Leave a wanted poster. Ask them about missing people. Yes."

Chapter 15
THE HOT AND COLD CRUSADE FOR SCOTT FREED

With his feet up on the windowsill of his rented room, Gunther leaned back in a wicker chair and opened a store-bought bound book with blank pages designed for diaries and journals. The thin, wooden covers were tied up by a red ribbon. The pages were not blank however as the first few pages were filled with notes and ideas from Gustav, along with a collection of missing people and their cities and counties, and what little he knew about them from gossip, intelligence, and the area newspapers that Gustav wisely collected.

"Sixteen people," Gunther muttered aloud, perusing the information.

Sixteen, all in Northeast Texas. There were men and women. A few ages listed, young to old. Two were obviously Indians. People always turned up missing with some frequency in rural areas, dead from an accident or old age, or disease. Animals would often carry off the carcasses. But, some of these people just disappeared from inside their houses. The sixteenth was poor old Noot. There was no easily identifiable clue connecting them all together. What of Oklahoma? Of Arkansas? Who was missing from there?

On the nearby tabletop was a stack of wanted posters for Scott Freed. He thumbed through the pile. He decided that while he certainly would investigate the missing person mysteries, and he would also try, if at all possible, to capture this murderer Scott Freed. Gunther already knew that Freed was once a petty criminal in Sherman, Texas, before he became a traveling dress salesman for a fashion company in Dallas. He sold his wares in Paris and all over in the area. But, drunk one night five months earlier, he killed a man in Paris in a fight at a county fair over some stupid squabble nobody sober would fight to the death over.

Freed fled. Authorities suspected him, and according to gossip, he'd picked up with various thugs in the region and was known to commit a series of big and small crimes like burglary, theft, and even robbery. He didn't care to rob banks, but rather, Freed robbed high-end department stores. He was forty-two and heavy-set. He wore glasses. He had black hair.

Inside Gustav's missing person's book was a check, an expense draft from the City of Paris. $20. There was a note attached with a paper clip.

"Dear Knight. Use this king's ransom from our coffers to fund your crusade. –Chief Gustav Henri."

"Crusade," Gunther said, with a chuckle.

He decided he would not let Scott Freed go scot-free. If he could, he would investigate missing people *AND* apprehend this Scott Freed.

Once Casey was loaded into the horse freight car, Gunther

and Stinky Moses walked across the rail station platform to the passenger cars.

"No news this morning on Eskimo Noot?" Gunther asked.

"No news. They are still searching. I reckon he's been gobbled up by wild pigs or something."

"Could be."

"Good luck to you, Gunth," Stinky said, looked off to the left of Gunther's face.

Gunther knew better than to try and shake his hand. Stinky checked his pocket watch.

"See ya, Stink. Keep Paris safe."

"Yeah. Uuh. Yeah. Yeah, well. I gotta go. There's been a report this morning of grave robberies at the Ojala Cemetery. I gotta ride up there and see what's what with what."

"Okay. *Adios, amigo,*" Gunther said, lightly tapping the side of Stinky's upper arm.

He didn't wait to see Stinky dust off the spot on his arm. He just knew he would. Gunther stepped up and in the 1:15 to Tulsa, Oklahoma. He took a seat and put his saddlebags on the floor by his feet. From the bags he pulled out a book, *Ivanhoe* by Sir Walter Scott. He picked up where he left off the night before...

"Chivalry! Why, maiden, she is the nurse of pure and high affection, the stay of the oppressed, the redresser of grievances, the curb of the power of the tyrant. Nobility were but an empty name without her, and liberty finds the best protection in her lance and her sword."

The train jolted forward, rocked and ground metal wheels on metal rails. His head bumped backward, and he looked out the window at Paris, Texas. He saw the transparent reflection of his face, and through it and beyond, he saw Stinky staring at the train from a distance. He rarely got a "face-to-face" with Stink, even this far apart. Then, he watched Stinky, his comrade in arms for many years climb on his horse. He was so tall that he could almost throw a leg over the saddle and not step into a stirrup. Gunther could not remotely guess at that moment, he wouldn't see his girlfriend, Ida, again, his friends, nor Paris for 20 years!

Tulsa in the Oklahoma Territory was a good place to start and he would work his way south, burg by burg. There was only one federal marshal appointed in the Indian Territory, E.D. Nix. He supervised about 150 deputies. Gunther was bound for their office in Tulsa. What would he find out about these missing people? Would he find Scott Freed?

When the 1:15 stopped in Tulsa, Gunther collected his saddlebags and stepped off the train. There, he spotted a familiar face!

"Zip Hollar!" Gunther declared.

"That's right, young feller," Zip said, shaking Gunther's hand. "I hear tell you have some work to do up here."

"I do, I do. Come down here and let me get my horse." And the two walked toward the freight end of the train. "What brings you to the train station?"

"You do, son. The Association has sent me here to help you."

"They have?"

"Yes. Listen, young feller, I might well be dead if it wasn't for your quick thinking back at the Sarasota spread. As you might imagine, Frenchie wired our headquarters and said you were coming up and you might need a local guide."

"I could always use a guide."

A pair of porter's walked Casey down the gangplank. The pair and the horse headed for the street.

"I'm tied up round front. I have an accounting office in Hugo, but it pretty much runs itself. So, I am here at your command, until they get all stonewalled and stymied about something. Where to first?"

"Marshal's Office. Know where that is?"

"I do, sir. I certainly do."

After a casual, twenty-minute ride through Tulsa, a large city with wide dirt streets, and numerous one- and two-story buildings, but mostly one story. They stopped at a single-story, dirty, wooden structure, with a narrow door and a few windows facing the street. A small, wood-burned, engraved sign graced the place with "Federal Marshal's Office, Tulsa. To the right of it read "US Post Office, Tulsa, Oklahoma."

They tied off their horses and walked into a lobby full of desks, Gunther toting his saddlebags. Zip seemed to know everyone, saying hi and shaking hands.

"There's Bill Tilghman right there. You know Bill?" Zip asked Gunther.

"Ah, no. Heard of him. One of the Guardians of Three."

"Three Guardsman," Zip corrected, speaking of the reputation of Bill and two other deputies, Henry "Heck" Thomas and Chris Madsen.

Zip grabbed Gunther's elbow and escorted him through the lobby. Gunther glanced over at a tall, older, stocky man wearing a too-small plaid hat, and a too-small suit sitting alone by the front wall.

"Bill, what you doing here?" Zip asked Tilghman.

"Passin' through, Zip. How the hell are ya?"

"Fair to middling. Hey, I'd like ya to meet somebody. This here's a deputy from Paris, Texas. Johann Gunther. He...he saved my life down there at that Sarasota Ranch shoot-out."

"Ohhh, I heard about that. Who hasn't? That is some mighty fine work, son. What brings you all the way up here?" Bill asked.

"Well, this, for one thing." Gunther dug into his saddlebag and pulled out a wanted poster for Scott Freed.

"Scott Freed," Bill said, "yeah, we heard of him. Killed a man in Paris. He's supposed to be up here now, somewhere, foolin' around in the Territory."

"Bill, we gotta go!" Another deputy shouted from the back of the office.

"Okay, I'll take this," Bill said, folding the poster into his pocket. "You got more, right?"

"Oh yeah. A passel."

"Leave em around. Good luck, fellers." He left in a hurry.

"Man's a legend," Zip said, watching him leave out the back door. Then he walked to a nearby desk.

"And here's less of a legend, Deputy Walker Stell," Zip said.

"Sit down here, you old fart," Stell said.

The men did sit and they talked about Scott Freed. Gunther noticed that Stell kept looking over Zip's shoulder at the man with the small, plaid hat.

"I wonder," Gunther said, "I wonder...do you have any missing people round here. People just up and disappearing? We just lost a railroad security guard off a Frisco yard down by me, and we can't find hide-ner-hair of em."

"Is he an Indian?" a man asked from behind.

Gunther turned in his chair to see two Indians, well dressed, with "Indian Police" badges on their suit jackets. They stepped around to the left of the desk.

"No, well, actually, an Eskimo."

"Eskeemo!" Stell declared. "From...up...up there in...ahh... Eskeemo...lands?"

"Yeah. Alaska."

"Might be the KKK. They're liken to kill anybody that ain't white these days," Stell said.

"Might be," Gunther said.

"We have had several people disappear on the Indian Territory," the man said. "I am Delaware Longhat."

They shook hands.

"We have several women and men," he continued. "A baby. We also had dead bodies stolen. People like to rob our graves, and they steal artifacts. Jewelry. Gold teeth. Weapons. Whatever they can find. They sell them up North. But in the last few months? They took some bodies too."

"These bodies been dead long?" Gunther asked quickly but didn't really know why he asked.

"No. Not really. A little while dead."

Zip spoke up with what he heard at the Anti-Horse Thief Association meetings, about some people missing all over the region. Gunther didn't take any notes. He would remember every word.

"It's the KKK, I tell ya," Stell said.

"But, a few of the dead are white folks too," Zip said.

Another deputy wandered over and joined in, "Last month Ella Bankstead lost her son. He was only thirty years old. Docs said some kind of disease. They buried him on the family plot on their farm. Old Man Bankstead heard some noise one night and saw three fellers carry off something from their little family cemetery. He got his gun and a torch and ran up there. They stole the boy, coffin and all."

"Grave robbers," Stell said.

"They took the whole kit and caboodle."

The Indian police nodded.

"Well, we'd best go," Gunther said after a bit. He handed the Indians and Stell the wanted posters for Scott Freed, and Zip and Gunther left the office.

They walked down the porch steps and over to their horses. They untied the reins from the front post.

"You know anybody in the KKK?" Gunther suddenly asked Zip. They stood between their horses.

"I think everybody knows somebody, somehow, somewhere in the KKK," Zip said.

"You know anybody that would sit down and talk to us?"

"Not without risking their life," Zip said. "But maybe...."

"I'm in the KKK," a deep voice came from the front porch of the office.

They turned and looked up. It was the big man in the small, plaid hat. He'd followed them out.

"I heard you in there," the man said.

"Who are you, mister?" Zip asked.

"My name is Christian Freed. I'm up here from Dallas, Texas. I heard you in there."

"Yes?" Zip said.

"You are looking for my son, Scott Freed," he said.

Chapter 16
PORK CHOP, PEACE PIE

"The lovers of the chase say that the hare feels more agony during the pursuit of the greyhounds, than when she is struggling in their fangs."

—Walter Scott, *Ivanhoe*

Gunther eyed up this Christian Freed, not sure if he might draw a gun on them. But he wasn't wearing a typical, visible gun belt, and his somewhat tight suit didn't show off a shoulder holster or gun belt. Maybe a derringer?

"Well, Christian Freed," Gunther said, "it's about dinner time. I'm starving. There's a pork chop house right across the street. What say we have a beer and a chop?"

"I'll be damned if I break bread with a man bound to hunt down and kill my son."

"Well now, hold on, Mr. Freed. I am not aiming to kill your son," Gunther said. "No. Not at all. I just want to bring him to court, bring him to justice."

"Justice?" Freed said.

"That's right. Justice."

"Justice in the form of a rope. A rope a breakin' his neck with a sandbag attached."

Gunther shook his head. What would Stinky say? Or Gustav?

"When a man kills another man, sir, there is a reckoning. A... call for...for an examination. That's why I am here. What are you here for?"

"I am here to find my son. To save him."

"Mr. Freed. Mr. Freed. Me too. If there's any saving, I am for saving. Now come on, why don't you join us across the street. You don't have to break any bread in two, just eat a pork chop. Okay?"

"I know this young feller, Mr. Freed," Zip said, "you can trust his word. You come on. Chops are on me."

Three beers and three pork chop dinners later, Zip lit up an ivory pipe.

"I am thinking of asking you to join us and look for your son," Gunther said. "You might be able to get him to surrender."

Mr. Freed rubbed his eyes. He was in his late sixties. Once his cap and coat were off, he revealed a receding, curly-gray head of hair and was quite overweight. His face was stubbled with ignored growth. His teeth were about half-rotted out.

"I don't know what I am gonna do. He was trouble as a teen. But the boy got a job with a clothing factory in Dallas, and he seemed to be okay. They started making and selling shirts, then pants, then ladies' dresses. I worried when they sent him on the road. He didn't do well on the road. He can... he, he loses control."

"He's a forty-two-year-old man," Gunther said. "Not a boy. It's not your fault. And he got real drunk the night he shot that feller."

"I know. I know. He is a drinker. He likes to smoke some kind of green, plant shit from Mexico too. Goddamn Mexicans. Look, I am retired. Mailman. Postal service. I don't have much to do with myself now. I sit around and think. And I can't get him outta my mind. I just sit around and hear stories and...his uncle lives up here near Tulsa. His favorite uncle. I had to come up here and see if he's here. I came here to ask the Federales about him."

"He's been seen in the area. This uncle...he in the KKK too?" Zip asked.

The man nodded, yes.

"Scott knows the country. He sold clothes all up through here," Freed said. "Far as Benton, Arkansas."

"What stories have you heard?" Zip asked.

He was silent.

"Klan stories?" Gunther guessed.

"Yeah. Yup," he said with a sigh. "I am a member. I don't do much. I don't do what all they do. But I hear a lot at our meetings...and down in Dallas it's not like big, official meetings, and we don't wear all that white shit. I don't. Just...there's just picnics and get-togethers in bars. Bible study. I heard that Scott was up here, making money doing something with the Klan."

"How does the Klan make money...doing something? Doing something...legal?" Gunther asked.

"Well, we have many businesses and we work together on business deals. It's a...society. A social group. But the barnyard talk is, he's up to no good, up here."

"Making money doing what? Robbery?" Gunther asked.

"No."

"Stealin' horses and cattle?" Zip asked.

"No. I...I don't know, but I don't think so. Something else."

The waitress came by.

"Darlin', three more beers," Zip said.

"Scott was close to my brother, and he lives around here, so..."

"What's *his* name?" Gunther asked.

"Luther Freed."

"You been there yet? His house?"

"No. He's got a place out away from the city."

"We need to ride out to Luther Freed's and see if your son is there," Zip said.

Mr. Freed stopped eating and gritted his teeth and squinted. It was a wet squint. He shook his head from side to side as if to say no, but instead he said, "Yeah."

"Okay," Gunther said.

"This has got to come to an end," Freed said.

"Okay."

They ate a bit and sipped a few more beers.

"We will go then. Tomorrow," Gunther said. "We'll stop nearby. We'll stop and you ride in first to talk...you got a horse?"

"No. I took a train up here."

"Okay, we'll get you a horse. You ride in first, see your brother. We'll wait a ways back. See if your son is there. We'll bring that deputy marshal with us we were talkin' to..."

"He's a good man," Zip interrupted.

"...he's got jurisdiction, and we'll just see if he's there. Okay? See what Luther says, if he's not there. But if Scott is there, you can talk to him, tell him to give up the goat?" Gunther said.

Freed nodded.

"You in a hotel?" Gunther asked, concluding so because Freed had no luggage with him.

"Yes."

"Okay. Tomorrow morning we'll do this. Listen, Mr. Freed, I don't mean to kill your son. Just arrest him. That is all. That is all I want to do. That's why I need you to talk to him if we find him. I am asking for your help."

"Okay."

The time was set to meet across the street at the Marshal's Office the next morning at 9 a.m. The three men stepped outside the restaurant. Freed walked off. Zip dug into his teeth with a toothpick like a gold miner.

"You trust him?" Zip asked.

"I don't know."

They watched him until he turned off at a street corner.

"I reckon..." Gunther said, "reckon what exactly goes on in a KKK, Bible study class?"

"Hell, if I know," Zip said.

"Seems contradictory. Hmmm. It is all very medieval," Gunther said.

"Medieval?"

"Chief Henri told me once when I hired on, that America was in its Medieval Times. The...era. Period. Ya know...times."

"Kinda so. But we'll crawl out of it, I 'spect," Zip said, spitting out the last small, chuck of chop.

"Hey, son, your horse is down over there!" Zip said.

"Yeah," Gunther said calmly. "He likes to lay down now and again. I left him too long."

Zip laughed. Casey was down on the dirt street, on his belly

111

and still upright beside Zip's horse.

"Rough on the saddle, ain't it?"

"I hook the stirrups around the pommel and keep all my good stuff on the right side. He usually always gets down on his left."

"Ha! Trusting soul?"

They started across the street.

"Casey, let's go!" Gunther shouted.

The horse's big head turned and looked at him, then he stood up and shook.

"I'm sorry I left you soooo long, Case," Gunther said, rubbing the horse's neck. "I'm sorry."

He threw the saddlebags over the horse, unhooked the stirrups from the pommel, and tightened the cinch. The horse just snorted and wildly shook his head fluffing everything right back into place.

Chapter 17
FATHERS, BROTHERS, AND SONS OF BITCHES

"As for man, his days are numbered, whatever he might do, it is but wind."

—Anonymous, *The Epic of Gilgamesh*

Christian Freed still remembered the way out to his brother's cabin, even though it had been many years. Stell and Freed sat up front in a two-horse team, buckboard wagon. Gunther was atop Casey, and Zip Hollar rode his horse. The ride out to Luther Freed's started out on flat bushland, but the trail turned into some rolling hills and trees soon enough. Freed was still garbed in that same tight, bad suit and hat, and Gunther could not detect an obvious weapon on him.

Gunther stopped their little caravan a ways out, and he rode in for a distant look at the property. It was beautiful, located down in a small valley with a backdrop of thick trees set the single-story log cabin, with a matching wood barn behind it. It was a large stretch, with manicured grounds and smoke lofting out of one of several chimneys. Some cattle and goats wandered in several fenced areas and well-kept fencing surrounded the living area. Gunther returned to the little troop.

"Zip," he said, "how about you swing wide around the north side and set up a watch. Just in case Scott is there and makes a run out the back into the woods, just in case."

"Okay."

"Fire, twice real fast in the air if he does."

Freed squirmed a bit in his seat at the word "fire."

Zip picked his way down a rough slope and ducked under some low branches before he disappeared. They gave him about five minutes, then the rest slowly rode into the small valley. Gunther unhooked the leather straps on the triggers of both his pistols.

"Hold it!"

A man walked out the front door holding a double-barrel shotgun.

"Hold it! Who goes there?" he repeated.

"Luther! Luther, it's me, Christian. Your brother," he shouted.

"Luther, I am Deputy Marshal Stell for the Oklahoma Territory," Stell shouted. "We sure need to talk to you."

"About what?"

Gunter looked at all the front windows for movement.

"Scott ain't here."

For Gunther, that was a wrong thing to say. How would he know they were there for Scott? Because his father was there?

"Have you seen Scott," Gunther asked.

"Who the hell are you?"

"I am a police officer from Paris, Texas, and we sure need to talk to Scott."

"Paris, Texas, huh?"

"Yes, sir."

"You got shit fer jurisdiction here as far as I'm concerned," Luther said. "You are just a Tex-ass invader."

"I'm his jurisdiction," Stell said.

"Is Scotty here?" Christian said. He got down off the buckboard and stood between it and Gunther.

"It would be nice if you would point that shotgun elsewhere," Stell said. "We mean you no harm, Mister Freed."

"Sheeet," the brother said.

And with that, two rapid pistol gunshots went off in the distance behind the house. As Gunther looked that way, he was suddenly airborne. Christian had reached up and grabbed his arm and yanked Gunther right off Casey. Gunther landed hard and face-first on the ground.

Luther lifted his shotgun at them and Stell rolled into the back part of the buckboard wagon. Pellets hit the wooden side but did not pass through.

Gunther was down and stunned, hat askew over his face. He rolled over to see Christian get aboard Casey! And Casey revolted a bit, stutter-stepped some, but the big man forced the horse off to the north. Gunther's two pistols, unlooped, were now gone from his holsters as he had turned nearly upside down during the fall.

"Casey! Sleep!" Gunther shouted.

The horse, in the beginning of a gallop, stopped cold. Christian flew right off. Feet over head. Casey laid right down on his side, as commanded.

Another shotgun blast at the wagon, as Luther marched forward, it was the second of a double-barrel gun. Gunther could see Luther break the gun in half to reload. He felt around in the grass searching for his guns.

Stell sat up, revolver out and raised up and poured lead into Luther. Luther crunched up, and then spread his arms and body wide like he was hit with a fit. Shotgun shells and the open gun went up in the air and then spun down.

"I've got to get my boy!" Christian said, stumbling to his feet. He started running with a bad limp to the north, around the fence.

"You alright?" Gunther shouted to Stell.

"Yeah! You?" Stell stood up in the wagon bed.

"I think so."

"Is your horse dead?"

"He's playing dead," Gunther said. "He's okay. Army horse." Gunther tasted a sudden rush of metallic flavor in his mouth. He rubbed his nose. It was numb and profusely bleeding.

"We got to get over to Zip," Stell said.

"I know...I know...here's one. Here's the other." Gunther found his guns on the ground.

Stell got back up in the front seat.

"Go! Go! Go!" Gunther said. "I'll be there. CASEY!"

The wagon took off north. The horse got up. Gunther assumed that he would be a better chaser in the woods on horseback and the wagon might get bogged down.

"Come on, boy," and the horse ran to him. Like a vet cavalryman he leaped aboard and took off for the north too, then east at a full gallop. He quickly passed the bouncing wagon on the rugged landscape.

Zip was gone. There were three trails into the woods. Gunther stopped Casey at the breakaway point.

A gunshot in the woods! Too deep and he couldn't tell which trail to take. Casey's front feet stomped like a frustrated racehorse.

They took off down the middle trail. It was a triple canopy growth path, dark from tall trees. And they raced and looked for any sign. He soon came to a clearing. Nothing.

"Zip! Zip!" Gunther cried out.

"Over here!"

Gunther saw Zip on his horse, waving a hand in the sloping clearing to the southwest. He seemed fine. He had Casey trot over to him.

"He's gone. He's trackable, but he's gone. Dead run out the barn. On a fast mount. I mean like a bat outta hell's cave. What happened to yer face, son?"

"Freed yanked me off my horse when you shot, and I gracefully landed...nose first. Freed got on Casey to...to get at his son, but me and Casey know some tricks. He's afoot back there. Luther came at us shootin' a double-barrel, and Stell killed him."

"Damn you say! I was a bit too far out watchin' the spread," Zip regretted. "First I saw of him, he galloped out the back of the barn. In this dense bush, he's trackable, but we need men to do it. He'll have about a 4-hour lead."

"What all's that way?"

"Nothin'. Woods. Woods to Arkansas."

Gunther nodded. He put a hand to his nose. He worked his jaw around.

"Here ya go, son," Zip said, and handed him a white hand-kerchief from a pocket. "I'll get back to Tulsa to get some men. I'll call out the local Thief Association, too. We got dogs. You and Stell clean up here," Zip said.

"Okay."

Zip took off at a fast clip, back by the cabin and back to town.

"Looks like Scott Freed got away scot-free, again," Gunther said aloud to Casey.

Gunther and Casey trotted back to the cabin. He saw Stell and Freed loading Luther's body into the back of the buckboard wagon. When Gunther dismounted, Freed acted sheepish.

"I..." Freed started to say.

"Just...no," Gunther said, waving his left hand at him while his right hand held the once-white and now-red cloth to his nose.

"Zip stopped and told us," Stell said.

"Yeah." Gunther said, and noted his jaw really hurt now. He looked the team of wagon horses over. No pellets had hit them.

"And now, my brother is a dead man," Freed said.

"I haven't shot a man in six years," Stell said. "And I am none too happy about it."

"Why do you suppose," Gunther asked, "he came out mean and gunnin' like that? He saw you."

"I don't know, deputy."

Reins in hand, Gunther walked down to the cabin. He let Casey free by the porch and stepped inside. He stood in the doorway and couldn't help but ask himself, "What would Gustav look for?"

The cabin was neat. Clean, with a hallway and two rooms. He walked into the other room, and it was obviously Luther's bedroom. Many personal artifacts. A rack of clothes hung from a wall. On the rack, in the middle of shirts, coats and pants, hung a clean, white pressed KKK outfit.

He stepped out on a back porch. There was bedding on the floor of it and leather bags. Gunther turned the bags over. Clothing. Ammo. Two pistols. Soap. Razor. Hair cream. Signs of a traveler. Scott Freed's baggage. He stuffed everything back into the bags, except for some papers, which he shoved into his vest pocket.

The back of the house was rutted with many wagon-wheel tracks, back and forth to the barn. He walked to the barn. There was an odd scent in the air. Once inside he could see that half of the building was a barn for horses and the other half looked like a workshop and office. All the windows were open. He walked in and was repulsed by a bad, powerful chemical smell. He clutched down on the handkerchief over his nose. He saw a large wooden table. But each corner of the table had long handles attached, like a medical stretcher he'd seen in the Army. There weren't many tools around of a carpenter, or a farmer. A small wooden wheel of thin hoses sat atop a desk. On another table sat six large glass containers of…Gunther stepped closer to read…

"Formaldehyde."

The source of the stink. He'd seen it, smelled it, and heard of it before from the doctors at Ft. Sill, Oklahoma. At times, when a soldier died and the body needed shipping home, the Army undertaker would flood the body with formaldehyde. His eyes started to water. He coughed. It was no wonder all the workshop windows and shutters were open, and this workroom had a big, back door. It too was open, along with the big double barn doors.

He walked out back. He saw a hand pump, water well. He saw large wooden barrels tipped over around the well. He stood a few up and looked inside. All were brown stained.

"Gunther?" Stell called out.

"Yeah, back here."

Freed and Stell walked into the barn.

"Whewieee! What's all this rank to high heaven?" Stell asked with a grimace, when Gunther came back inside.

"Did this Luther work as an undertaker? Work at a funeral home?" Gunther asked.

"Not that I know of," Stell said. "But folks out here will do anything to make a little money. But we deal with all the city undertakers, and he wasn't one of them."

Gunther looked at Freed and Freed shrugged his shoulders.

"Your brother ever in the Army?" Gunther asked.

"No."

"This stuff here, formaldehyde. The Army use it to suck out the blood and pump it into dead soldiers to ship them home. It stops bodies from decomposing for a while. Embalming. They called it embalming. I don't know of any other use," Gunther said. "Farming? Ranching?"

"Nope. It stinks like...well...like nothing I ever smelled. Paint? Turpentine maybe," Stell said. "Round here, people keep their dead in their homes, in their parlor rooms, for a showin', then bury em right away. So there's no need for much preservation."

"Yeah," Gunther said, still looking around. He opened a desk drawer. He found syringes inside. He took one new syringe, put it in a case he found and put it in his pocket. "Yeah, stinks. Luther was in the KKK, you know. You killed a KKK man."

"Shit!" Stell said. "That'll be some kind of trouble."

"Is that some kind of trouble?" Gunther asked Freed.

"Ah, it is. Yeah. It could be. Depends on where you live. Up

120

here? Could be."

"Shee-iiiit," Stell said.

Gunther pulled a pocketknife out and carefully carved a label off one of the glass containers. The formaldehyde was shipped from Atlanta, Georgia. That label, too, went into his pocket. He cut a small section of the hose from its reel.

The three walked out and over to the back porch of the house, Gunther picked up Scott's two leather bags and stuck his face in each.

"What?" Stell asked.

"Smells a bit…like the formaldehyde."

"My son sold dresses! My boy was no doctor," Freed said.

"No sir, that he wasn't." Gunther wished he could sit down and talk with Gustav right away.

"Here," Gunther said, shoving the bags into Freed's hands. "Here's your kid's bags."

"My kid's bags," he mumbled.

"We gotta get outta here. Get back and warm up a posse," Stell said.

"Yeah, you two go on. I'll catch up," Gunther said, and he sat in a rocking chair on the back porch, pinching off his nose.

Freed and Stell started to leave, but Freed stopped.

"I'm sorry that I…"

"Nope," Gunther said staring off at the backwoods, line of trees, with his right hand up and holding the bloody handkerchief like a small flag. "Just, just nope."

Chapter 18

THE DOCTOR PRESCRIBES DEATH

"...having once seen him put forth his strength in battle, methinks I could know him again among a thousand warriors. He rushes into the fray as if he were summoned to a banquet. There is more than mere strength—there seems as if the whole soul and spirit of the champion were given to every blow which he deals upon his enemies..."

—Walter Scott, *Ivanhoe*

As Gunther rode up to the Marshal's Office, the men and bloodhounds were about ready to leave for the hunt. Christian Freed was standing up on the sidewalk, watching the preparations.

"Comin'?" Zip asked.

"I've some things I *have* to attend to here, Zip. I got to wire the Chief..."

"And we need a signed statement about the shootin'," Stell interrupted.

"I'll do that right now," Gunther said as he tied off Casey

and stepped up the stairs.

"Use my desk," Stell said. "Witness statements, top right drawer."

The posse tore off.

"They won't let me go with them," Freed said, standing on the sidewalk.

"I wonder why?" Gunther said sarcastically and walked by him and into the office.

He took a seat at Stell's desk in the lobby and pulled open the drawer. He found a "Federal Marshal's Office, Witness Statement" form and a fountain pen. Gustav told him that the British and French police used the "who, what, where, when, how and why" questions to write a police report. Answer them. Gustav said to always use short sentences. Gustav also said never use pronouns, use nouns *every time* to identify people in each short sentence. He wrote down what had happened at the Luther Freed property. Short. Concise. Detailed.

Then he wrote out an even shorter telegraph to his Chief.

Chief. –(Stop)

Hunted Scott Freed in Tulsa. –(Stop)

His uncle Luther Freed tried to kill us and deputy marshal shot the uncle –(Stop)

Posse chasing Scott Freed now –(Stop)

More missing people up here –(Stop)

Formaldehyde and funeral items found at Freed cabin –(Stop)

Formaldehyde purchased at Hillary Brothers Chemists in Atlanta Georgia –(Stop)

Sold to farmer Luther Freed, not an undertaker –(Stop)

Mystery to me and investigating this –(Stop)

KKK involved with Freed family –(Stop)
Wire back at this Tulsa Office –(Stop)

He scratched out the KKK line, realizing several, telegraph personal would be reading, prepping and sending the message. He wished he could call Gustav, but there probably wasn't a telephone in Tulsa yet and, even if so, there were none in Paris.

Gunther blew the ink on the paper, then waved it in the air. He walked over to an older marshal and laid the statement on the desk. The man nodded. He eyed up Gunther's bruised face and caked blood and smiled a wry grin. Gunther folded the wire announcement into his pants pocket.

"You might wash off a bit there, Paris. Yer face is one big scab," came a voice from the left. It was Bill *Tilghman*. He pointed toward a back room.

Gunther did. He washed off his face and enjoyed the cool water upon it. He looked in the mirror. Big scrape and bruise on about one-fourth of his forehead down to his nose. Maybe a broken nose? His upper teeth hurt, but they were all there upon his inspection. He almost threw Zip's handkerchief away in a trash bucket, but saw that it was embroidered in a corner. He'd ruined it for sure, though. He soaked it. He squeezed it out, but the brownish-red stained deep into the fabric.

When he came out he found Tilghman waiting. He draped the handkerchief over Stell's chair back to dry.

"Heard you had a helluva morning," Bill said. He put the statement back down on the desk.

"We did. Where is the biggest funeral home in Tulsa?"

"Nelson's. Four streets south of here on 12th Street," Tilghman said. "Turn right on Connector Avenue, right there, you'll see the big sign. You can walk it. Put yer horse in our stable round back. Tell ya what. I'll walk with ya because I have to pass by there."

Gunther stepped outside and guided Casey around back. The horse needed some oats and hay anyway. A well-dressed Indian took Casey and promised to brush him off. Then Gunther met up with the famous lawman out front. He knew Tilghman had been a buffalo hunter, gunfighter and lawman in Dodge City and a friend to Wyatt Earp. Bill had survived the infamous Gray County War.

"I figure it might be more helpful around here if I went with ya, you being from Texas and all."

Gunther told Tilghman more of what happened and what he'd seen at the Freed house.

"That is very strange; let's see what they say at Nelson's."

When they entered the business, Tilghman guided Gunther through the lobby of coffins for sale and into the head office.

"Well, hello, Bill," Mr. Nelson said.

"Hello. This is Deputy Johann Gunther from Paris, Texas. He's hunting down a murderer, and he has a few questions for ya."

"Oh? A murderer," Nelson said. They all sat down. "I...well... what can I do for you?"

"What do you make of this?" Gunther said.

He pulled out a section of the hose he cut off, the syringe he found and the label off the glass container.

"When I was in the Army, the doctors and undertakers used formaldehyde in bodies when they had to ship them home," Gunther said.

"Yes. Where did you find all this?" Nelson said.

"At Luther Freed's barn. We were hunting a fugitive, his nephew, this morning and we had to shoot Luther."

"Dead?"

"Dead," Tilghman said. "He shot at them with a double-barrel."

"Oooooh."

"They already brought his body into your back room a little while ago. Jackie has it downstairs."

Nelson nodded. He looked over the items on his desk.

"That's...that's unusual," Nelson said.

"What do you make of it all, Eddy?" Tilghman asked.

"This is embalming equipment. This is what we use to ship bodies home to relatives. This Luther Freed...I know him, his wife died about five years ago. But he is no undertaker. Maybe taxidermy."

"Taxidermy?" Tilghman said.

"Taxidermists use chemicals such as alum and borax. Draws out the moisture. Maybe, formaldehyde. You can't preserve and eat any food with any of that in it. I wouldn't. You wouldn't use any of this to preserve foods. But in taxidermy? Maybe. Yes."

"Anything at Luther's that looks like he was a taxidermist?" Tilghman asked Gunther. "Heads? Antlers? Hooves of any sorts? Those hooves are popular coat hooks these days?"

"No."

The three stared at each other for a few seconds, then Eddy Nelson stood up. Tilghman and Gunther stood too. They thanked Nelson and stepped outside.

"Well Paris, I'm going that-a-way," Tilghman said, as he pointed away from the Marshal's Office. "Good luck with everything. Need any help? Let us know."

"Thank you, sir."

126

"And oh...just so you know," Tilghman said, "since yer runnin' into the KKK here, that Nelson feller, he's some kind of Grand Realm leader, or some such title, of the KKK here."

Gunther just stared at him. Tilghman tipped his hat and walked away.

As soon as the lawmen left, Eddy Nelson mounted the stairs of the funeral home to the second-story apartments above. A door stood open and he walked in. A lanky man in a red smoking jacket sat on a couch reading a thick book.

"Doctor," Nelson said.

"Good afternoon, Ed."

Nelson motioned for the man to walk over to the windows with him.

"See that young man walking there? He was just in with Bill Tilghman. He's a deputy up from Paris, Texas. He said they shot and killed Luther Freed."

"Luther? Good God, why?" the man asked.

"Don't know exactly. Didn't want to ask too much. Chasing a fugitive, the Texan said. It'll all be in the newspaper tomorrow, so I didn't want to sound too needy."

Gunther crossed the street and the man got a look at his profile.

"He found the embalming fluid, the hoses and the needles out at Freed's. He was asking about why Luther Freed would have such a rig."

"Oh. Oh my, did he now? What does Tilghman know?"

"Nothing. I think he was just helping the kid out and walked him over. I told them that maybe Luther was doing taxidermy."

"Brilliant," the man said. "Henceforth, methinks we

should leave a taxidermy book at every one of our sites. Quite brilliant, Eddy."

"He strikes me as young, smart and stubborn. Ex-Army. He actually had a label off of a formaldehyde jar," Eddy said quietly, watching Gunther walk into a restaurant. "I think we ought to kill him."

"Hmmmm," Dr Trafalgar said. "We could use a tall, young blond man on the list. Yes."

Chapter 19
THE MUMMY MAN

Gunther ordered a cup of coffee and pulled out the Scott Freed papers he'd collected from Freed's clothing bag. One was an old letter from his mother. Next was another letter from a woman, a religious and amorous letter of sorts, dated two years earlier. Another was a list of names. Single names, and a city beside each one. There was a line through about six names, the most recent one being "Scotchey's—Tulsa." He'd seen that name before, when he was riding into town. It was a big, two-story brick store. The next name, unscratched, was "Williams and Son—Guthrie." Guthrie, Oklahoma. Gunther bet it was a clothing, dry goods store, as all the names had that ring to them.

The waitress brought the coffee.

"Thanks, ma'am. You have a store here in Tulsa…Scotchey's?"

"Yes, we do."

"And… was it robbed? Lately? Do you know?"

"Yes, it was," she said. "About…ohhh…two weeks ago."

"Masked men, I reckon?"

"One man. He did have a mask."

"Are you the son of a bitch that shot our friend?" Came a growling voice.

The waitress backed away. Gunther glanced up and looked three men over. Three big men, in their forties or fifties, dirty, unshaven and badly dressed, each wrapped in gun belts, had strutted in the front door and stood a few feet from his table. Gunther sighed with an air of tired disgust.

"I myself did not shoot your friend, no. But he came out of his cabin with a shotgun and started shooting at us. Without barely a word spoke."

"Who's us?"

"A federal marshal, and his very own brother."

"What marshal?"

Gunther slid his seat back and leaned back in the chair. In doing so, the sides of his jacket flipped open, exposing his two pistols. All three men looked down at them, then back up at his face. Bruised and freshly scabbed, he looked like death.

"Fellers, we are in a very dainty place here where normal people come to sup on lunch and dinner. This ain't no border town, or bordello, to spin up a mess in. Whatcha want?" Gunther said, reaching for his coffee cup with his left hand.

Silence. What would Gustav say? What would Gustav do?

"Now we can all have a seat here and have some coffee, and I'm buyin'..."

"We ain't drinkin' with you, you son of a bitch. What marshal was it?"

"You could read about it in the newspapers tomorrow. Or... march your little chain gang down to the Marshal's Office and ask them."

130

"I'm askin' *YOU*, peach fuzz!"

Gunther stood. He stood so fast the chair slid back inches. The men flinched but did not touch their guns. Gunther noted that lack of reflex.

"Peach...fuzz..." Gunther half smiled and chuckled, then got real serious. "I've seen and done more in my peach fuzz lifetime than you've seen or can even imagine. For one thing, you know how many times some dipshits came around me looking for revenge over some other dipshit they knew was shot?"

Their eyes widened.

"A lot. Most...died. Now, this has been a very...long...day already. You three can do something. Right now! Or leave."

The three men stood still, eyes cutting to one another.

"Yeah," Gunther said. "Three stupid, bully boys. Walk in here. No plan. All big talk and big mouths with bad teeth."

The three backed away a bit.

"You'd..." one said.

"*Huh?*" Gunther said, goading...

"You'd...you'd better leave Tulsa."

"Fact of business is I *am* leaving Tulsa. Tomorrow. And it ain't on account of you three turds."

They left. Gunther realized that everyone in the place was looking at him. The three men stood outside the glass door and windows, arguing. He sat back down but cleared his jacket sides of both guns, unhooking the leather straps over the trigger. He watched them. Barely blinking. He made ready to flip the table over. Were they planning a return? Or resigning to leave? Their head shaking and grimaces made them look like they were resigning. He heard one yell, "He didn't do it, Chris!"

Then, they walked out of sight. He took a breath. He was

steaming with a tired, impatient anger. He guessed if they'd left and there was no shooting in the end of a confrontation, that is what Gustav would have wanted. Quell it. Quelled. But deep inside, he wanted to shoot them down. Was this the...the "gun burn," Gustav warned him about?

The waitress poured him more coffee.

"You know them?"

"Yes," she said. "Bobby Dunlap. Chris Ritchter. Winston Dolittle. They live around here."

"Bobby Dunlap. Chris Ritchter. Winston Dolittle," Gunther repeated. He would tell Stell about them before he left. Tell him to watch his back, with some names attached.

"You're right, they are bullies," she said.

"I'm sorry, folks," Gunther said aloud to people at the other tables. "Some leftover police business." He opened his jacket to show them the badge on his shirt.

He looked back down at the list on the table for a few moments. He opened another piece of paper. Handwriting.

"Two white. Two black. One teenager," signed "Doc T."

White and black? Black and white? He then drank a gulp of coffee and dropped a nickel on the table and left.

Retracing his path from yesterday, he walked the Tulsa streets until he spotted Scotchey's. It was certainly a fancy place, and his guess—the nicest store in town.

"Good afternoon," Gunther said to the well-dressed ladies in the lobby, as he removed his hat. "I wonder if I might talk with the manager, or the owner?"

They could see the badge on his shirt, under his jacket. Gunther browsed a bit, and in a moment, an older man with wild, wiry hair appeared.

"Weeell, laddy, what have yee?"

"Are you…"

"Scotchey. Allen Hilderbrand, but they call me Scotchey."

"Scottish."

"Indeed, what can I do fa yee, laddy?"

"I'd like to confirm that you were robbed recently?"

"Hell yeah, we were robbed, laddy. The bastard came in here, with a shotgun and his face wrapped like a gadamn, Egypt mummy. Scared me ladies here. I mean, who robs a clothing store when there's maybe…maybe fifteen banks aboot?"

"Scott Freed?"

"Whatcha say?"

"You remember a Dallas dress salesman named Scott Freed?"

"Ahhh yeah."

"Could it have been him?"

"Yes," one of the women interrupted. "It could have. I am the buyer, and I've dealt with him the most. He was as tall. Same… same chest and, and shoulder size."

"If it's him, he's been a busy bastard. Aboot every two weeks he's robbed a clothing store in the Territory."

Gunther pulled out Freed's list and showed it to him.

"Well, I dunno aboot all of them, but there's mine, and the two before. We've been hit like dogs."

"Okay. What day was it? What time of day was it? Was there any reason that day was picked?"

"It was a Friday afternoon," the buyer said. "No special reason."

"You don't have extra money on hand then, for some reason?"

"No."

"Okay."

"Who buggered up ya face like that?" Scotchey said. "Say, you from around here? New lawman here?" he asked.

"I'm up from Texas."

"TEXAS!"

"Yup."

"I've never met a Texan that made any sense."

"I've never met a Scot I could understand. But I've made sense here, and I understood every word you said. Somehow."

"HA!" Scotchey said, but it wasn't a laugh.

Gunther smiled at the ladies, winked (which hurt), put on his hat, and turned for the door.

"I'll tell the Marshal's Office about this," Gunther said. "But a posse is out looking for him now. For murder in Texas.

"I hope they snare the mummy bastard."

Gunther stood outside on the busy avenue. He thought about holding a rag full of ice on his head. Even his hat hurt him. He headed for his hotel, with one stop at the telegraph office he'd seen on the way.

"Hello, sir, can you send a wire to Paris, Texas, for me?"

The clerk looked at the badge and said, "I certainly can, deputy."

Gunther took out his prepared message and laid it on the counter. There was a small, stained, wooden box with pencils in it, shavings and a closed, straight razor for pencil sharpening. He grabbed a pencil with a cleaved good point. He crossed out the city of Tulsa in the last line from Tulsa and changed it to

Wire back to Guthrie, Federal Marshal's Office, Oklahoma *–(Stop)*

Chapter 20
THEY BE DEAD

Williams and Son Department Store
Guthrie, Oklahoma

"Mr. Williams," Gunther said, looking at the older gentleman. Then he turned to his right. "Mr. Williams," he said to the younger gentleman. "I am here today in your office, at Williams and Son, asking to become your store detective."

The father and son looked at each with quizzical expressions.

"You are quitting your lawman job in Texas?" the son asked, as Gunther had just, seconds earlier, introduced himself as such.

"No."

"Then?"

"I have reason to believe that a former dress provider of yours, a salesman Scott Freed..."

"I remember Scott," the son said.

"...will wrap his face up in a bandage and rob your store within the week. As he has robbed numerous others he tended too, about every two to three weeks."

Gunther pulled a piece of paper out of his pocket with a modified list of stores and robberies and handed it to the father. The son left his chair, came around the desk and read it too.

"As you can see, your business name is next on the list," Gunther said.

"But we can count on the Federal Marshal's Office here in Guthrie to..." Williams Senior said.

"Already been there all day yesterday. They helped me with this list. Scott Freed killed a man in Paris, Texas, for which I am after him. And he is on a robbery spree of his old haunts. He just escaped us in Tulsa. Then he escaped an eleven-man posse, with bloodhounds. I mean to catch him here. At your store, sir. I suggest that I linger around your store for the next four or five days on the lookout for him. Marshal E.D. Nix himself said he could not spare any men to sit here, all day, watch over you, and wait it out every day. So, I volunteered to do so."

"We've never had a store detective," the son said.

"I understand."

"We can't pay you," the father said.

"The City of Paris is already paying me. At least for the next few days. Then I must return to Texas. I will dress like a store detective and wander about, watching the store and the exits and entry points. Tell your employees I am here for general security, which is not a lie. If he shows up, I will do my best to see that no innocent people are harmed and you are not robbed."

"There seems to be better places to rob than our little store," Williams Senior said.

"This is not a little store, sir. It's a three-story, brick building full of expensive, big-city merchandise. But you are right. It seems, however, that this Freed feller wants to rob what he knows. I guess he's seen your safe. Knows where it is?"

"He has," Williams Junior said.

"We have to move it somewhere else," Gunther suggested.

"Okay!" Williams Senior said, slapping his hand on the desk. "You're hired. Er...so to speak. The least we can do is befit you in an appropriate suit to walk around here. Son, take Mr. Gunther to see Lars in Men's."

"Lars is all the way from Sweden," the son said, waving a hand toward the office door. "He is quite the tailor."

"As long as he can tailor space for my guns, I'll be a happy man," Gunther said.

On Thursday morning at 10 a.m., Gunther showed up at Williams and Son. He wore his new four-button, sable frock coat (a three-quarter-length cut, that fell to the knees), matching pants, matching vest, white shirt, black tie, black shoes, and a dark-brown derby hat. The look, however, was ruined by a somewhat stained, two-gun belt, mostly hidden from view, except for the tarnished buckle, which showed up when he was not sufficiently buttoned up.

He introduced himself to the ladies and men that worked on the first floor at the jewelry and perfume counters and various other departments.

"Johann Gunther, your new store detective. At your service," he told them, each with a doff of the derby.

These visits included a bit of lingering in the presence of the more attractive women who were adorned in all the latest fashions.

"Whatever happened to your head, Johann Gunther," a darling brunette, selling face cream and lotions, asked him.

"I fell off my horse."

"Why, you don't strike me as the clumsy type."

"What if I told you I was chasing a vagabond, murderer, and I was jumped?"

"Why, I believe you would be fibbing me."

"Well, ma'am, that's the best story I can tell."

She giggled. He giggled.

"I might have some lotion here that could soothe some of that pain," she said.

"If I could only bear the pain of rubbing it in," Gunther said. "It is very tender to the touch right now."

More giggling. Her name was Darla, and she was known to slip off her shoes and work barefoot, well, stockinged foot, behind the counters whenever she could.

When customers appeared *en masse* before lunch, he stepped outside the double front doors onto the brick entryway and looked around. He leaned and half-sat on the black, wrought iron railings.

Gunther spotted a brass plaque on the brick wall –

"Williams and Son, Established January 1889."

"That's a few months after the Oklahoma Land Rush," Gunther thought. Guthrie was an amazing city. A boom town. A bit of a dusty nothing until the 1889 Land Rush, when some 50,000 people showed up in the area to trace off and claim land. On April 22, at precisely high noon, thousands of would-be settlers made a mad dash into the newly-opened Oklahoma Territory to claim cheap land. First come, first served! Settlers could run off and claim 160 acres of public land and receive a title to the property after five years if they lived on and improved the plot. All this had happened when Gunther was stationed at

Fort Sill, Oklahoma, where wild stories, tales, and newspaper reports flooded his imagination. Then, the L Troop of the 5th Cavalry of Sill, which somehow helped "supervise" the mad Rush, returned from Fort Reno with even more tales.

At 11:50 a.m. that April morning, soldiers called for everyone to form a line. When the hands of the clock reached noon, the cannon of Fort Reno boomed, and the soldiers signaled the settlers to start. With the crack of hundreds of whips, thousands of what they called "Boomers" streamed into the territory in wagons, on horseback, on bicycles, and even on foot.

Oklahoma's Indian Territory was already a catch-all for scores of displaced tribes. As many as forty tribes, including the Chickasaw, Choctaw, Cherokee, Creek, Cheyenne, Comanche, and Apache, had relocated there from their traditional lands. Suddenly, 50,000 people arrived and squeezed in and shoved in, and at times fought with the Indians. Gunther and his D Troop became part of problem and part of the solution in these lawless lands—hunting, arresting, and sometimes killing roving crooks, settlers, and Indians.

Within a few months, Guthrie and the surrounding cities exploded with growth. Electricity. A water system. Public transportation. Stores. Restaurants. Bars. Hotels. Cattle. Trains. Hospitals.

The Williams and Son department store sat on a corner lot downtown, and the front doors were right at the corner of the building, giving the store a triangular look when one entered. The receiving docks were in the back, with a dirt road running behind it as a service road for all the neighboring stores on the avenue.

"Where would a robber on horseback tie off his getaway

horse?" Gunther wondered. He slowly walked the perimeter of the establishment. The neighboring dentist office was separate from the store, giving the store four untouched sides. Gunther decided that the best place to hide a horse was out back on the dirt, service road. It was unkempt, bushy, and full of crates and company coaches and wagons. Freed could stash a steed anywhere, front or back, but the back, a concealed and handy place, was most likely.

The back, elevated loading dock of the store had a large wooden door that opened and closed, up and down with a pull rope. As Gunther walked by it was open and two men sat out on the dock at some beaten up table and chairs. Gunther stopped, walked up to them and sat at the table. They just looked at him. He pulled a wanted poster of Scott Freed out of his vest pocket.

"Gentlemen, my name is Johann Gunther. I am a deputy from Texas. And for the next few days, I am also your store detective. This man shot and killed somebody down there in Paris and I am looking for him. There is evidence that he will try and rob this store in the next few days."

Bewildered, they looked at the drawing.

"Which is why I am here, bothering you. My guess is he will enter the store through the back, through this door, if it's open, or that door beside it over there, if it's unlocked."

"You reckon?"

"I reckon."

"But I also reckon he will ride around this place a time or two before he does, without a mask. All his other robberies of stores, he was alone, on horseback." Gunther pointed up the service road with his thumb. "I Suspicion he will tie off his horse up there by the bushes and the garbage. Wrap his face up in medical bandages, come through these doors here, and do the deed."

"Do the deed."

"Yeah, that deed being robbing this place and maybe killing a few more folks. Such as yourself."

That caught their attention.

"Mr. Williams Senior hired me to stop him. Can I get you to keep an eye out for this man, or any man, circling the store, spying over this back area? He has been inside before as a traveling salesman. Can I get you to keep the doors closed and locked when you are not out here...working?"

"You can also get me to bring my .45 Colt to work and leave it hangin' nearby."

"That would be fine, sir," Gunther grinned. "'Cause, I don't care in the least who shoots him. Me or you."

"Sez here there's a bounty of fifty dollars on him. But it don't say dead or alive nowhere."

"If you catch Freed dead or alive, I will see to it that you get fifty dollars."

"I'll beat cha to it," the other man said to his compadre.

"Then you can have it," the other said.

Gunther stood.

"Mr. Williams would appreciate it if you would close those doors and lock them, when you ain't looking or working."

"He can count on us."

"Good day, gentlemen."

He first workday ended quietly. Then Gunther wandered down to the Marshal's Office. Marshal Nix was the head of not just the local Guthrie office, but also of the entire Oklahoma Territory of some 150 deputy marshals. Nix offered to stable

Casey in their backyard barn for the duration of his stay. Gunther wanted to check in with Nix, and then visit Casey.

The office was buzzing with activity. Marshal Nix stood over some men talking very seriously. Gunther came in, took a seat and listened in.

"Roberts and Lucas says that the gang is using Ingalls as their headquarters," Marshal Nix said, "and I believe him. They are always in Vaughn's Saloon. If I can get news they are indeed there, we will make a run on the place. I sent Reginald out there to see what he can see."

The men agreed with shouts of "hear-hear" and hoots and hollering. Their meeting adjourned. Nix spotted Gunther and walked over to him.

"Quiet day at the department store?"

"Quiet day," Gunther said. "What's going on, sir?"

"No doubt you've heard of the Dalton gang and the Wild Bunch gang..."

"I have."

"The last of them have teamed up and are giving us hell all over the Territory. Robberies. Shootings. Murders. We hear tell that they are holed up in Ingalls, Oklahoma. If I can get a reasonable confirmation, we are gonna beat hooves out there and catch em. It's about forty flat, dry miles away. We have two deputies there now, undercover as a railroad men, to spy. Ingalls got a telegraph office, and they'll tell us what's what. There's no lawman in Ingalls. So, the gangs think they've found em a real hidey-hole."

Gunther nodded.

"You hold down the fort, you hear?" Marshal Nix said with a smile and walked off to his office.

Gunther felt like Nix thought his gambit in the store was a long-shot plan. Gunther checked on Casey out back where he found his horse sound asleep and snoring down on his side in his stall. Gunther wouldn't wake him. The Indian stable man grinned when he saw Gunther.

"Sshhhh," the man said, putting his finger to his lips with a smile

Gunther walked to the local bookstore which, thanks to a large population of over 10,000 people, was quite well stocked. He bought an Edgar Allan Poe book of stories, seeking the particular tale he'd heard about, *The Premature Burial*. It was about a man with catalepsy who in a fit feared he would be assumed dead and buried alive, only to awake in his coffin, six feet underground. Gunther ate dinner, went to bed in the hotel and fell asleep reading Poe's story about waking up, six feet under, in a coffin.

The next day, late in the morning, Gunther roamed the store, with several visits with Darla, the cream and lotion saleswoman.

"So, where are you from?" she asked.

"I was born in Germany. Where are you from?"

"Virginia. Germany! My, is that as romantic as it sounds?"

"Absolutely it is."

"Faraway places. Hmmm, hmmm," she said, staring at his face. She put both hands on the glass counter and leaned forward. "What is the most beautiful place there...the most romantic in Germany, that you have been?"

"As a boy, my parents took me Lake Alpsee. In Bavaria..."

"Bavaria," she sighed slowly.

"Yes, the Bavarian Alps. Snow topped." Gunther looked up at the ceiling and waved his hand high in the air as though gazing at them that moment. "And at the lake there was a boat ride. A flat-bottomed boat ride. No top. So, once out on the lake you could see all the castles surrounding..."

"Castles!"

"Oh yes. Castles. Amazing and old, from...Medieval Times.

"Medieval," she said. "The times of ladies and knights."

"Yes. There were five...I don't remember...maybe seven, amazing castles lit up at night with fires and torches. Flickering. If you go, you must go at sunset or at night. And on the boat, they serve drinks and dinners. But I was just a boy and could not drink the apple wine."

"What did you drink then?"

"A water that has a...a fizz like a soda, and some chocolate milk."

"German chocolate milk," she said, slowly. "Perhaps someday, some gentlemen might escort me there?"

Gunther leaned in also, his elbows on the counter.

"Perhaps..."

"Mr. Gunther!" came a voice from the rear of the store.

Gunther turned to see one of the two dock workers he spoke with yesterday standing at the store back door that led to the storage rooms and loading dock. His eyes were wide and his jaw slack. Gunther walked over to him.

"They're here," the man whispered.

Gunther pulled him away from the sales floor into the back.

"Jerry peep-eyed them a riding by the back and looking in. Then Jerry went down to the dirt road once they passed. He peep-eyed them tying their horses off—just where you guessed—and they started wrapping up their faces to hide them like masks."

"They you say? How many?"

"Two."

"Two," Gunther repeated.

"What you want us to do?"

"You run down to the Marshal's Office and tell them to get over here."

"Okay," and he took off, about as fast as an old man could go.

Gunther jogged back to the lotions counter.

"Darla! Darla," Gunther said to her in a loud whisper. "Tell everybody on this floor to get outta here. Now. I mean now. There might be a robbery."

Gunther pulled both his pistols and dashed back to the double doors of the storeroom. He could not let these men enter into the store area with customers and sales crew. He peered around the corner for a view of the loading dock. He saw Jerry standing just inside the open loading dock door.

"Jerry!" Gunther whispered.

He turned. Jerry had a big pistol in his hand, as he had promised.

"They're a coming," he whispered back. "Should I shut the door?"

"No! Gunther said, "they would just come in the front then. Too dangerous. We have to stop them here."

"Oh, okay."

"Get over to one side. And get back a bit," Gunther said. "Get behind something, huh?" But there was nothing really there to get behind that would actually stop bullets. As they said in the Army, "Cover stops bullets. Concealment doesn't, but concealment is better than nothing."

Gunther closed the interior doors and stepped back to the opposite corner of Jerry. He caught a glimpse of two masked men, their faces wrapped like mummies with a cowlick of black hair sticking up and out at the top of both their heads, running into view, then out of his sight at the sides of the big, open door. There was no mistaking their intent.

Seconds passed. No sounds. Then the two appeared up on the dock and then in the doorway, holding long guns high and pointed at the store doors. One held a big, empty canvas sack, for the booty inside, no doubt.

Gunther did not hesitate. With a Colt on each, he blasted away, riddling their bodies. Five or six bullets into each one! They danced at the impact, the dance of death in the air, dropping their rifles, gasping and writhing, as rounds perforated their faces, necks, and chests. Then, they quivered away down on the wooden floor, just barely inside the door.

Gunther dashed over to Jerry, and snatched the unfired gun from his hand. This was quicker than reloading. The weapon pointed, he slowly walked over to the dying men. He kicked the long guns away and took the pistols from their gun belts.

"They be dead?" Jerry asked.

"They be dead," Gunther said. "Or will be, in a second or two."

"Should we help em?"

"Naaah. Don't think so. They reap what they sow," Gunther said.

He reached down and yanked apart the wrapped bandages on one. It was not Scott Freed. But, it was one of the men who confronted him in the restaurant back in Tulsa. He did the same with the second man, pulling off the mask. This one was Scott Freed, the man in the wanted posters.

The doors behind them swung open and three deputies barged in, pistols brandished. Marshal Nix walked in behind them.

"Scott Freed, I presume?" Nix said.

Gunther pointed to Freed's body.

"The other one is from Tulsa. Either Bobby Dunlap, or Chris Ritchter, or Winston Dolittle."

"I guess, you have $50 coming to you," Nix said.

"Give it to Jerry here," Gunther said. He was my look-out and…and he brought me this gun." Gunther held up the pistol, then walked over to Jerry and handed him back the pistol. Jerry stood frozen, dumbfounded.

"Good work, son," Nix said.

Williams Senior and Williams Junior ran in next, shocked, and looked over the mess.

"I needed Freed alive, to ask him some questions," Gunther said. "But I couldn't risk the two of them getting into the store with those rifles."

"Thank you, Jesus, then…" Williams Senior mumbled. He looked up at Gunther, his eyes wet with appreciation.

"They're bleeding all over the floor," a deputy said. "Let's toss em outside."

Gunther and the deputies tugged the corpses out the door.

"Somebody summon the undertaker," Nix said. "You fellers be around till they get here. Tell Rolando we need a photogravure of that other man. We'll send it to the Tulsa office."

"Send it to Stell in Tulsa," Gunther said. "He'll know him."

The store employees returned inside and gathered at the

doors, gawking.

"Well, Deputy Gunther, we have some paperwork to do," Nix said.

"Yes, sir," Gunther said. He shook his hands around in the air a bit. Was that some leftover *gun burn* that Gustav warned him about? He loaded his two pistols.

They walked through the store, and Gunther stopped for a second by Darla.

"And it was a pleasure meeting you, Miss Darla. Goodbye."

"You're...you're leaving?"

"Yes, ma'am. I must return to Texas."

And he walked out of the store with Nix. Gunther knew it was unlikely that Darla would ever forget this violent, unusual day, and the mysterious man from Germany.

Gunther sat at a desk at the Marshal's Office and began another "who, what, where, when, how and why" statement.

The front doors opened and a red-headed, pig-tailed girl of about twelve, wearing a leather apron, ran in, holding a piece of paper.

"Marshal Nix! Marshal Nix!" she cried out.

"What is it, honey?" Nix said, appearing from his office.

"Telegram for you."

"Thank you, dear," Nix said, taking the slip of paper. He smiled and waited for the girl to leave the office, then shouted, "The gangs are there in Ingalls."

The men in the office jumped up and gathered some gear.

"Hickson," Nix shouted," "How many men do you have for a posse?"

"We have me, four deputies and two Osage Indian police.

Five volunteers promised, marshal," Hickson said. "I think some of Perkin's officers will help."

"That's...not enough," Nix mumbled.

"I'll go," Gunther spoke up.

"You...you are busy, and..."

"I'll go," Gunther insisted. "I am done with Freed." Gunther could simply not sit still if major gangs could be rounded up. He had to help.

"Okay, then. Hickson is the ramrod. That number will have to do. Okay, Johann, go get yer horse ready."

Chapter 21
LE MORTE D'DEPUTIES

Central Great Plains, Oklahoma
1895

The posse did not run full out, but rather paced their horses. The August daylight was hot, but the evening air wafted in and cooled things down. Gunther was already getting itchy in his fancy Williams and Son suit, and the short brim of that derby was not helping him with the uninterrupted sunshine.

They did a few more hours and took a break, resting the horses and having a quick meal. As they sat on the dry dirt ground, drinking coffee and eating jerky, Gunther took the opportunity to speak with the deputies about any mysteriously missing people in their area. He mentioned their missing Eskimo Noot case and others in the region.

"Yes, yes, we have," James Masterson said. "When folks disappear, there's usually a story to it. And we usually find the bodies. Eventually. Sometimes it's a hunting accident, a kidnapping, a drowning. But we have had a few men...and women…just vanish, as if by the hand of Merlin the Magician."

"Who is Merlin the Magician?" The Osage Indian police sergeant asked.

"Merlin the Magician worked for King Arthur, and the Knights of the Round Table," Masterson said. "He did magic tricks and so forth, and was an advisor to the King."

"Like a medicine man?" the sergeant said.

"Yeah, exactly," Masterson said.

"Round Table?" the Indian repeated.

Masterson made a horizontal circle in the air. Coincidentally, the men were all sitting in much the same type of a circle.

"Knights like braves. Warriors. Advising the Chief—the King Chief."

"King Arthur. England."

"Yes," Masterson said.

"*Le Morte d'Arthur,*" Gunther chimed in.

"Yes," Masterson said, smiling at Gunther.

"Read it as a kid," Gunther said. "I grew up in Germany."

"Then you are very familiar with knights!"

"And wars. All kinds of wars," Gunther said.

"Tough times," Masterson said.

"Members of the Gunther family left Germany. Some went west, to the 'Wild West,' some stayed in New York City, and some went to Brazil," Gunther said.

"Brazil!"

"There's a bunch of Germans in Oklahoma and Texas," Masterson said.

"You know," Deputy Shadley spoke up between mouthfuls, "a woman walked out of her house to pump water for dinner in Cedar Valley. The husband waited and waited. The kids waited and waited. The husband looked outside. The empty bucket was laying on the ground, not spilled, and nobody has seen hide-ner-hair of her since. It'll take Merlin the Magician to find her!"

A few other deputies added some odd incidents they'd experienced too, building a case in Gunther's head.

Then, the posse cleaned up, mounted up, and continued at a walking pace, grateful for the evening breeze. Outside the city of Ingalls, at a certain rocky landmark known to Deputy Hickson, they veered off the trail between the cities of Perkins and Ingalls. They turned a few breaks and saw two covered wagons and a campsite, near a brisk creek.

The team greeted the three waiting men, as well as the sight of moving water. Eventually, Hickson introduced Gunther to the three.

"This is Perkins City Marshal Dick Speed. And Doc Roberts and Red Lucas. This is a deputy Johann Gunther from Paris, Texas. He happened to be in town, killin' robbers this morning, and he actually volunteered to come."

They shook hands.

They eyed Gunther's fancy suit and derby hat.

"Bit...overdressed?"

"I didn't have time to change."

"Gunther was playin' store detective and he shot down two robbers with rifles," Hickson said.

"He'll do," Shadley offered a vote of confidence.

"Doc Roberts is not a doc," Hickson added. "So, don't get shot tomorrow."

A raid plan was devised around the campfire after dinner. Red Lucas would ride in at sunrise, get breakfast, and scout the town. He'd come back and report any sightings. If most of the Wild Bunch and Doolin gangs were there? They'd all advance into town, in the two wagons, from two different directions, jump out and surround the Ransom Saloon. Gunther didn't like it much and would have preferred a more cavalry approach. Individuals on horseback. What if some escaped? How could they give chase in a Conestoga wagon? What would Captain Latisimo back at Fort Sill say? But he was the youngster in the group. And he knew that a platoon of men riding in on horseback could cause early and unneeded attention as well. The wagons would at least conceal the men. Maybe one wagon up front and the others on horseback?

"Mind if I ride in on my horse?" Gunther interrupted.

All the men turned to him.

"Why?" one asked.

"Well, I am a cavalryman, sir. Fort Sill. And….and I shoot well from the saddle, and…we might need to chase somebody." Gunther had more tactical reasons but did not reveal them, for fear of sounding like a smarty pants.

Hickson remained quiet, and all the men looked to him.

"I guess that's fine," Hickson finally said.

"Yeah," another deputy agreed.

Also, Gunther did not want to leave Casey tied up with the other horses out there by the creek. What if they were all killed in town? What would become of Casey and the other horses if no one knew they were there?

Shadley's eye caught a movement down by the creek.

"What the…"

There, ankle-deep in the water was a small boy in rolled-up jeans and a dirty, white undershirt. Just as surprised, the boy stared at the men and their wagons.

"Hey there, boy!" Hickson said. "Howdy!"

The boy took off. Some of the deputies took off after him. They encircled the lad and snatched him up by the waist, hauling his wriggly self all the way back to the campfire.

"What's yer name, boy?" a deputy asked.

"Barney."

"Barney what?"

"Barney Clements."

"Where you live, Barney Clements?"

"Yeah, I live here. Just outside of Ingalls."

The men looked at each other.

"How old are you?" Masterson asked.

"Nine."

"Nine. Well, Barney. Are ya hungry?" Masterson asked.

The boy looked over the steaks and beans in the frying pans. He sniffed the air.

"Yeah."

"Have ya a seat, then."

While the others spoke with the boy, Hickson walked off with Masterson. Curious, Gunther followed them to listen in.

"We can't let him go," Masterson said. "Everybody in Ingalls loves the outlaws and covers for them. It's like the gangs are the main source of prosperity. Those sorry asses livin' there have been snitching on us and hiding them out for years."

Hickson nodded.

"We keep him here?"

"We have too," Masterson said.

The three walked back to the campfire. The boy was chowing down.

"Barney," Hickson asked, "what would happen if you didn't get home tonight?"

"My maw and my paw and my granny would be sick. They'd think I was dead in a wash somewhere. Gotten by a rattler."

"How far away is yer home?"

"About...I don't know...two miles."

"You roam far."

"It ain't far fer me."

"We are on a...a mission...and it's secret and...so, you have to stay with us tonight."

"A secret? Yer gettin' after the gang, ain't cha?" the boy mumbled while chewing.

"No."

"Yes."

"No. We are just passing through to Missouri, and no one can know we are on the way."

"I see all those badges yer wearin'. Yer here to get the gang boys."

"You are gonna have to stay with us tonight, kid. That means a dinner. A breakfast. Buttermilk. Eggs. Bacon. Biscuits. A soft bed in that wagon. And home in the late morning for lunch."

"We don't eat no lunch. Just biscuits in the morning and supper."

"Well, then, you'll be home for supper."

Gunther wandered over to the creek as they argued with the boy. He knew the raid was getting messy.

Saturday morning.

"He's gone," Tom Houston said, peeking into the wagon bed. "The kid's gone."

The other men rousted out of their bedrolls.

"Well, shit," Masterson said.

"Whatcha think?" Hickson said. "Still try it?"

"Well, there's a chance he's warning Doolin."

"I'm still a goin'," Red Lucas said, hauling his saddle over to the horses.

"We adhere to the plan, then," Hickson said.

An hour later, Red Lucas trotted his horse into Ingalls. He ate breakfast, visited the saloon for another morning coffee, and left unnoticed. It was another hour before he returned to the wagon camp with the news.

"I saw Doolin, Newcomb, Waightman, Clifton, Dalton, Bitter Creek, and Tulsa Jack in the Ransom Saloon. I didn't see Arkansas Tom anywhere. If true to their habits, they stay there all day and night even."

"Then let's go," Hickson said.

The lawmen climbed into the wagons, Gunther climbed on Casey, and they started out for Ingalls. It was a tense ride and Gunther anticipated an ambush on the way. Here and there he rode ahead of the wagons like an Army scout to spy upon the trail. But no ambush came.

Just outside the city, they split up to enter from both sides of the main street. Gunther stayed with Hickson's wagon. Dick Speed drove the other wagon. Red Lucas told them all that the saloon was midway on Oak Street and that they would see the whole length of the street and easily read the business signs. The whole city of Ingalls was hardly a city at all, just about twenty somewhat-scattered wooden buildings. Only the run-down OK Hotel had two stories. Gunther thought the hotel should have been called the "Not OK" judging from the exterior.

Hickson saw the signs ahead and pulled his wagon over by some trees in front of a doctor's office, a Dr. Pickering. Gunther made a note of Pickering as it might be handy to remember a medical location. He could see Speed's wagon stop down on the far side of town and the lawmen dropping out of it and dash over to some hiding places besides buildings and brush. Gunther stayed on his horse for a higher look. He saw Dick Speed walk into a livery stable about mid-town.

There was a man walking a horse on the street, and soon he would come upon all these lingering men on Gunther's side of the posse.

"Shitfire, that's Bitter Creek Newcomb of the Wild Bunch," a deputy near Gunther whispered.

Speed stood beside a local teenager at the barn door of the stable. The teen pointed at the walking man. The man saw this pointing and stopped. He pulled a rifle from his saddle's scabbard. Speed raised up his rifle. And all hell broke loose…

Speed shot first. It was clear to Gunther that the bullet hit Newcomb's rifle by the way it splintered and how the man could not hang on to it. Part of the bullet must have dug into his leg because the man's left leg immediately buckled and he crumbled, knee first to the dirt. The horse bucked. Speed shot again as Newcomb got up, pulled a pistol and shot back at Speed while as he tried to crawl on board his spooked, stutter-stepping horse. With a numb leg, it was no easy task.

Just then a bare-chested man appeared with a rifle in a second-story window of the OK Hotel and shot at Speed. Once, twice, Speed was hit and knocked down. It looked fatal to Gunther, and Speed was still in clear range of the sniper. Speed was badly shot yet again. Meanwhile, Newcomb got up on that wild horse and galloped away as just about all of the posse shot after him. Gunther fired too, but at the hotel window, as the Wild Buncher ran this gauntlet, but then he turned sharply into the livery stable. Gunther had turned his horse to chase but stopped. He thought surely the man was hit several times.

"Don't go, Gunth!" Hickson hollered. "We need you here!"

They did. About fifteen people ran out on the street from Ransom's Saloon. And all the officers just opened fire at them. The man in the window still fired away too. He even shot down an innocent customer running away down the alley. Horses out front fell, as the deputies spread out to cover the saloon, as well as hide from the hotel sniper's gun. The man in the window shot another deputy off his feet. Gunther dropped off of Casey and pulled him into a wide space alongside the doctor's office.

"Sleep, Case," he ordered, and the horse lay down.

Gunther ran to the corner of the neighboring building, reloaded his long gun, and knelt down with his rifle at the ready. He lever-actioned five rounds, with three-second intervals into the hotel window, for to him, their biggest problem was that bare-chested sniper at the OK Hotel. This created cover for about fifteen seconds or so, and lawmen took to better cover, but some didn't. Gunther cussed their stupidity.

The men from the saloon, still shooting, either ran back in the saloon or scattered to the nearby livery stable and within minutes, some burst from the back and front doors of the stable on horseback. Gunther dropped his empty rifle—wishing he had a military sling—and with his two pistols poured a slow flow of lead into the hotel windows as cover for the open-filed deputies. A few more dangerously entered the street to shoot at the fleeing desperados.

Gunther reloaded his pistols, then slow shooting with seconds in between, he ran across the street for the hotel front doors. He shoulder-bashed them open, ready to kill anybody inside with a wicked eye and a gun. A few people inside screamed and dived for the floor.

The pale clerk peeked over the desk counter and said, "It's Arkansas Tom, in Room 22."

Gunther reloaded yet again from the box of shells in his coat pocket. He'd never heard of Arkansas Tom but would kill him anyway. Gunfire still erupted out on the street. Two deputies charged into the lobby. Gunther's six guns were loaded.

"He says it's an Arkansas Tom up there. Room 22," Gunther told them.

They nodded and acted like they knew him. And just then Tom himself appeared at the top of the steps for an instant, still bare chested, wearing pants, as though he was trying to escape or get to the gunfight on the street.

"There he is!" one of the deputies shouted.

The three raised their guns to shoot, but Tom ducked back down the hallway and out of sight. The gunfire out on the street diminished a bit, then stopped. Only the sounds of the wounded men and horses wailed on out there.

"Who you got in these other rooms?" a deputy asked.

"Just Tom up ere!"

"Get outta here," the deputy told the clerk and two women in the lobby. They ran out.

Gunther led the way up the stairs, his gun barrels aimed ahead. There were only two rooms on the floor. Rooms 21 and 22. He and the deputies passed 21. He stayed on his toes to keep his boot heels from scuffing the floor, but one of the deputies...had spurs on.

Gunfire. Holes were punched and rounds roared and ripped through the thin walls, across the hallway and into the far wall. The three men lurched back.

"Come on down!" a man ordered from below. The three lawmen descended the stairs backward. They exited the lobby and saw several of the deputies were outside, in the middle of the street, aiming rifles at the upstairs window.

One of the deputies with Gunther said, "It's Arkansas Tom."

Gunther surveyed the street. It seemed like about eight horses were shot. Several human bodies lay out there too. A teenager sat up against a fence holding a bloody shoulder.

"Tom!" Masterson shouted. "Tom, I got a stick of dynamite in one hand and a match in the other. You come down outta there or I'm gonna blow you up to pieces."

"Oh, sweet Jesus..." the clerk muttered from across the street. "Not my hotel."

Gunther stepped back far enough so as to not be blown to pieces.

"Tom?"

A rifle flew out the window and it hit the dirt roadway.

"One damn minute," a growling voice came from above.

They waited. A lawman ran behind the hotel to make sure he wouldn't run off out back. And in one minute, Arkansas Tom walked out the front door, hands in the air.

Two deputies ran to up him, holstered their handguns and beat him off his feet with their fists. Under about ten fast fists Tom fell gagging and cursing onto the wooden sidewalk. Masterson put the explosive in his pants pocket.

Dick Speed was dead. Shadley was dead. And Gunther could see some of the men tending Deputy Tom Houston up the road. They shook their heads. He too was dead. Gunther walked over to the teen by the fence to maybe get him to that doctor's office.

"Hey, kid. Kid!" Gunther said.

He got closer.

"Kid!"

The boy was propped up. But dead too. His hand was still stuffed inside his shirt at the shoulder. His empty eyes stared at Gunther's face as he lifted the kid's head by the chin to look at him.

Some of the townspeople wandered out of the few buildings.

"This boy's dead over here," Gunther yelled to them. "He's dead."

He walked over to the Ransom Saloon with a Colt in his hand. He pushed open the door with the barrel and walked in. It was a ramshackle, hammered together place that could barely stop the rain or a good wind. An unarmed, wounded man in a dirty apron over his dirty clothes sat on a chair against the far wall.

"I own this place," the man said.

Gunther nodded.

"I'm shot!" The man's upper arm was bleeding. He held a filthy towel on it.

"There's a doctor's office down the street."

"That old, scum-sucker!" The man said. "I don't know what's worse, him cleaving on me, or this bullet in me."

Gunther walked over and lifted the towel and hand. The arm looked like hell. Bruised black and blue with a dark hole and oozing blood.

"I think you should select the cleaving," Gunther said.

"You fuckers of mothers shot my place up. And shot me too."

Gunther nodded again. He went behind the bar, grabbed a bottle of whiskey and poured a shot into a glass. His hand was steady, no shakes, and he took note of that. He looked at the glass and at his fingers. Gun burn, he thought. Gustav's gun burn. Must burn through the nerves. Must make for a steady hand.

"They say, you've been harboring these fugitives here for months," Gunther said.

"Fuck you if I have," he said.

"Well, fuck this city if you have, and it has been fucked."

Gunther swallowed the whiskey in one gulp.

"That'll be five cents," the man said.

"Fuck you," Gunther said.

"Fuck *you!*" the man said.

Gunther walked out.

"I will see you all in court!" the man yelled.

"Not if you don't get that arm looked at."

Gunther stepped outside. It was apparent that almost all the outlaws got away. He heard the sound of horses suffering. Whinnying. Gurgling. Gasping for breath in deep heaves. He looked over the downed animals. He found two, still alive, and shot up multiple times from pistol and rifle rounds.

"Hello, stranger. Hello," he found himself saying to the face of one.

It was something his Army sergeant, Callahan Reginald, an old, calvary vet, would say to a dying horse. Sgt. Callahan would then pet the dying horse's neck and shoot the horse in the head. It had to be done to their four-legged friends. It just had to be done.

Gunther pulled his pistol, like Callahan, and shot the horse between the eyes and just a bit higher. All the men in the street jumped at the gunshot. He walked up to the second horse and looked it over.

"Hello. Hello, my stranger, friend," he whispered to the horse. On its side, its visible eye giant and wide, its labored breath...then, boom!

He walked up the street to Masterson and Hickson.

"The man at the livery said that that little boy we lost this morning ran into town and told the gangs we were coming here to get them," Masterson told Hickson.

"Damn. Why didn't they leave town, then?" Hickson said.

"He said, they packed up their horses *to* leave..."

"And they didn't?" Hickson said.

"They didn't, he said...he said, they just changed their minds. Decided to...to play cards, stay and wait."

"What the hell? Then, that's how they ran out so fast. Horses packed and ready. Ready to go," Gunther said.

"The bold, arrogant bastards," Masterson said.

"Yup. They decided to go back to the saloon and wait for us. And play cards. God almighty!" Hickson said.

"Yeah. Arkansas Tom over there has the flu, and he stayed in bed," Masterson said.

"Damn that little kid," Hickson said.

"Gentlemen," Gunther interrupted. "Well, there's not much else for me to do here. I think I'll get my horse and head on back. I still have to report to Paris and..."

"Okay, Johann," Hickson said. "Tell Nix what happened, first thing."

"First stop. I certainly will."

"And thank you for your help, son. Don't think I didn't see you save our asses by shooting at Tom's window. You kept him down. I will put that in my report."

"Yessir. Thank you, Johann," Masterson added.

Gunther tipped his derby and walked off.

There was another dead man beside the bar door. He looked like a customer. No gun belt. City clothes. Older fellow. Gunther looked him over. His big hat was on the sidewalk beside him. Gunther took off his derby and propped it on the dead man's bare head with a tap to secure it and picked up the big, brimmed hat. He put it on his head. A decent fit. It was a long, sunny ride back to Guthrie.

He walked over to the wagon, looked in, and grabbed a can of beans and a can of peaches, one for each side pocket and turned for the doctor's office. The doctor was peering out his front door.

"Hello, Doc!" Gunther said.

"What the..."

"Just a little outlaw round-up. Say, your bartender is bleeding to death in your luxurious saloon. Might check in on him."

The doctor ducked back inside.

"Get up, Case!" he shouted as he got close to his ride. "Let's go."

Casey stood up.

He hugged the horse's neck and got into the saddle and they stepped out on the one and only main street. The doctor hustled by in front of them with a small black bag in his hand. Gunther looked it all over one more time. He saw the beaten-down Arkansas Tom, now in shackles, huddled on the dirt road. He saw the wounded and dead men and dead horses strewn about.

"Costly," he mumbled.

He headed back to Guthrie.

Chapter 22
THE PRESENTIMENT

Guthrie, Oklahoma
One Day Later

Gunther sat across from Marshal Nix and explained what happened in Ingalls. Several other deputies and a large black cat that jumped on Nix's desk and sat looking at him like a black, porcelain statue, listened in. Gunther related the incident step-by-step.

Nix scratched and shook his head when Gunther was done.

"Helluva deal," Nix said. "Hey, you got a telegram from yer boss."

He opened a drawer in his desk, pulled out the paper, and handed it off. Gunther stood, took the envelope, and stepped outside Nix's office into the lobby to escape the heated and emotional conversation about Ingalls that followed. He opened it and read the message.

Dear Knight –(Stop)

Good progress –(Stop)

Went to Sherman to telephone Atlanta as I was curious about what you reported, and company admitted they ship a great deal of that chemical to Tulsa –(Stop)

More than normal for deaths and city that size –(Stop)

Something is not right –(Stop)

This is not our jurisdiction but check Tulsa railroad lines for amounts of coffins shipped or maybe even large, narrow boxes like coffins –(Stop)

More worried about this and you must take extra care now because I fear something big is going on so return to Paris as soon as you can –(Stop)

Chief Henri

Gunther folded the wire up and put it in his pocket. The men filed out of the office. Some very grim as they had to take death messages to the wives of the dead. Nix came out and put his hand on Gunther's shoulder.

"I have to report this to the governor, but I'll wait until Hickson returns. We need a written report from you, but not right now. Get out of that fancy suit. Take a hot bath and eat a steak. Get some rest. Come on back in the morning. They'll take good care of your horse round back."

Gunther smiled and nodded.

"Then what's next, son? Home to Paris?"

"Yup. But, by way of Tulsa. I have to finish up some business in Tulsa. Then Paris."

"So, your police chief down there was an actual Paris, France, police detective, was he?"

"Yes, sir," Gunther said with a smile. "He's very smart."

166

"I'll bet there's a helluva story about that."

"Oh, there is, sir."

Tulsa, Oklahoma, two days later

The railroad men led the horses down the ramp at the Tulsa Station, and Gunther fetched the reins for Casey. He tied the horse off out front and walked back into the station, to the manager's office.

"Howdy," he said to the men in their Frisco Line uniforms. "My name is Deputy Johann Gunther." He opened his jacket and tapped the badge on his shirt. "Is the manager here?"

"Whatcha need, deputy?" a heavyset man said. "Come on in my office."

They sat at a worktable. After some formalities, Gunther quickly go to the point. He asked to see the shipping manager.

"I'm the shipping manager, and..." the man said, "the manager of everything. I even clean the lavatories sometimes."

"Do you ship a lot of coffins out of here?"

"Coffins?"

"Coffins."

"We...we ship coffins, yes. A fair to middling amount."

"Do they stink?"

"I think they all stink."

"I mean stink of chemicals."

"Yeah, yeah. They bathe the bodies in some chemicals to ship them."

Gunther nodded.

"Do any other...boxes...other wooden boxes, stink too? Stink the same?"

"Boxes can stink. Fertilizers, oils, and such. Even new

clothing can sometimes stink."

"Do they stink of formaldehyde? The coffin smell?"

"Well, yeah. Sometimes shipments of new clothes come in and they smell something like that. Ya know, new clothes smell. They can stink too."

"Where do many of these coffins and stinky boxes go off to?"

"We send coffins everywhere. Big cities. Other...stinky... boxes, well, I don't rightly know."

"Do you think there is an unusual number of coffins? Since most people are buried right around here?"

"That's true. I hadn't thought much about it. We send everything outta here. Chickens and machine parts—you name it, we ship it. But we have a lot of new residents from all over from the land rushes. Even Europe."

"Yeah. You reckon most of the coffins come from...."

"Well, Nelson's. Nelson's Funeral Home. Only one we got here and it's growing. Thanks to the ...."

"Land Rush. Uh-huh."

"They started out in woodworking years back," the manager said, "then started making coffins. Then they became a funeral home. They still make furniture and fence planks and fence posts in the back."

"And they ever ship their woodworks?"

"All over."

"Big cities?"

"Yeah. New York! Omaha! Kansas City. Chicago..."

"Huh. Imagine ordering fences all the way from Tulsa? Seems like folks in Chicago could make their own fences and furniture. Lots of people die here in Tulsa? And get shipped out?"

"I don't know. Some. I guess. But the funeral business is growing. And a lot of people came here from other places. So, their families live far away."

"That's, that's perfect," Gunther said.

"Perfect? Perfect for what?"

"Perfect. Thank you, sir."

"Why you askin', son?"

"I don't know. Might…" Gunther stood. "…might open up a funeral home."

Gunther rode over to Nelsons. But he didn't enter the front doors. He rode around back and passed by it slowly. Collar up. Hat pulled down to his eyebrows. The back doors were open and several men, covered in sawdust were working with saws and hammering away on various projects and on some long boxes. He made the circle, then took a look around the area. Being an old Army scout, he saw a break between two, single-story buildings and a rise in the land with some grass and scrub brush behind it. A future observation point. Then he took off for the Marshal's Office.

He stumbled into panic at the Tulsa Marshal's Office. When Gunther walked in the Chief Deputy Marshal Halbert Greenway was yelling orders and deputies seemed to be moving everywhere.

"What?" Gunther asked one.

"Stell is missing."

"Missing?"

"He didn't show up yesterday. We didn't really notice. His girlfriend came in this morning and said he'd missed their dinner last night. He's not been at home. And he's not here again today."

Greenway walked up to Gunther. "It's probably those three fellers you told us about last week."

"I just killed one of them in Guthrie," Gunther said.

"Then, we're rounding up the other two, now."

"Anybody going to Stell's house?"

"I am," shouted a deputy from across the lobby.

"I'll go with you," Gunther yelled back. He turned to Greenway, "In some way, this is all my fault."

"Bullshit, cowboy, yer just doin' yer job," Greenway said.

"Mike Tothers," the deputy said, shaking Gunther's hand.

"Johann Gunther."

"You out back?" Tothers asked.

"Yup."

"Let's go."

They got their horses ready and galloped to Stell's house. Deputy Stell's little square, single-story, wooden house was on a quiet side street, full of houses that all looked the same. It had a short, white picket fence, suitable for tying off horses, and they did.

"Stell!" Tothers sounded off, as they walked up to the front door. A single horse coach drove up, driven by a stout woman with curly brown hair. She stopped, yanked the brake, and jumped out.

"He's not here. I've been looking for him here and everywhere. I am his girlfriend, Patsy. Go, go on in. I unlocked the door this morning. I got a key."

"Was the front door locked this morning?" Gunther asked.

"I...I don't know, I just stuck the key in the lock and turned it."

"Okay."

Kitchen. Dining room. Bedroom. No Stell.

Gunther looked at the bed. It was messy. A gun belt with a gun was on the floor by the bed.

"He make his bed?" he asked.

"Not always," she said.

"What's different?" Gunther asked.

"I don't know. I don't come here much. I live with my sister and my mother."

"Come on, let's take a good look around," Gunther said.

"No coffee made. He makes coffee every morning," Patsy said.

There was no sign of any cooking either.

"Oh my God," she said suddenly.

"What?" Tothers said.

"His boots." She pointed by a worn, leather chair in the parlor. The boots were lined up on top of a newspaper.

"He ain't got but one pair of boots?" Tothers asked.

"That's them. I'm on him about it. He needs a pair of shoes too," she said. "Oh my God, this is not at all right."

They continued looking.

"He has…." She took off for the bedroom, her gaze scanned the floors. "He has him some slippers. Gray slippers. And… they're gone. They ain't here, neither. Oh…"

Gunther stood by the bed again and took a real hard study of it. He laid on the floor and looked under it. He got back up. He looked at the configuration of the sheets and blanket, trying to detect a ghost of sorts, a story of a sleeping man, or the evidence of an abducted man, pulled from it.

"Anything?" Tothers asked.

"Nothing," Gunther said as he leaned in and smelled the pillows and sheets not touching them.

No blood anywhere. He walked to the back door. It was unlocked.

"That ain't right," Patsy said. "It's always locked, day and night."

Gunther walked out back. The yard was empty but for an outdoor cooking spot, some tree stumps used as chairs, and a wash line. The outhouse door was open and the small room was empty. He walked the fence line and then he saw it.

"Y'all come out here," Gunther said. They did.

Gunther pointed to a slipper. Upside down by the back fence.

"That's his," Patsy said in a gasp.

Gunther took out his pistol and with the barrel, flipped the slipper over. The toe was muddy.

"Dragged," Gunther said. Like Gustav might have done for him dozens of times, Gunther ran his pointed finger from the back door, then with two fingers covered the probable dragging path.

"Oh, my poor baby," Patsy cried out. "Is he still alive somewheres?"

"Don't know."

Gunther looked over the yard to see the sporadic signs of two feet dragging. Then they all looked toward the sparse woods behind the house and to the next, distant street over.

"We've an Osage Indian policeman that is the best tracker we have, ma'am. I'll get him out here," Tothers said. "And we got a real good dog."

"Patsy," Gunther said, "would you please go to every door on this street and that street over there and ask people if they saw or heard anything last night, and get back to the office and tell us what you found out?"

She took off.

The lawmen walked to their horses and mounted up.

"Those men that threatened me last week were most likely in the KKK," Gunther said.

"That don't surprise me."

"Let's get back to the office and send for that Osage tracker and the hound dog, but I'm gonna go somewhere else real quick," Gunther said.

"Okay. Where's that?"

"Nelson's Funeral Home," Gunther said.

"Why there? Nobody would kidnap a deputy, kill him, and take him in fer a proper funeral."

"I just have a feeling. Trust me on this. My chief would call it a 'presentiment.'"

"What's that?"

"It's French for…a hunch."

Chapter 23
THE DEVIL'S WORKSHOP

Gunther rode up to the back doors of the funeral home again, only this time he stopped and stepped off Casey. He tied him off by a pile of metal cans and walked in the open back doors. The men were hard at work and paid him no mind. Gunther counted five of them. He paid special attention to what they were making. Some were indeed making some fence pieces. One, a table, and one, painted a stencil on a few long boxes with a blackened paintbrush.

Gunther stopped to read the painted letters.

"Dr. Milton Trafalgar, Nelson Funeral Home, 111 Lockhart St., Tulsa, Oklahoma."

Was this the "Doc T" at the bottom of Justin Freed's list? He lifted the lid and the long box was empty. The painter just looked at him.

"If'n you got a new body, Agnes is in the front office," the man said, looking at Gunther's badge.

Gunther winked and smiled at him, which is what Gustav would do for a stall, and then he briskly walked around the whole first floor, looking in every room and every closet. No one was there. He found the embalming room with that strange smell again. No bodies. No Stell.

He spotted a stairway and marched up it. There were five doors down a hall. He opened the first one and barged in.

A lanky, older man was standing in there, in a suit, no tie, wearing eyeglasses and greased-back hair.

"And to whom will I be speaking?" the man asked, taking off the glasses.

"Whom...is Johann Gunther. Deputy," Gunther said.

"Ahhh...hmmmm. Johann GoonTAH," the man said, trying to sound German.

"To whom be you?"

"My name is Milton Trafalgar, doctor of medicine that is, and at your service. And what might be your service be?"

"I am looking for an Eskimo from Texas," Gunther said. "That, and a missing deputy marshal named Stell."

"An Eskimo from Texas! My, my, Mr. GoonTAH, that is unusual."

"He was visiting Texas from Alaska."

"I see."

"But Stell works here in town."

"I see. And are they dead? This is a funeral home. You know, they are just developing the name 'parlor' here in the Americas. Funeral...parlor. Not home. So many people display their dead in the parlors of their homes for a funeral. Disgusting habit, really. The word 'parlor' originated denoting a room in monasteries in Medieval Christian Europe, a place where church officials could converse in a relaxed manner. I believe you Westerners use the term 'parley' when making deals and negotiations, and such. This is a funeral home away from home, so to speak. A parlor away from a parlor. Thus…funeral parlor."

"Lots of people seem to be embalming and sending bodies far away from here. Not too home-y," Gunther said.

"A trend, Mr. GoonTAH. I predict that soon, it will be unpalatable having those who have slipped their mortal coils, stretched out in one's parlor rooms, near the kitchen, for several days. Burying them here, there, and everywhere will be the future cricket, first for the rich, then the near poor." Trafalgar intently lit a cigar. "These funeral *homes*, the very idea of them, is a recent invention. A service for mankind!"

Gunther stared at the man.

"Cigar?" Trafalgar offered.

"No, thanks."

"Do you know why people are buried six feet underground, young man?"

Gunther shook his head, no.

"It's from my country, actually. England. London officials and medical practitioners back in 1665 thought that deceased plague victims could still spread their diseases, and that burying these bodies so deep would help stop the spread of the disease. They were mistaken. Have a seat. Six feet deep, it's a rather, medieval idea, don't you think?"

"Medieval," Gunther agreed. Gunther turned his wing-back chair in such a manner that he could see the doorway. He swept off his Stetson and sat down.

"Medieval ideas seem to…to stick around, don't you agree?"

"What brings you to Tulsa, Oklahoma?" Gunther asked.

"In an odd way, these Land Rushes bring me here. But I am on a constant quest for medical research. A Land Rush brings

176

many people in. Diseases. Sicknesses, hitting all shapes and sizes and origins of people. Diseases normal for one land are deadly to another. I am also a great follower of *Anopheles Quadrimaculatus*. Do you know what they are, sir?"

"No."

"The mosquito. 'General' Anopheles. Commander-in-Chief mosquito. It has killed more humans than any other force in history. Shaped and decimated civilizations with its diseases. A military genius, this general. Anyway, HA! I also follow its migrations as best I can."

"So, you practice medicine here?"

"Abstractly."

"Abstractly."

"Whiskey then? Tea?" Trafalgar asked.

"I'll pass. So, have you seen an Eskimo?"

"Dead or alive? As you…Western fellows like to say."

"Dead."

"Can I help you?" Owner Ed Nelson interrupted, striding into the room.

"Nooo," Dr Trafalgar said, "Mr. GoonTAH and I are just chatting about the missing and the dead. And the mosquito."

"What brings you back here, deputy?"

"We are missing a deputy marshal, and I thought just maybe, someone might have brought his body here for an… embalming."

"Who?"

"Stell."

"Stell. I know him. A funeral? And he's still missing? Not dead?" Nelson said, acting confused.

"Stranger things have happened around here," Gunther said.

Gunther stood and put on his hat. "Stell is still missing. Curiously, he shot that Freed feller they brought in here last week."

"Oh," Nelson said.

"Death upon death," Dr Trafalgar said, "it's a *booming* business."

Gunther walked to the door.

"Such a booming enterprise, Deputy GoonTAH..." the doctor reaffirmed.

Gunther stopped, turned, and looked back at them.

"Booming in that someone such as yourself..." Trafalgar said, eyes wide, his hairy eyebrows bobbed up and down, "might entertain joining the death business?"

Gunther half-smiled and said, "I think I am already in the death business." He left the room.

"Good luck finding your *Eskeeemo* from Texas!" Trafalgar shouted after him.

Nelson and Trafalgar looked at each other after Gunther left the room. Nelson shut the door.

"I thought he was gone back to Texas," Nelson said. "But today's newspaper reported he'd just gone to Guthrie, then off for a raid of the Dalton Gang and the Wild Bunch."

"Busy, busy boy. Well, he's back, and we most definitely need to exterminate him. He does a good dance-around, but he's getting more of the notes down to the song. Sloppy death is fine," the doctor said, sitting back down.

"Yes, sir," Nelson said.

Gunther got on his horse and rode to the telegraph office. In the lobby, he prepared a wire with a pencil and paper.

A Doctor Milton Trafalgar from England is here in Tulsa, doing something, working or living at the Nelson funeral home –(Stop)

Train station reports a lot of shipped bodies in caskets and boxes to rail stations in major cities –(Stop)

Can you inquire on Trafalgar with your international police connections –(Stop)

He walked Casey a few streets down to an outfitter's store he'd seen earlier. He tied the horse off and walked inside to find a store with farm and ranch gear. He picked out black pants, a black shirt, and he found a black scarf.

"Bit hot for a scarf, ain't it?" the clerk said when Gunther paid for the clothes.

"It's an early Christmas present," Gunther said.

"I see. I see." The clerk folded the garments, wrapped the clothes in brown paper, and tied the square package with a white string.

Gunther walked Casey to the Marshal's office and stabled him around the back. It almost seemed like the other horses were noisy and glad to see him. He took his telescope from a saddlebag along with his rifle and canteen. Then he walked in the back door to the office. Nix was there sitting on a desk talking to some deputies.

"Any luck?" Gunther asked.

"None," Nix said. There was a creek about 100 yards beyond the house and the tracks ended there. Looks like two men nabbed him in his sleep, clubbed him and dragged his body out."

"We walked the far side of the creek quite a ways," Mike

Tothers said. "We couldn't pick up a trail. There are a hundred horse tracks over there. Picnic grounds. Fishermen. The tracks lead everywhere. Whatcha find out?"

"I don't know," Gunther said, sitting on a lobby bench. "There's a strange British doctor living in the Nelson funeral home. Looks like he's living there on the second floor. Milton Trafalgar. Seen him yet?"

"Nope," said Nix.

"Nope," said Tothers.

"Nelson is in the KKK?"

"I certainly think so," Nix said. "He might be an uppity-up in it, too. He seems to boss a lot of men around that don't work directly for him."

"I sent word back to Chief Gustav in Paris about this Dr. Trafalgar," Gunther said. "If anyone can find out about him, my police chief can. He knows police all over the world. He'll contact Scotland Yard. Trafalgar is in all this somehow."

"In all what?" Nix said.

"This," Gunther said, waving his left hand. "All these missing people around here. Stell. The KKK. All of it."

"Ya think?" Tothers said.

"I think."

Nix scrunched up his face, sighed, and walked to his office. Gunther stood. Tothers unfolded his arms.

"See ya tomorrow," Gunther said, and walked out the door with his outfitter's package under his arm.

"Get some sleep!" Tothers said.

"Not likely," Gunther muttered to himself.

Back in his room and when the sun set, Gunther changed clothes into his new, store-bought dark outfit. He already had a dark brown hat, gun belt, and boots. He wrapped the scarf around his neck, shoved the telescope in his pocket and hung the canteen of water on his shoulder. He left the hotel and slowly walked down the main streets, then took some side streets. He wandered around near the Nelson Funeral Home. He found his way to the small hill he'd seen earlier. He sat among the brush and grass where he had a clear view of the back of Nelson's. He put the scarf around his face, pulled his hat down and watched.

The back doors were still open and men worked into the night, hammering, sawing and painting. Then about 1 a.m. they quit. They gathered up their belongings, stopped and talked out back a bit, and then all walked off. The rear doors remained open. He thought about sneaking in.

It was a long, warm night. Not many gnats or mosquitos, but several waves of lightning bugs, hundreds of them, if not thousands roamed by, making the long night out almost worthwhile just to see their flowing magic. At 7 a.m. a new crew of four men showed up. At 8 a.m., a covered wagon showed up. The wagon rolled up, drawn by two horses, and the men started loading wooden crates and boxes into the wagons. They joked and cursed. Nelson and Trafalgar walked out, holding coffee cups, and entered into the conversation. Trafalgar wore a short black cape with bright red interior and a black top hat.

Once loaded with large and small wooden boxes, the old wagon lumbered and creaked off, and Gunther crawled down the hill and stood, jogging his way around the large look-out mound and into the back streets. He caught up with the wagon, spotting it again and followed it, hoping it wouldn't travel too far, or worse, leave town. It didn't. It stopped at the railroad station. The driver leaped down from the wagon onto the elevated sidewalk and walked into the shipping office. Gunther walked by and sat on the platform. He watched as the Frisco Line workers and the shipping manager he spoke with days ago come out and helped unload the boxes and crates. Once the wagon was empty, the driver climbed aboard, released the brake and wriggled the reins across the horses' backs. Off they went.

Gunther walked into the shipping office.

"Hello, deputy," the manager said, eyeing up his black clothes.

Gunther walked right past him and found the biggest, longest wooden crate. Stenciled on top was the return address: Dr. Milton Trafalgar, Nelson Funeral Home.

"Where's this going?" Gunther asked.

"Main Chicago railroad station," the manager said.

Gunther looked around and grabbed a hammer on a table. He stuck the claw end into a plank and wrenched it open.

"Hey!" a man cried out.

Off came three long boards, and all three men looked inside.

"Run down and get Marshal Nix," Gunther said. "Nobody else. Just Nix. Tell him I found Deputy Stell."

Chapter 24
THE CHICAGO RUN

"The big knight fell heavily to the ground, and lay there, as nearly dead as possible. His servants came running from the castle and took him in. He got better in the end, but nobody cared much about that."

—Roger Lancelyn Green, *King Arthur and His Knights of the Round Table*

Nix and Mike Tothers glared into the wooden box.

"Did he die, and Nelsons is shipping him to kinfolk in Chicago?" a clerk asked.

"Naked?" Nix said. "And no, no one knows fer sure he's dead yet. And he has two daughters that are the only next of kin, in Pine Bluff, Arkansas."

"Oh."

Gunther turned the body and examined it for injuries. He turned it on its right side, then left, then face down. Nix joined in the inspection. They saw no obvious damage from gunshots, clubbing, or knife wounds. Stell's hair was pretty long, and Gunther set into it like a monkey grooming a monkey.

"He was smacked in the head," Gunther said. "His skull is mushy on the right side. And...and...looky here. There is just a tad of dried blood in the hair here. He has been cleaned up, but not completely."

"Who is this being delivered to?" Nix asked.

The manager looked at the manifest and said, "It just says here, 'Chicago Platform.' Whoever it is will just pick it up with the right paperwork."

The three lawmen looked at each other.

"We going to Nelsons?" Tothers asked.

"No." Gunther said, before Nix could answer. "This is a gang caper of some kind. Doing something and we need to find out exactly what."

Nix listened.

"Let's re-box Stell up. I'll ride to Chicago on the train with him. See who picks him up. Then we'll see just what in hell is going on here."

"There's a woman in this one," a Frisco man cried out, almost in agony, almost tearful. He'd opened the other body-sized box.

She was about thirty years old. Naked. Beautiful even when dead. Gunther picked up the boards removed from the top and saw that name again. Return address, "Dr. Milton Trafalgar."

"Missing any beautiful women?" Gunther asked.

"Not yet!" Nix said with a sneer. "Mike, you go to Chicago with Gunther." He turned to the men in the shipping room. "I swear to Jesus if you tell anybody about this? I'll put you in jail on bread and water fer a year."

"When does the train leave?" Tothers asked.

"In seventy minutes. It goes to Omaha, Nebraska, then you switch trains to Chicago."

"Marshal will you…will you tell my wife I've been called off fer duty?" Tothers asked.

"I will, Mike. I know it's sudden. I know. But the less people know about this, the better."

"Get us tickets for Chicago and back, and orders for Stell and this poor dead woman to come back here with us," Gunther said.

"Charge my office, Randy," Nix said.

"Yes, sir."

"Marshal, will ya take my rifle and canteen?" Gunther asked, unslinging his shoulder weapon and canteen.

"Sure, son. Be at the office," Nix said.

"The World's Fair itself is a goin' on in Chicago. Maybe you all can see it?" A younger worker said.

Gunther did not answer, and Tothers was not thinking about this as a vacation trip. Trying to make things look normal, the freight workers went back to their normal duties. Gunther and Tothers walked outside on the platform with other customers. They walked over to a small shop called Amherst's and bought some coffee and cakes. Then they sat at a nearby table. Afterward, Gunther walked into the platform's news store and looked over its small newspaper and book racks. He saw one book by Jules Verne called *Claudius Bombarnac,* a story about a train ride through Asia by a bored travel writer, made exciting by a sudden transport of a Mandarin mummy and the gangs of awaiting thieves, eager to snatch the remains. Seeing the similarities of his pending journey, he chuckled and bought it.

A milkman, dressed in white, wearing a white cap and gloves, pulled his dairy wagon up to the back of Nelson's.

"Boss man here?" he asked the crew, leaping down.

"Yeah."

"Best get em."

Dr. Trafalgar and Nelson joined the milkman and the workers standing around him.

"I just saw Gunther and that Deputy Tothers drinking coffee at Amherst's on the train platform," the milkman said.

Trafalgar and Nelson stood silent for a few seconds.

"Think they know about Stell and the lady?" A worker said.

"How?"

"That Gunther is a nosy bastard. I don't know," Nelson asked.

"Naaah," one said.

Trafalgar walked in a few circles, then spoke, "He's already been on a raid with the local constabulary. Perhaps he's on another mission. Know or not, we could catch him out of town, crack his skull, and dump him off somewhere between here and Omaha. I like that. I like that idea very much."

"Mike Tothers too?" one asked, almost sympathetically.

"Maybe," Nelson said. "If need be. Mike is just a...good ol' boy. Does his job. Simple feller. Not with us, though. Let's try and leave him be. Hurry out and get Archie, Happy, and Zeke. Get them armed and on that train. They're at the wizard's house. Tell em to get there, and if they make the train? Kill Gunther and if need be...Tothers too. Make him disappear in prairie dust."

"Disappearing in the prairie dust," Dr. Trafalgar repeated. "I like that. A song title maybe?"

One of the workers ran off. The milkman got back on his

wagon and with the clanging of glass bottles, took off for the rest of his route. They all watched him leave.

"It's now official. Open season on this bloody Texas Deputy Gunther," Nelson said.

The Frisco train to Omaha lurched off, nearly one-quarter full of passengers. This run, with a stop in Omaha then on to Chicago, would take about a day. Hungry, both Gunther and Tothers went to the primitive dining car for sandwiches, more coffee, and maybe some cake or pie. Tothers told Gunther his life story, how he'd grown up in Tulsa, worked on a farm, went to college there in Tulsa, and was hired by Nix as a deputy.

"How many years?"

"Seven years. You?"

"Army four years. This'll be my fifth year in Paris."

"Curious work," Tothers said.

Tothers saw numerous Tulsa residents come in and out of the dining car, but he was none too happy to see the next three men. The men barely looked at them and sat far in the corner.

"Don't look over there now, but, those three cooters that just walked in?" Tothers said.

"Yeah?"

"Archibald Clox, Happy Podashay, and Zeke Engal."

"Yeah. What of it?"

"Those three have no business going anywhere, least of all Omaha, or any other foller-up location. Like a world's fair."

Gunther tipped his hat back, sat back to lift a cup of tea for a sip, and glanced at them.

"They are KKK," Tothers said. "They are under Ed Nelson's reign of the funeral home. The KKK is their full-time job. Most

187

others have a regular job and a family and KKK once a week or so. These boys are on full-time staff."

"Full timers. What do they do?"

"I don't rightly know what a full-time KKK man does, but they is, no doubt, up to no good," Tothers said.

"Are they here guarding the bodies? Or what?" Gunther asked.

"Don't know. Could be."

"Or, just here to kill us," Gunther said.

"More n' likely," Tothers said solemnly, shaking his head.

After eating, they made their way back to an empty car at the rear of the line and stretched out, swearing not to sleep. Gunther got up after a few hours of reading Jules Verne, he needed to stretch and decided to check on the crude, crate coffins in the freight car.

"Goin' back," Gunther shouted to Tothers in a seat up ahead.

They were the only two in this whole car. Tothers did not turn around but rather waved a hand in the air. Gunther walked through the freight area and talked for a few minutes with the freight man, an older man from Southern Illinois. Bored, he stared out the back platform for a while, and the Indian Territory faded away into darkness. Then he decided to return to his seat and his new book, worried that the lighting might not be bright enough to read.

Wobbly, Gunther shook side to side and walked back to his car. The train was noisy, and when he slid the back door open of his car no one could hear him, least of all the three dangerous men Tothers had previously pointed out.

The three were seated right behind Tothers, crowded into their one bench. With all the empty rows of seats there was no reason for such a cluster, except…trouble. Tothers sat perfectly upright in the seat in front of them. The three leaned forward talking to Tothers. Gunther could not hear what they were saying until he got very close and he saw one of the three had a large pistol out and held low.

The next thing the four of them heard was two pistols cocking right behind all of them. The two men flinched at the feel of cold metal on the back of their necks. The third man in the middle sat still.

"Yup. Guns. Fixin' to disconnect your heads from your necks," Gunther said in a growl. He sat on the bench behind the three, with his two big guns out, touching the napes of the two men at the ends.

"In case you in the middle might be wondering what in hell is going on, I've got two guns right on the necks of yer partners here. I have an idea why you are sitting here bothering Mister Tothers, but I really don't exactly care why for the moment. You three are gonna drop yer guns on the floor. And right now."

They did, and Gunther kept a careful count. The thuds cleared Tothers to stand up, turn, and pull his pistol on them.

"Now GET up!" Gunther said.

They did.

"Let's go," Gunther said, standing up himself and jerking his left-handed pistol toward the back of the car.

He pistol-point shoved them out the back, outside, on the open platforms between the cars. He instantly kicked one right off the train. The man yelped in surprise, desperately. Gone in a second. The other two, stood and watched, astonished.

"Oh my God!" one of them cried out.

"Let's go, you skunk fuck," Gunther said.

The second man crouched, then jumped off the moving train. Gunther looked at the last man.

"What is going on here? Where are those bodies going?"

"I don't know nothin' about no bodies," he said.

Gunther shot him in the foot. He screamed and almost fell off the deck.

"What is going on?"

"Fuck you."

"What is going on!" Gunther demanded.

"FUCK YOU!"

Gunther shot the other foot, and the man couldn't stand and fell right off the train. He yelled, but he and the sound disappeared quickly.

"Damn," Tothers said.

"I shoulda killed each one of them for sure," Gunther said.

"You might have! This is a moving train at its highest of all speeds," Tothers said. And they're in the middle of nowhere. With nothing. And now Zeke has two shot feet."

"Yeah," Gunther said, looking over the flat, dry land. He smiled slightly. "It's hell being in the KKK, ain't it."

They walked back inside the car, and Tothers shook his head, "You don't fool around none," he said.

"I woulda shot all three of them in the feet. Make em talk. But under the circumstances, I think we will find out all we need to know in Chicago. And, where do you think they would have put us? Shot us in the head and chunked us right off this train, too."

"They asked about the coffins and why we were here," Tothers said. "They said that Ed Nelson was just doin' his job, shipping bodies, and what business was it of ours."

"That tells us a lot right there. I reckon we're alone now. Let's get some rest and see what tomorrow brings," Tothers said.

"How did they get behind you?"

"They walked in, and Archibald, seein' on how I was alone, pulled his gun on me right away. Then they sat behind me."

"I never should have left the car," Gunther said. "I'm sorry."

"...and they piled in behind me, talking smack. They told me that I might be alright if I behaved. But you? You had to go.'"

"Had to go."

"They said they were on orders to kill you. Not me if I behaved."

"Beeee-haved," Gunther drawled and plopped down in the empty, three-seater where he left his book. "Well, they had to go, and I think we're safe."

"I think so," Tothers said, laying back in his seat too.

In another four hours, the train stopped in Omaha. They could see the big signs at the station for the Chicago World's Fair, officially called the World's Columbian Exposition, to celebrate the 400th anniversary of Christopher Columbus's arrival in the New World in 1492. This same train would switch tracks and continue on to the big city, and they need not change lines. Gunther spent the layover time sitting in the freight car keeping an eye on his deadly cargo. The train loaded up with World's Fair tourists, and off it went for the remaining seven-hour leg.

It was morning in Chicago, and the main station was busy. Giant banners for the World's Fair hung everywhere. Gunther and Tothers stood around the freight car. The freight men knew nothing of their cargo, except that the lawmen were there to see who tried to pick it up, and then they were to haul it all back to Tulsa. The workers carried all the shipments out on the business dock, and Gunther and Tothers waited in folding chairs. If no one came in three hours, the two were to stay in Chicago until someone did and return the next day. So, they sat. And sat.

After two hours of delivery pick-ups, a large wooden wagon drove up and two burly men walked to the dock area. Gunther stood and wandered off to the right to read on the side of their wagon—"University of Chicago Medical School." The foreman spoke with the two, then called Tothers, who was closer, over. Gunther walked over.

"...and these men are here for the crates," the foreman told Tothers, as Gunther approached.

The lawman showed their Texas and Oklahoma badges. The workers looked surprised.

"Do you men know what's in these wooden boxes?" Tothers asked.

"Ahhh, bodies, usually. Probably." one man said.

"Bodies."

"Yeah, the college buys em for research and, and autopsies," the other man said.

"We can't release them to you. I'm sorry," Tothers said.

"Looky here, Tex, we are ordered..."

"I'm the Tex one," Gunther interrupted, "and these people were murdered in Oklahoma. This is a murder investigation, and we were sent here to see who these bodies were being sent to."

"Murdered? Looky here Tex, we don't know nothin' about murders. We are here to get the coffins. We do this all the time," and he made a move toward the crates.

"Nope. Not gonna happen," Gunther said, stepping in the way, "you pick up these bodies from Oklahoma a lot?"

"About once maybe twice a week."

"How many?"

"Two. Three. Four at a time. I need those bodies for my delivery job. Look, do I have to get the Chicago police?"

"That would be a great idea," Gunther replied to the man's threat.

One of the men jogged off inside the station to find some local police.

"Who at the college gets these bodies next?" Gunther asked.

"It's all under Doctor Wellsbrook. He's a dean. He is no murderer. We all think these people have died from something and the...I dunno, the family sends the body to us for doctors to learn on..."

"Dr. Wellsbrook. Okay. This name right here look familiar to you?" Gunther pointed to the name stenciled on the coffin crate.

"Dr. Trafalgar. Yeah," the man said." That's the guy in Oklahoma who sends us the bodies."

"You know him?" Tothers asked.

"No."

"Always from Tulsa?" Tothers asked.

"I think so."

The other delivery man walked up with three Chicago policemen in uniform. Gunther told them the story. Then, the officers approached the two university workers, with Gunther and Tothers in tow.

"Boys," a Chicago officer said, "go back to the school and tell em that they can't have these bodies..."

"But they paid for them..."

"I know, I know, but they can't have em. It's an Oklahoma murder investigation. One of the bodies is a murdered federal deputy, for Christ sakes. The other is some missing woman."

"Oh."

"The college is gonna have to settle this some other way. But these bodies here," the officer threw a thumb over his shoulder, "they are going back to Oklahoma."

"Okay then, okay," one said. "We...we tried." The two walked back to their college wagon.

"Sorry, fellers," Tothers shouted out to them.

"Good luck with your case," the Chicago patrol sergeant said. "It looks like a lulu to me. Listen, that medical college is always buying bodies for research. They come out to our morgue all the time, find out the names of the dead, contact the families, and try to buy the bodies for...for training and research."

"Fer a lot of money?" Tothers asked.

"I think so," the other officer said. "I don't know how much, but I hear it's a pretty good coin."

They turned to leave the dock.

"Thank you, officers," Gunther said as they walked off.

Gunther walked over to the train freight workers.

"Goin' back," Gunther told them, and they started putting the two coffins back on board.

Tothers stared at the closest giant World's Fair poster. Gunther walked up next to him.

"No chance for this, huh?" Tothers said. "Bet it's magical. Someone like me, my wife and kids, we'll never see anything like this."

"That ain't true. You can plan and do whatever you want, But, nope, we're going straight back. But now we know those sons of bitches are killing people, on order, all types, and selling their bodies to medical colleges. Probably all over the country." Gunther said. "And this damn British doctor—this Trafalgar—Is the key. The key murderer."

"And the Klan. Killers. Using the immigration of Land Rush people as cover to send them all over," Tothers said.

"We have time to tell Nix by telegraph. Right away. Run and telegraph him. You know this medical college will be telegraphing Trafalgar as soon as those delivery men get back."

"Will do," Tothers said, and he headed off inside the station.

"Tell him to telegraph my Chief too!" Gunther shouted, and Tothers waved an acknowledging finger in the air.

Gunther stretched out in an empty three-seater and tugged his Stetson down over his eyes. Tothers was across the aisle and the two coffins were back in the freight cars. Southbound to Omaha. He added up the events and the total was murder. Dr. Milton Trafalgar was running a murder gang of KKK killers, operating out of Tulsa, Oklahoma. They were killing people of all shapes, sizes, and races for medical universities, for their medical research. They were using a funeral home of a new, highly-populated area to cover up the murders. The colleges either didn't care or didn't know. Gunther thought for a moment about poor Eskimo Noot, thought about the last time he saw him, shopping for food in a Paris store. He'd nodded hello to Gunther. All the way from Alaska. A college graduate. A railroad worker. There was no telling what medical school, where, cut him up into pieces for a classroom autopsy. "Looky here at the Eskimo! What a specimen."

The three KKK men he'd kicked off the train had probably

limped on home by now, if they could limp. Or they died from injuries? He expected trouble the minute the train stopped at the Tulsa station, maybe even the Omaha station, if Trafalgar and Nelson had time to run some men up there. The trouble could start in Omaha.

Just as the train rolled into Omaha, he and Tothers jumped off onto the platform and Tothers studied the few people waiting to board. Tothers saw no one suspicious from Tulsa, at least. They nodded to each other and climbed back on the train seconds before it hissed off.

Chapter 25
SIEGE AT CASTLE TULSA

Night. Dark. Fog. Quiet, but for crickets. A few streetlights flickered. The Tulsa train arrived late, a little after 10 p.m. The few passengers got off the train. A burly conductor finished up his work. Two railmen helped. An anxious deputy waited for them.

"Still alive? Deputy Anthony Grimaldi," the man said, introducing himself to Gunther. He was a stocky man with thick black hair under a tipped-back, brown leather hat.

"Still," Gunther said. "Johann Gunther." They shook hands.

"Tothers."

"Hi, Anthony."

Gunther scanned the station and the empty streets. A fog settled in about a foot off the ground. It rolled around in patches and in slow motion waves.

"The train will be locked up till dawn. We'll get the bodies out of the car then," Grimaldi said.

"Trafalgar?" Gunther asked.

"Gone. He's gone." Grimaldi said.

"Gone how?" Tothers asked.

"Don't know. Wagon? Horse? Not by a train from here. He disappeared this morning. Probably after the College in Chicago contacted him."

"Nelson?"

"In jail as of this morning. He ain't talkin'. He says we're crazy. He says there will be hell to pay for jailin' em."

Gunther walked to the edge of the platform. The darkness. The fog. A hellish feeling.

"I don't like this," he said eyeing the streets. "Where we going?"

"I'm going home," Tothers said. "Get my horse and go home."

"I wish you wouldn't," Gunther mumbled.

"You ain't," Grimaldi said. "Both a ya are going to the office, and we'll sort it all out come mornin'. Nix's orders."

The few passengers were met by family and friends. Laughter. Happiness. Hellos. And they left in a few coaches and on horses.

"Walkin', I reckon?" Gunther said.

"Walkin'," Grimaldi said.

Gunther grimaced and said, "Tell ya what, let's not walk the easiest way."

Grimaldi held a rifle in his hand and laid the barrel upon his shoulder.

"Whatever you say, Tex," he said. "Every shot you've called has rung a bell so far."

The three stepped down to street level and instead of taking the obvious, main avenue, Gunther took a right turn to a side street. The deputies followed. Then they took a fast left down the next avenue. Gunther stopped suddenly, and they bumped into him. Gunther quickly peeked around that last corner behind him. He could spy the railroad station and the main avenue.

"Shitfire," Gunther whispered.

"What?" Tothers said.

"Two men came out across the street and ran down the avenue, as if to run parallel with us."

"They just folks leaving the station?" Tothers asked.

"Their faces...are wrapped in white cloth. Masks," Gunther said.

"Well, shitfire then," Grimaldi said.

Gunther backtracked up to the main avenue. The other two followed. He peered around that corner. He saw the two masked men wave to two other masked men in an alley across the street.

"Ambush," Gunther said. He looked all around and saw no quick solutions.

Tothers and Grimaldi peeked around the edge too and spied the backs of the four men. The four were hunched over, in dark clothes with white cloth masks, as they crept up the avenue, likely hoping to catch sight of the lawmen at the intersections of the side streets, anticipating their path.

Gunther first thought of hiding, but then the dark roadway and its rippling fog had an odd glowing red flicker, moving, growing closer, and they heard voices coming their way along with it. The three darted back to the railroad platform and went knee high, half-covered in the fog, watching.

Three men in complete, white KKK robes appeared. The red flicker on the fog came from one of them carrying a wooden torch. They walked brazenly down the middle of the street and right past them, as if to catch up with the other four searching ahead.

"Seven," Tothers whispered.

"So far," Grimaldi said. He slowly opened the lever action on his rifle and slipped a small piece of metal into position on the action. This would hit the trigger if he closed the lever all the way. This metal attachment would cause an instantaneous firing when the lever closed alone and would do so with every subsequent lever action for a really rapid fire. Grimaldi would not have to squeeze the trigger, just work the lever action.

There was a subtle scuffling sound right behind them, upon the elevated platform.

"He's back here, Colonel!" shouted a gravelly voice from the rear.

The lawmen spun their heads to see the train conductor, shaped like an ogre, waving his arms to get attention. In one hand he toted a huge metal wrench. The ogre heaved it at Gunther's head, then he jogged away with a limp. The heavy tool hit the side of Gunther's head and shoulder, knocking him right off his knees, onto his back and down to the dirt. Tothers and Grimaldi got lower in the fog and spread out.

At first, Gunther's head felt numb and he thought nothing of the blow, but in seconds, a pain, a grogginess, and nausea befell him. He tried to sit up and felt dizzy. He laid back down, flat on his chest, partially covered in fog

The seven men collected on the street. Most near the sidewalks, but the man with the torch and in a white hat and robes stood in the open, fearless in the middle of the empty street.

"Tothers! Grimaldi!" the man in the white robes said. "We have no quarrel with you. We just want the Texican."

Silence.

"And we want Ed Nelson," the man said. "He's done nothing but dispatch dead people off to the hereafter. He's hurt nobody."

"Then who hurt Deputy Stell? Who killed Stell in his bed?" Grimaldi shouted.

"It wasn't Ed Nelson," the Colonel said. "Come on out and we can treaty about this."

"But you will kill the Texican, Gunther!" Tothers said.

"That's neither here-ner-there and not your concern!" the man demanded.

Gunther almost vomited. But he pulled a pistol and sat up, his back resting against the platform for support fog swirling around him. Tothers' handgun was already out.

"Let us pass," Grimaldi said.

"Give us the Texican."

"We gonna stay here all night?" Grimaldi asked.

"No. No. We will treaty...or you all will die here," the Colonel said.

And with that word "die," Gunther shot the Colonel right in the face with his pistol. The hood flapped in red. The torch flew, tumbling in the air. The body dropped and the six men with him were in a shock for a second.

Grimaldi worked the lever action and the .32-40 rounds poured out like a Gatling gun. Tothers fired and rolled, fired and rolled. As the masked men were shot, they ran, and they shot back at the gun flashes from under the foggy platform. Gunther tried to move but couldn't. He fell flat in place. He could shoot, but he just couldn't move. Then the dark night went black all around him.

His arms were over his head. His head back. Hat gone. His

butt and legs dragged on the dirt. A boot ripped off his foot. The hustling sounds of grunts and steps churned on either side of him.

"Wha..."

"You're ok," A familiar voice said, out of breath. "You're gonna be ok."

"Ok," he repeated.

"You are...?" Then he passed out again.

His head hit the hard floor. He opened his eyes. Men ran around him.

"Wha..."

"You're ok," Tothers said, leaning into his face. "You're shot. Twice. In the arm and the leg. And you got conked hard on the head."

"When?" Gunther knew he was now on the wooden floor of the Marshal's Office. "What am I...?" Men blew out room lights and crouched by windows, holding guns.

"We got em," Grimaldi said.

"They're either dead or scattered," Tothers said.

"Who...got?"

"The men. The KKK. You'll remember. You'll remember in just a minute. Don't worry about it."

Crouched over, Nix ran through the lobby and looked Gunther over.

"Get em back here," another man said.

They dragged him over to an interior wall.

"I'm Longo Prosper, Deputy Gunther," a man said, whose face loomed into his view. "I am a doctor. A surgeon..."

"Longo'll do ya good," Nix said.

Gunther tried to focus on the man's face. He was about sixty years old. A beard. Glasses.

"I'm gonna have a look at your wounds, now, son. See what's what."

Gunther vomited again, but the doctor never missed a step. In fact, he chuckled as he wiped his face.

A rag went over Gunther's mouth. The smell was horrible. Like varnish. Like they were painting his face. He…

Gunther woke again bellowing like a bull in a rut from pain. Two men held his arms. This doctor hovered over him with a small silver knife. There was blood. There was branding iron heat! Then the rag covered his face again. He gagged. Coughed. Yelled. The smell. Horrible. He…

He woke yet again. He was lost. Where was he? The doctor sat cross-legged, beside him.

"You took a bullet in the back of your arm, by your shoulder. It went in and out near your elbow. You took a bullet in the top of your thigh. It went in and out your thigh by your knee. Your knee and elbow are okay, son."

Gunther stared in shock at the doctor. He coughed and looked around the room. Deputies were still kneeling by the windows. Men were shouting outside. Nix bent over, ran to him, and sat on the floor.

"They are laying siege out there on us," Nix said.

"Siege," Gunther said. "Siege like a castle?" Gunther imagined Gustav's face next to Nix.

"Like a castle. I reckon, they want to kill you… they want us to turn you over…"

"They...?"

"The KKK, Johann! You shot their leader in the face and you broke up their murder gang. They were killing people on speculation. Selling the dead to medical universities for teachers to teach new doctors."

"Yeah, yeah, they...they..."

"Now, more of em are dead. You have dispensed more justice around here in one week then we have in years. They think they can threaten us and fix it all."

Gunther was mystified.

"You, Tothers, and Grimaldi killed all seven of them by the station. You shot their leader. More piled into town within an hour," Nix said.

Gunther tried to remember. He tried to sit up.

"No, no, no, no," Nix said, pushing him back down.

"Is Tothers and..."

"They are fine. They hauled you back here."

Gunshots. Broken glass. Pounded wood. Splinters flew.

"Send out the Texican!" A voice bellowed from outside. "Send out Ed Nelson!"

"What is the...water. Is there any water?" Gunther asked.

The doctor gave him a glass of water.

Another man knelt beside Gunther.

"First, we are gonna get you the hell outta here," Nix said. "This is Jason Pelster. He's the postmaster."

"Son, we are next door," Pelster said. "Through that room there, there's a door there to the Post Office. I am sure nobody knows about it. It's never used, but they built it when they built the federal building here. We make a postal wagon run to Oklahoma City every morning to deliver and distribute the mail."

Gunther's eyes shifted over to Nix. Nix nodded.

"We have a secret compartment in the floor of every wagon," the postmaster continued. "In case we have… money… or, or certificates, or other valuable cargo. We're gonna put you in there, seal it up and at 6 a.m. we'll run the wagon, like we do six mornings a week, to Oklahoma City."

"What time is it now?" Gunther asked.

"4:15."

"In the morning?"

"In the morning."

"Good God, I've caused you all so much trouble…"

"Just doin' yer job," Nix said. "We'll get you outta here. Then we'll wait them out for a few hours. Then break the bad news that you is gone. Yeah, we'll stall for hours. Then I'll talk with them. No one has been shot on either side since your hullabaloo at the station. And they're all dead! All we have here so far is damages and threats. I'll talk with em, let em leave, maybe. We may or may not arrest em all eventually. If they remain, if they persist, they will be met with the full fury of the law."

"Ed Nelson?" Gunther asked.

"He stays with us. He's got a lot of explainin' to do," Nix said.

"Our drivers are no lily-livers," Pelster said. "They ride with shotguns and many were with Wells Fargo in the wild 70s and 80s. We'll take you to the federal territory hospital in Oklahoma City," the postmaster said. "Well also get backup down here from Oklahoma City to help us."

"This your idea?" Gunther asked Nix.

"It is."

Gunther sipped the water. He looked at the bandage on his arm and the bandage on his leg.

"All this stop bleeding, doctor?"

"Fer the most part. Seeping a little," Doc Longo said, putting up his tools.

"Seeping. Hey, I need my guns!" he said and tried to look around.

"You'll have em," Nix said. "We took em when the doc was cutting you up."

"Standard practice," Gunther mumbled. "Oh, my Casey!"

"We'll take care of your horse, Johann."

"Okay. Okay. He sleeps a lot."

"Yeah, we noticed."

"What time is it now?"

"4:16. A whole minute has passed," Pelster said.

Gunther looked around on the floor and set the water glass carefully down, trying to look confident.

"You mind if I sleep now?" Gunther asked with a slur.

"Not a bit," the doctor said.

Gunther's head drooped.

"All that's gonna hurt real bad, real soon," Longo said to Pelster. "And that's gonna be a rough ride in the bottom of that wagon. He'd better be real quiet when he's first getting outta here. Stuff a rag in his mouth or something."

Pelster nodded.

"I won't utter...a sound," Gunther mumbled with his eyes closed.

He was lifted and startled awake. Four men held him, two by the arms, two by the legs. They passed through the back room, through a door and into the postal building. The postmen stopped their sorting and packing and looked at him. They laid him on a stack of canvas bags. He hurt. His head. His leg. His arm. Dr. Longo Prosper followed them and took another look at his bandages.

"Hmmmm," the doc said.

"Hmmm what?" Gunther said.

He just nodded his head up and down and walked off.

The four deputies stayed with him. The postal men slid open wooden double doors. An enclosed, fairly new looking postal wagon with a four-horse team was a few feet away and sideways to them. Gunther watched the postmaster and another man open the side doors of the wagon and pry open the floor.

"Okay," he told the deputies.

Another man ran up with four seat cushions and laid them in the hatch as the men lifted Gunther out the door, the few feet to the wagon, and inside. They laid him on the seat cushions. One deputy handed him his two-gun belt. Gunther winced and nodded thanks. He laid the rig on his chest.

"Okay, son?" Pelster asked.

"Yup."

"Now, be quiet. No one can see us in the stable. It's gated. They have circled around us, the whole federal building, and they may try to stop us. Jerome here is riding shotgun and he takes no guff. Just be quiet."

"Quiet," Gunther repeated.

Pelster and a worker put the hatchback on the floor. It sealed and Gunther laid in total darkness. He got sick to his stomach but held his guts in. What sounded like bags hit the wooden floor above him. Could he breathe under all this? But on his new ceiling above him, inches away, he saw thin red and yellow reflections from the floorboards, bouncing off the ground from the torches moving outside. Air!

Then the wagon shifted from side to side, deep right to deep left then level, all in such a way Gunther thought two men climbed aboard the perch. The horses moved off and now he really felt sick. He heard a wooden gate like a fort open and the wagon proceeded forward.

"Hey there. Stop!" ordered a voice.

"Halt!" came another.

Outside and atop the wagon, the two postal men still sat. A driver and Jerome the shotgun rider.

"What?" Jerome said.

"We are looking for somebody."

Three men with rifles stood in their way. Two more were ten or so feet to the right and another three were off to the left. Some of them wore white masks. Some didn't.

"What in hell is goin' on here?" Jerome asked.

"There's been a shootin' and we want the man who done it," one said. He held his rifle aimed high.

"You aim that thing at me again and there'll be another shootin' right here. I'll kill ya right now where ya stand," Jerome said.

The man lowered his gun.

"Is the shooter in the Marshal's Office?" the driver asked.

"Yeah, he is."

"You wanna hang em or something?"

"Yeah, we do."

"Well, we're the Post Office and we don't know nothin' about all that. We have to deliver this mail to Oklahoma City," the driver said.

The men looked at each other.

"Open er up," one commanded.

Three of other postal workers were still at the open back gate. None of them were armed. The deputies were across the yard, hiding behind the postal dock doors.

"It's locked," the driver said.

"Why is it locked?"

"It's the mail!" Jerome growled.

"Mister mailman, you ain't goin' nowhere till we see what's in that wagon. You all are government men in cahoots with each other, and we don't believe any of ya."

"Carpet baggers," another man said.

Jerome winced at the pejorative and signaled for a man from the gate to approach the wagon. He tossed the man a set of keys. The man unlocked a padlock, unlocked the doors, and opened them. Buried inside and under the floor, Gunther slowly pulled both his pistols from the holsters on his chest.

"Step aside, yank," a man said and looked inside, rifle first.

The interior held six dirty canvas bags of mail. He poked at them with his rifle, probing as best he could in the pre-dawn light. The man stepped back and shook his head side to side.

The worker shut the doors and started locking the wagon.

"Yank? Carpet bagger?" Jerome repeated, "When's all that shit over?"

"It's never over," another said.

The worker chucked the keys up to Jerome. He shoved them in his jacket pocket.

"Get out the fuckin' way," he said to them. And they did.

The wagon rocked off. The postal men shut the back gate. Gunther holstered his two pistols. That done, he started to feel the pains in his arm and leg.

About thirty minutes later the wagon stopped. Gunther heard the wagon door unlocked. He pulled his gun again.

"Johann?"

It was Jerome's voice. He heard the bags slip across the floor and the hatch opened.

"How ya doin', kid?"

"In a foggy...fog," Gunther said.

He sat up and looked around.

"We made it far enough out. I figured you needed out of this here coffin."

"I do. I do."

Jerome climbed in and helped Gunther out of the secret bay so he could lay on the wagon floor. He plucked out the seat cushions and laid them on the floor and helped Gunther slip onto them. The driver stood outside looking in. Jerome opened a woven picnic basket and pulled out a glass jar of water and handed it to Gunther. Then he unfolded a plaid cheesecloth and handed Gunther a sandwich.

"Ohhh, thanks. I need this."

"Okay, we're gonna get goin' again. Hang on to something."

"The doc said you're gonna need a lot of water."

They shut the door and locked it. Gunther settled in between two big mail bags for the ride to Oklahoma City, nibbling on a beef sandwich. He carefully unscrewed the jar for sips of water.

Hours later, the wagon stopped. The door opened. Gunther heard Jerome shout.

"I've got a deputy out here! He's been shot. Not in the brisket but in the arm and leg, but he's still gonna die."

Jerome opened the wagon door. Nurses ran out, shoving a bed on wheels. Gunther was very dizzy, exhausted, and on the verge of unconsciousness.

Four of them and Jerome inched Gunther out of the wagon and onto the bed. Jerome put his folded gun belt on his lap and shoved a paper satchel between his legs.

"Nix told me to give you this."

"What is it?"

"Telegrams from yer boss in Texas."

Gunther nodded.

"We will tell the Marshal here that you are in the hospital. He'll take care of you now."

Gunther was whisked off.

"Thanks. Thank you, boys," Gunther shouted over his shoulder. "I…"

And the men and wagon took off.

He was put on a table and two doctors looked him over. They peeled off all his nasty clothes and bandages.

"This looks pretty good. Who worked on you?" a doctor asked.

"A feller named Longo Prosper? Prosper Longo? Something like that."

"We know him. Good man. He even cauterized these wounds very well. This must have hurt?"

"I don't remember."

"Well, then yer lucky, young man."

Naked, Gunther was next wheeled off to a bathing room. Two nurses set him on a wooden bench in a large metal tub filled with water. They bathed him with sponges leaving his injured arm and leg hanging out over the side of the tub to avoid getting his wounds wet. They scrubbed him with soft brushes, poured water over his head, and then scrubbed him again. They drained the tub and started all over once more. He wanted to make some funny remarks about this situation but didn't have the strength and didn't trust his slurred cleverness. The hot water burned but he did not complain. They lifted him out, dried him carefully to avoid disturbing the wounds, then applied new bandages. Then they put a long, clean sleep shirt on him, wheeled him to a private room, and hefted him into a bed. The bed was fresh, clean, and seemed like a special, beautiful, new heaven to Gunther. Once flat with his head on a pillow, with nurses tucking him in, his eyes filled up with tears.

"I...can't thank you ladies enough, for...everything...I..."

They just smiled.

Another nurse walked in with his gun belt, his wallet, and that paper satchel Jerome handed off. Gunther saw that his badge, once on his shirt, was now pinned to a side of the belt buckle. She placed the belt with the badge and the wallet in the bag and put the bag on a chair beside the bed. She said, "Your clothes are filthy and bloody. You only have one boot! We are going to throw them away. The marshal will be here later today to look in on you, and he'll arrange to bring you a nice, new suit."

"I don't have much money."

"I am sure the government will pay for you, deputy. Get some sleep."

He nodded. He started to reach for the satchel, to read the telegram, but suddenly fell fast asleep.

Hours later Gunther awoke to see the satchel back on the chair. A nurse must have set it there. He opened it, and there was but one piece of paper. It read:

I contacted my friends in Scotland Yard –(Stop)

They report that Milton Trafalgar is a renegade doctor, wanted in England for murder, rape, robbery –(Stop)

Sending inspectors to Tulsa to begin an investigation and hunt –(Stop)

Marshal Nix reports that you have been an outstanding help and almost single-handedly cracked Trafalgar and his KKK gang of killers, grave robbers, and body sellers, as well as solved other store armed robberies and cornered outlaws –(Stop)

Outstanding work –(Stop)

Police Chief Gustav Henri, Paris, Texas Police Department

Just after Gunther finished a dinner of pork chops, beans, and fried apples, two well-dressed men in suits walked into his room. They were followed by a lesser-dressed Hispanic man, carrying a suitcase.

"Deputy Johann Gunther. My name is Marshal Jim Braddocks," the older man said with an extended hand.

"My name is Bass Reeves," the other said, a black man with a gigantic mustache.

"I run the office here and Bass works out of Arkansas office but covers this territory too."

"Some 75,000 square miles," Bass said with a smile.

"Thunderation!" Gunther said weakly, inching himself to sit up more in the bed. "Well, sir, I think I have heard of you."

"It's possible," Bass Reeves said.

"Manny, come over here," Braddocks said to the third man. "This is Manny from our office. He is going to clean your guns and badge up shiny, and polish up your gun belt. It has come to my understandin' that you only have one boot! And your clothes is a mess."

"I believe so."

"Manny will take care of all of this. He works in our office and can get, clean, and fix any and everything."

Manny nodded. Gunther nodded back. Then Manny opened his suitcase to display well-organized, gunsmith tools, cleaning supplies, and leatherworks. He sat on the floor by the bedstand and lifted Gunther's rig off of the chair and onto his lap.

"Have you heard anything from Nix and what happened after I left?" Gunther asked.

The two officers pulled up chairs and sat, hats off.

"I have, I did," Braddocks said. "They arrested some of the siege. Ran the others off. Ed Nelson is still in jail and is talking his head out of a noose. What of exactly, I don't know."

"They have to question the four or five men that work in the funeral home. They know it all," Gunther said.

"It is apparent you have cleared up many mysteries in Arkansas, Oklahoma, and Texas."

Bass Reeves nodded.

"The governor of Oklahoma," Braddocks said, "had a mystery of his own. His wife's sister disappeared outta nowhere about eight months ago. He is now of the belief that these men, this Trafalgar and his cohorts are responsible for her odd disappearance, thus bringing a quantum of closure to his wife and a grievin' family. He is indebted to you."

Gunther nodded.

"And the governor and the Marshal's Office of Arkansas also thank you," Bass Reeves said. "This has shed a light on some missing people reports."

"And now, I have the most depressing news for you, son," Braddocks said.

Gunther's eyebrows shot up, "Oh no, who's been shot?"

"No, no, not like that. It seems that there is a bounty on your head. A $1,000 bounty on your head, from the Klu Klux Klan. And said bounty has already been broadcasted throughout the Southern United States and continues to be, by telegraphs, handbills, and newsletters."

Bass Reeves grimaced along with Gunther.

"$1,000!" Gunther whispered. The amount was astonishing.

"I fear, that we fear you are no longer safe anywhere you go south of the Mason-Dixon Line. You shot and killed one of their beloved leaders. As witnessed by a KKK railroad engineer or conductor."

"The conductor. That's the son of bitch that hit me in the head with an engine tool," Gunther said touching the black and blue side of his face.

"The governor of Oklahoma and the governor of Arkansas have come up with a solution for this, for you. And they have spoken to your Chief Henri by telephone."

"What kind of solution?"

"We have all agreed that we need to get you the Hades outta hear."

"Outta...here?"

"Way up north. Protected. For years."

"Years?"

"Yessir. The two governors of which we spoke, you see, are empowered to make recommendations and appointments to various prestigious positions. The two of them, and this has been confirmed awaiting your approval, have worked together and secured a slot for you at the military academy in West Point, in New York."

"West...Point," Gunther said. "Can they not get me another police job up North?"

"No, they cannot, sir. They have no such influence. Now you were once in the Army, which helped said appointment. The school is four years long. A military college. You would be safe behind their walls for four years. And we believe that $1,000 will fall by the wayside by then. Or we will have arrested or killed off the ones who would pay such a fortune. You are familiar with the academy?"

"Well, I am. But I was just a, you know... troop. A horseman in the cavalry. I am not cut from the same cloth as these cadets. These officers."

"Who says?" Bass Reeves said. "You have faced killers and murderers. Without hesitation. You have kept the peace, worked with Indians. And solved many problems. Everyone thinks you're a real smart kid."

"And your police chief says you are a reader and a good student of history and the law." Braddocks said.

"He thinks I should go?"

"He does, Mr. Gunther. He does. He knows also that it will keep you safe. Keep you alive. You will not be safe in Paris, Texas, or, for that matter, anywhere in the South."

"In this whole region," Bass Reeves said.

Gunther stared at the blankets folded over his chest. He sighed.

"I suggest you pull that sword from the stone, because you can, and get your ass up to West Point. What say yee, King Johann?"

"I am shot to hell. I need help holden my own self up just to take a piss in the room right over there. But it seems I have no choice? Then…yes."

The men stood. Manny remained on the floor, working.

"Excellent. I will have two deputies guarding you now twenty-four hours a day. I will have one escort you all the way to the academy in New York State and hand you off to the Army at the front doors of West Point."

"When?"

"The next class starts in four weeks."

"Can I go back…."

"…back to Paris for a visit?" Braddock anticipated. "Good-byes? Hell no. You'd be a dead man. Right now, no one knows where you are, boy. They will think you are headed back to Paris. You are safe here for a little while. Then we'll get you north. Your police chief is gonna tell everyone you've gone back to Germany. Just to keep the peace in his little burgh when they come a lookin' for you."

"No Paris," Gunther said, disappointed.

"No Paris. New York. West Point."

PART II
CRUSADE 2

CHAPTER 26
MUDDY WATERS

Remedies Detective Agency
Fort Worth, Texas
March 1916

"Gunth."

Gunther stared out of the window of his meeting room.

"Gunth!" Jefe repeated.

"Yeah?" he turned to his friend. "I was just thinking about how I met Stinky and Gustav. Back in the 1890s. And the last time I saw them. You know, I've never been back to Paris, Texas, since. Since that one afternoon I rode out on a train to Oklahoma for what was to be a 'short' trip, collecting information, hunting for a wanted man."

"What will you do now?"

"Stinky and I will go to Paris and see Gustav."

He sat back down at the conference room table.

"Gustav quit writing to me, early on, during my first year at West Point. He quit after he got all the details of the shootings, and the mayhem in Oklahoma I was involved in. It was really the old Wild West up there, back then. I kept getting into all these fixes."

"I cannot imagine," Jefe said sarcastically.

"He wrote me, that he thought I was becoming a...a killer. He said I was a killing machine. Too quick to draw. Too quick to shoot. 'Gun burn' as he used to call it. He said it was all his fault because he taught me to shoot and fight. He said a peace officer should first solve things peacefully. That last letter from him was quite a letter. Quite the composition. Quite the thrashing. I have it somewhere. He said...he said he was disappointed in me."

Jefe stared at him.

"*He* was a violent man," Gunther said. "*He* shot people and... and *he* beat them up too. Yet *he* thought *I* was too violent? One time I shot two men trying to rob a department store in Oklahoma. I was his deputy then, and I believed one of our murder suspects was going to rob a big store. Later, when he heard the details, he said that I should have staked out the store, stopped, and arrested the two men outside. Instead? I shot and killed them inside. I was alone. I couldn't sit in a bush in the backyard for six days. What if the robbers went in the front doors and what? What then? I am out back sitting in a damn rose bush? I had to improvise. Plus, I did not want these killers getting inside the store full of customers and salespeople."

Jefe nodded.

"A policeman, he said, kills as a last resort. Anyway, I never wrote back to him after that. I never wrote to anyone really while from West Point. I...never had anyone to write to."

"Dhis was the sad young life you have lived," Jefe said.

"Yeah, maybe."

"Maybe he wanted you to be better than him."

"Maybe. Stinky…Now, Stinky's way was always perfect for him. Stink worked with people when they had problems. He knew how to do it all. All the time. But when it was time to pull the trigger, Stinky pulled."

They sat quiet.

"Anyway, Stinky and I will go to Paris. I will protect Gustav. He might turn out to like a little of my gun burn after all."

"I'll go too," Jefe said,

"Nahhh. We have cases here to work, and this is my old problem."

"You are *my* oldest problem."

"You can't risk going," Gunther said. "You risk enough. You risk enough as it is. You…"

"I know, I am married. The children."

"Exactly."

"You don't have to go, either."

"Funny. Gustav was always talking about European history. Knights. Medieval history. The times. Our nickname at West Point was the Black Knights, and West Point looks just like a giant castle on a river in Europe. Black knights from the black uniforms they gave us. West Point. A few mottos. Ideals. Loyalty. 'Bear true faith and allegiance to your unit and other soldiers.' Duty. Fulfill your obligations. Loyalty. I have to go. Stinky was like a brother to me. Gustav like a father. I am…I am like, like a bad son. Stinky and I will leave in the morning."

"We will pack up dey Chevy Baby Grande," Jefe said.

As I recall, it's about 150 miles from here to Paris, or thereabouts. The roads will be good to Sherman, then some kind of rough ride onward to Paris, but the Chevy will be fine. But I don't know how long I'll be gone. I'll just have to see how things are when we get there."

"Okay."

"You know," Gunther continued, "I was escorted all the way to West Point from Oklahoma City by an Oklahoma federal marshal, to see that I arrived at the gates safely. I was still a mess of wounds and pains from the gunshots. But I planned on giving the marshal my Paris police badge at the gates, so he could return it to Paris. They all wanted me to keep my law enforcement status up to the very end, in case something happened to us along the way to West Point. But I forgot to hand it off. I kept it. I still have that Paris police badge in my things upstairs somewhere. I believe I will take this badge back to Gustav in person."

"He is no longer the police chief," Jefe said.

"You're right about that," Gunther said. "I still might do it though."

"Symbolic," Jefe said.

"Yeah, yeah. Symbolic."

Morning. "Quite Some," was Jefe's favorite cousin from the Philippines, imported by Jefe ten years earlier from the islands to run the Remedies stable of horses and two coaches, behind their office/residence. But in the last decade, the agency had collected two automobiles, causing Quite Some quite a bit more work to do. Jefe insisted his cousin take some auto mechanics classes from the Fort Worth Chevy dealership to better maintain and keep the vehicles running. Quite Some became a handy mechanic for friends and family.

Their main company car was a 1916 black Chevy Baby Grande, a 2,500 lb., Model H-4. 171 cubic-inch, 4-cylinder, 3-speed sliding transmission. Electric lights. A 5-seater. Two in the front, three in the back, with a convertible top.

Stinky, Jefe, Gunther, and Quite Some were loading the back seat with gear, luggage, and food. They tied three large cans of petrol on the back. Jefe's kids were running about, and Maria and Gunther's personal maid-assistant from India, Mesha, stood watching them in the courtyard. There was the usual sense of doom and gloom when either Gunther, Jefe, or the two of them were loading up their horses or cars to run out on a mission. Jefe's children, of course, maintained no real sense of danger.

Quite Some was about to crank the car.

"Hold on. Hey, Stinky," Gunther said, "You know how to do this?"

Stinky shook his head, no.

"Come on around here as you may have to do this."

Stinky lumbered over to the front of the car by Quite Some, and watched as Quite Some gingerly circled the hand crank starter trying to catch the crank just right and start the car.

"Y Jou hab to feel it," Quite Some explained, in a thick accent.

Stinky, as still as a statue, watched. Quite Some quickly started the engine.

Gunther waved goodbye to Maria and Mesha as they forced half-smiles and waved back. Mesha's monkey sat inside on the windowsill, looking out at them. Jealous.

Gunther approached Jefe. He put up his hand, but they always grabbed each other on the forearms instead of shaking hands.

"My friend," Gunther said.

"My friend," Jefe said.

Jefe could detect just a slight air of excitement about Gunther. A new journey. A new adventure. Jefe shook his head from side to side. This air will surely lead to their deaths someday.

"Peace be with you," Jefe said.

"Not this trip," Gunther said.

With that, Gunther and Stinky climbed aboard the Chevy. Stinky checked his pocket watch. Gunther hit the horn, clearing the kids out of the way.

"Adios!" they yelled.

"Ingat! Ingat!" Gunther yelled back.

And out the back gates they drove. Jefe slowly walked to the gates, stepped out, and watched the Baby Grand leave.

"Crazy," he muttered. "Crazy." He helped Quite Some shut the gates.

"You have lots of friends here," Stinky said, a tad more relaxed when away from people.

"Yes, I do," Gunther said.

"How did you meet them?"

Gunther slowly explained his history from West Point on. Cuba. The Philippines. China. Assignments and jobs from President Theodore Roosevelt. How Mesha saved his life in Afghanistan. Why there was a pet monkey roaming the office. How and why he and Jefe started a detective, problem-solving agency. This conversation ate up many a mile. Stinky stared, face forward, never changing his expression. Gunther knew however, he was absorbing every word, memorizing them in fact, as was…Stinky's way.

"When did you leave Paris?" Gunther asked.

"4:33 p.m. April 23rd, 1909."

Gunther smiled.

"Why did you leave Paris?'

"Chief Gustav retired. 5 p.m. April 1st, 1909. And I decided at 5:23 p.m. I would not work for the man the city wanted to be the new chief."

"He still there?"

"Yes."

"What's so bad about him?"

"His name is Garrison Drill. He has worked in many police agencies and offices in Oklahoma and Arkansas. He makes a very good first impression, by which he tricks people into thinking he is smart. But he cannot last anywhere for more than six months. He has a troubled head. He cannot help but make trouble. Small and big troubles for people. He makes big mistakes in investigations. He usually suspects the wrong people."

"Seems like he's been in Paris a long time."

"I don't know why. Many good men have quit from him. New good men hired. Then they quit. Only weak men remain. Stupid and weak men. He makes enemies of good people. He makes alliances with bad people and stupid people. Untrustworthy people."

"Oh. I see," Gunther said. "Can we count on him for help?"

"His help will only hurt. That's the way I see it. There is always a problem."

"Why did you become a federal, deputy marshal? Way out in West Texas."

"I had no job. I needed money. I knew the marshals around Paris. They like me. They got me the job. This reminds me,

Gunther. I can make deputies in emergencies. I can deputize you. I might need to deputize you in Paris. Are you prepared for that?"

"I reckon I am."

"I reckon you are."

Stinky still had not turned his head once to look a Gunther.

"You ever get married…or anything?" Gunther asked.

"No."

"You?"

"No."

"I started working as a marshal 9:02 a.m. May 1st, 1908."

"You like the job?"

"Yes. No. Yes. We cover lots of land out there. No good fishing."

"That's a problem," Gunther said.

"Muddy. Muddy waters out there too. You can't see in the water. This bothers me, Gunth."

"I quit fishing," Gunther said.

And for the first time, Stinky turned and looked at him, aghast.

"I got too busy. Not enough time," Gunther explained.

"I suppose you eat fish only from a restaurant, then?"

"Or from a store. I just don't have time to go fishing."

"A store. We'll go fishing in Paris," Stinky said. "The water is clear there in Paris."

"We'll go fishing like we used to," Gunther said, "at Lake Crenshaw."

"Yes. The last time we went fishing was 5:25 p.m., June 17th, 1896." Stinky said staring ahead.

"Did we catch anything?"

"I can't remember."

Stinky can't remember? *That* made Gunther squint and look hard at Stinky.

They made it all the way to Sherman without a single flat tire. They spent the night in the Aberdeen Hotel. The next morning the temperature had dropped into the low forties with a gusty wind and a depressing, overcast sky. They put on several layers of clothes, rolled the rooftop over the cab, and continued northwest on the rougher road to Paris, Texas. They arrived in the city limits within four hours.

A sign read, "Paris, Texas. Population 15,000."

"Wow," Gunther said. "15,000."

"When you left it was 6,347. When I left it was 11,017. Turn here," Stinky said.

"Turn here," he said again minutes later.

"It's there. Gustav's house."

The single-story house did look like a French cottage. The land was flat and well-treed. They drove up to the front of the house. Gunther became nervous with the first signs of meeting his old mentor considering the many year "gun burn" grudge between them. But the house windows this gray day revealed only a dark interior.

Stinky got out and knocked on the door. Nothing. He peered into the front windows. He hustled through the cold wind and back to the Chevy.

"They ain't there. Let's go to town."

Small icy droplets landed on the windshield and whipped in the openings of the canvas rooftop and cab. Within minutes, they were downtown and, for both men, much had changed.

Much had developed. Some cars, some horse-drawn carriages, some folks on horseback, and quite a few people meandered along the avenues and streets. Gunther parked in front of the city police department. They walked inside.

"Can we help you fellers?" a large, older female with a cigar in her mouth asked from behind a front desk in the lobby. The name plate on the desk read "Maisy Morris, Station Administrator."

Gunther and Stinky took a good look around their old digs. Gunther tipped his hat back and peeled off his gloves.

"Yes, Mrs. Morris..."

"*Miss* Morris," she corrected.

"Miss Morris, we are trying to find our old police chief, Gustav Henri. And we'd like to talk to the new chief about some trouble that is brewing for Henri."

"Our?" Miss Maisy Morris said.

"Ah yes," Gunther replied. "We both use to work here once. It was years...."

"And can I help you?" came a bellowing voice from the chief's office. It was Garrison Drill in the doorway. He was a tall, thick-necked, fat man, bald, thin-lipped, with a double chin. Almost cross-eyed. "I am Chief Drill."

"Johann Gunther. This here is Deputy Federal Marshal Stinky Moses. We both worked here years ago."

Drill looked Stinky over, from Stink's boots up to his 6'9" head.

"I know you. I remember you." He said to Stinky with a grimace, a bobbing head, and with almost a tone of disgust. He waved his hand for them to enter his office. He sat behind a desk, and they sat in chairs. He stared at them, which Gunther took as an act of intimidation. Gunther stared back.

Finally, Drill said, "Lookin' fer Gustav Henri?"

"Yes. We've been told there's some men coming to kill him. Revenge. Vendetta."

"What's it to you?"

"Oh, he's just an old friend and might need some help," Gunther said with almost a smile.

"You think he needs help?"

"Might."

"You use to work here?"

"Yup."

"When?"

"1890s."

"1890s? Well, this is a very quiet city now. Since then. We have no trouble here. I run a quiet city. A tight city. Nothin' happens here I don't know about." He pounded his desk blotter with a fat finger.

They waited.

"I don't like the looks of you two coming in here...you wearin' guns?"

"I am a Federal Deputy," Stinky said, finally looking up at him. "I sleep with my guns."

Gunther opened his jacket. He had a 1911 .45 semi-auto in a holster on a stout, yet thin belt, not a Western-style gun belt.

"I don't like people coming here with guns, lookin' to shoot this place up..."

"We are not looking to shoot any place up," Gunther said.

"Yer old police chief was in here with his 'problem.' I told Henri to get out of town if he thinks somebody is coming to kill him. He came in here and told me some cockamamie story about some Chinks comin' *all the way from China* just to kill

231

him. I told him he was dreamin'. I told him even if it was true, I want no such thing to happen here. And I ordered him to *geet* outta my town!"

"Is he still here?" Stinky asked.

"You're that weird, giant fucker that use to work here," Drill responded. "People liked you and said you were a good police officer, but I know you fer what you really are." He glared at Stinky.

"You don't know me," Stinky said slowly. "And what am I really?"

"Is Henri still here?" Gunther interrupted.

"Is he still here? Yeah, but only until I feel like running his Frenchy ass off."

Gunther chuckled.

"And that is funny to you?"

"How well do you know Gustav Henri?" Gunther said.

"You know I got you figured out too," Drill said, changing the subject again. "You come in here with that expensive jacket and pants, and that spring-loaded gun. I know you through and through."

"Where is Gustav?" Gunther asked with a poker face.

"That French bastard is down the street in the Ascot Hotel. That French Huguenot wife of his is hiding out with her parents at their house. Still in my town. He says he is staying there till the Chinks show up."

"There are eight of them, we are told."

"I know how many Chinks."

"If they show up, are you going to help us stop them?" Gunther asked.

"Hell no. I told him to take his troubles and leave Paris. I

232

won't lift a hand to help him. I won't get any of my men hurt on some stupid old blood feud from a million miles away."

"8,026 miles," Stinky said.

"If he stays here and gets killed, I'll piss on his grave. And I will remind you. This is America, and Chinks can come and go as they please in it."

Gunther noticed that Stinky was now staring at Drill.

"Why doesn't yer weird-ass, giant friend here call for a company of federals to...to swoop in and save yer old boss?"

Gunther stood. Then Stinky stood. And it took a long time to unfold himself fully until finally he towered over the fat man in the chair. Gunther smiled a big grin, chuckled, and shook his head side to side.

"You think yer funny?" Drill said.

"Nope. I think you are funny."

They left the office. Gunther winked at Miss Maisy as they walked by. They left the station. You couldn't see the drizzle in the air, you could only feel it. Gunther put on his gloves and wiped the windshield.

"I guess everything you said about him was true."

"I know," Stinky said. "I know people that know him. He is an asshole. Always been one." He stepped around front and cranked the car with one easy swing. Gunther smiled.

"I guess you got the trick to that," Gunther said, as Stinky climbed in.

"Jou hab to feel it," Stinky said, with a perfect imitation of Quite Some's pronunciation. Stinky...almost...smiled. Gunther smiled for him.

"If they haven't moved it, we remember where the Ascot Hotel is."

Within minutes they pulled up out front of the Ascot. The front had been redone and once inside the two saw the complete refurbishing. It looked like a Dallas hotel. The Pyramid Room was gone and replaced by a sprawling restaurant area. And none other than the original owner, William Serani walked up to them.

"Bill," Gunther said with a broad smile and a handshake.

"Stinky and Johann, my, my God," Serani said. "Together again! You two are, I hate to say it, it's like seeing ghosts! My, oh my. It has been almost twenty years? And I am afraid that I know why you are here."

"It's great to see you, Bill, and…and this place!" Gunther said.

Serani knew not to shake Stinky's hand.

"Where is he?" Gunther asked.

"He's out back. We have an outdoor eating area now, attached to the restaurant, and he just sits out there a lot. He's…I guess he's waiting for those foreign men to show up."

Gunther looked through the lobby, past the ornate glass doors that revealed the flag-stoned outdoor eating area. Part of it was partially covered by a rough-hewn cedar pergola covered with dormant wisteria. At the moment, the outer tables and chairs were collecting a thin dusting of icy snow. The chairs were tipped forward onto the tables.

"Early for this weather, but it is Paris, Texas. Tomorrow it will be sunny and hot. I gather you boys are here to help him?"

"Yes, sir," Gunther muttered.

"No one else will. That ragweed of a police chief won't. And there is no one around that much remembers or much cares what he has done for our community. You two were like a little Army anyway. And the three of you? My God, when I think back to the 90s, you've seen a lot of...a lot of...ahh..."

"Shit. Shit is the word you're searching for," Gunther finished it for him, staring out the back windows.

He nodded at Serani and started for the terrace.

"You men want some coffee?"

"Yeah," Gunther said. "Black."

"Root beer for me," Stinky said.

And they walked right up to the glass back doors and paused. There, in the far right corner, at a table, back to the stone wall, sat former Paris, France Detective, Devil's Island Warden, and local Police Chief Gustav Henri, alone in the cold, wearing a big jacket and wrapped in a blanket, staring out into the backyards of scattered houses and then into the fields beyond the hotel. Gunther and Stinky looked at each other, opened the doors, and walked outside.

At first, Gustav appeared speechless. Then he said, "Is this a vision from the past that I see before me?"

"Chief," Stinky said.

"Chief," Gunther said.

There was no handshaking, Gunther knew Stinky didn't want to and maybe Gustav wouldn't want to shake his hand anyway. Gustav remained seated.

"Why are you here?"

Gustav stared at Gunther.

"Why are *you* here?" he repeated.

"Stinky heard word that you were in trouble," Gunther said.

"I know he knows. Why are you here?"

"You told me. I told him," Stinky said.

"You did?" Gustav returned to staring out at the fields.

Gunther sat in a chair. Then Stinky sat. Gunther eyed up

Gustav. He was still stocky, strong-looking, but with an older, kind of meaner face.

"What is your plan?" Gunther asked him.

Gustav didn't answer right away, telegraphing annoyance. Then he spoke up.

"I am told that eight men are coming from Indochina. They landed in New Orleans two or three days ago. The marshals thought they were coming into Galveston. There was a whole bunch of Indos coming into New Orleans and the marshals think they got in with them."

"And yet, here you sit?" Gunther said.

"Well, Major Gunther, what am I to do? If I leave, they will chase me down. If I stay, I end it. I end me. Or I end them."

"End all eight of them. Yourself," Gunther said.

Gustav's head bobbed a bit, a yes and a no.

"Where is Lucy?" Stinky asked.

"She is with her folks on the north side of Paris. These skunks will not hurt her, just me. It is their gangster way."

A waiter came out with coffee and a root beer.

"More coffee, Gustav?"

"Yes, please. Thank you, Stanley."

"Will the Sheriff's Office help?" Stinky asked.

"No. I don't know any of them there, anymore. All my old friends are gone. They told me that they only cover the county areas, the spaces between the cities. They leave the city policing to the city police. The police here are a worthless lot of conniving cowards. They presume the innocent guilty and the guilty innocent. If you heard all the sad stories you would cry out loud."

Gunther noted that Gustav still had a bit of that

French-American cadence to his speech.

"Chief Drill is an idiot," Stinky said.

"Chief Drill thinks you're an idiot," Gustav said with a sudden laugh.

"Then he is wrong again."

Gustav smiled. Stinky did not. He looked mad.

"Your friends at the Marshal's Office in Sherman won't come. They said that they can't sit around here, watch me pout, and wait for trouble. They are too busy. Aren't you too busy?" Gustav asked of Stinky.

"I am on vacation," Stinky said. "I never take vacation and I have a lot of vacation saved up."

Gustav slowly spun the coffee cup on the table in circles. He said, "I have an archenemy if you will, named Saw Walawarman. I may have spoken of him to you two in years past. I shot him in France in a police raid. I sent him to Devil's Island. Then I was sent to Devil's Island as a sub-warden. I supervised him there. I stopped him and his wicked plans again and again. Somehow, eventually, he has sent word to French Indochina to kill me. It is a criminal, family honor vendetta. I think maybe some of the French government…may have helped him. As you may recall, I created quite a scandal years ago with the Dreyfus incident. I helped set Dreyfus free."

"They finally set Dreyfus free?" Gunther said.

"Yes, they did. My discovery of forgery set him free. Yes."

"After so many years," Gunther said.

"Yes. Now, because of Saw, I am in these troubles. My oldest friends with the French police knew this revenge was going to happen. They warned me. I still have friends over there, you know! After all these years. But none are here to help me here and now, are they?"

"You have two here," Stinky said.

"Friends and enemies. Now you, Mister Gunther? Major Gunther?" Gustav asked. "Do you have any archenemies? Are they still alive? Have you caught up to the mastermind Dr. Trafalgar yet, whose case you so aptly cracked, sending you, at once, off to the Army and off to wars around the world?"

"No, I have not caught him. Scotland Yard came over and tried to track him down. He showed up back in England. Then Norway. He tried the same dead body fandango in the States again, at various Gold Rushes and Boom Towns. Then Brazil. He is, was, they say, at large. He might be dead by now from old age," Gunther sipped his coffee. "But I have a few enemies. Yeah. There is a corrupt Texas Ranger named Chester Winch in Fort Worth."

"And how is it you have not shot all of them dead, yet?"

"You know, Gustav," Gunther said impatiently, "the moment has not been right yet."

"I see. The *right* moment. And how do you define the right moment?"

"The same way you do."

"Ahhhh. I see. This is your answer. I have taught you how to kill at the right moment."

"No," Gunther said with an impatient sigh, "the Army taught me to kill. *You* taught me to be a good police officer and a detective."

"And you two are here to save me? At the right moment," Gustav said.

"We are here to *help* you," Gunther corrected.

"And you feel the need to...help? I need rescuing? Help? With all your, your special Army skills at killing Indians and foreign people?" Gustav was looking right at Gunther.

Gunther's lip curled just a bit at the remark, then said, "Yeah, that's about right."

"Yeah, that's about right," Stinky repeated.

"I'll bet you learned some more special skills at West Point." Gustav turned to Stinky. "So, you snaggled him up and brought him up here with you."

"I did. On my way."

"You ever get married? Have any children," Gustav asked Gunther.

Gunther hesitated for only an eyeblink, then said, "Not in this life, sir."

"Hmmm," he growled, as though confirming an expectation.

"So, you are going to spend your time downtown," Gunther said. "Sitting here. Hoping a confrontation will happen here?"

"I believe they will first show up downtown. Ohhhh, I see," Gustav said. "That does that not suit your extensive, Army battlefield experience?"

"It might, but I have to think about it. For one thing, how will they arrive? By train. By coach, do they still have a stage-coach line here?"

"Yes, they do," Gustav said. "A coach line."

"Train. Coach. Horseback. Auto. When they get here, they have to look around. Ask around to find you. And I hope they don't know that you know they are coming?"

"I am inclined to think, they believe, they are going to surprise me."

"Stinky, we need to use your status as a marshal," Gunther said. "You need to tell the railroad people to watch out for such a group and contact you. You'll need to tell the coach office. I guess I'll…I'll walk the streets and see who comes in and…"

Stinky slid his chair back and reached into his pocket. He pulled out two badges and laid them on the table.

"I hereby officially deputize you both in this emergency."

Gustav winced and groaned. Gunther cut his eyes to Gustav, then back to the badges.

Gunther reached to pick it up.

"You signing on for all this," Gustav asked.

"You mean, all this…Medieval stuff?" Gunther smiled.

"Yes," Gustav said.

"Yes," Gunther said. He picked up the badge.

"I never wanted to do any of this again," Gustav said. He picked up the badge and rolled it around in his right hand.

"Raise your right hand," Stinky said, raising his right hand. "Repeat. I promise to…do the right thing."

Gunther and Gustav had to smile a bit at each other, for the first time in some twenty years, at that oath of office.

"I swear to do the right thing," they said in unison.

"By the powers invested in me by the United States Federal Government, you are now Deputy Marshals."

Gustav put the badge in his pocket. Gunther pinned the badge on his shirt under his jacket.

"Yet another nice shirt ruined with puncture holes from these damn badges," Gunther said. "These gangsters—you think they will speak English?"

"They will surely speak French and Chinese. But they'd never come over here without some sort of an English translator."

Gunther nodded. "They're gonna need a story to nose around here to find you. Pretending a…what? A business trip?

A…hunting or fishing trip?" Gunther said.

"There's an outfitter company here that runs hunting and fighting trips now," Gustav said.

"We'll have to contact them. Stink and I will get a room in another hotel. I'll visit the outfitters. Stink, you go to the railroad and the coach line. Gustav you…you, I guess you just sit in the corner of the lobby, huh? There's a good spot by the front windows, and see who comes and goes, and lay low."

"That all, Major?" Gustav said, not knowing whether to be disgusted or impressed.

"Well, well now, birds of a feather," said Police Chief Garrison Drill, marching up to them, with an overweight deputy in tow. "Aren't I lucky to catch the three of you together in one net."

The men said nothing. Drill stopped at the table.

"I think you are a danger to this city," Drill said, wagging a finger at Gustav, his thin, bottom lip and chin protruded.

"You and yer two birds…get your shit and get out of Paris, Texas."

The three looked up at him.

Stinky stood up.

"Deputy!" Drill barked, suggesting an intervention. But the deputy's eyes widened as Stinky reached his full towering height.

"I am a federal law enforcement officer," Stinky said calmly. "And you cannot order me to do anything."

Drill moved back a step, trying to make a meaner looking expression.

Gunther opened his jacket, displaying his badge.

Gustav smiled, and pulled the badge from his coat pocket. He held it up and shook it a bit.

"In fact," Stinky said, "In a matter of law, a point of law, I can order *you* to leave the city." He sat back down.

"Ahh!" Drill said in a cough, in an exasperation, "Deputy!" To his underling.

His man bowed his chest out, rocked his head back and forth and stepped up, trying to make a meaner face too.

"Mister Huff and Mister Puff," Gustav said.

"I would suggest that the two of you, leave, as your presence here is useless," Stinky said.

"I will be...I will be contacting the county attorney about this," Drill said.

"I, too, will be here and available for legal commentary," Stinky added, sounding like a big city lawyer.

Gunther and Gustav smiled at each other again. Old times, and such was Stinky's perfect way.

"You three fuckers have not seen the last of me! I know how to handle your type!" Drill declared.

The three men said nothing. Drill and the deputy left the patio.

"Your deputizing occurred just in time," Gustav said.

Stinky opened up and looked at his watch. "My timing is usually exceptional."

Gustav raised his coffee cup and held it over to the center of the table. Gunther did also and touched Gustav's cup with his own.

"All for one," Gustav said.

"And one for all," Gunther said.

Stinky looked confused but knew a toast when he saw one. He touched the cups with his glass of root beer.

"The Three Musketeers," Gustav told him.

"*Dumas*," Gunther told him.

Now the new Deputy Federal Marshal Gunther went to Lamar County Outfitters and asked for a phone call notice if such a group of Asians showed up for a hunting trip. Deputy Marshal Stinky Moses went to the coach office and the train station and asked for a phone call if a group of Asians showed up. Gunther and Stinky set up their rooms and headquarters at the Tree Top Hotel, the second largest hotel in Paris. Gustav remained at the Ascot, whiling away the hours looking out lobby windows and reading.

Gunther was reading too. He found the new city library and since he could not sign out books as a non-resident, he sat on a couch inside. He'd never read his old boss Teddy Roosevelt's *The Naval War of 1812,* and he saw it on a shelf. He otherwise strolled the streets, eating here and there, and sat for periods with Gustav, where their conversations became more friendly and normal. Gustav anxiously asked him many questions about his experiences and became fascinated with his past. He told Gustav about Cuba, the Philippines, China, Africa, India, and Afghanistan, as well as life as an investigator in Texas.

"It is all fantastic," Gustav said.

"But you too have led an amazing life," Gunther reminded Gustav.

"Yes, some might say so. Sleeping can be difficult at my age and when you awake. In the dark." Gustav confessed, "So many memories, good and bad. When you are young you have no such clutter. No experiences. Then, your head at night is just full of dreams of the future. But now? Now I have only this, this clutter of horrible sights and mistakes. I'd take those future dreams over ones of the past."

The national news in the city's one newspaper was ominous. The Great War was on in full in Europe. Millions of soldiers were dying over there in a stalemate. And the Germans had started shooting and sinking American merchant ships. President Woodrow Wilson was still avoiding the US entry into the war. Gunther's old commander Teddy Roosevelt was all over the country stomping for war. But life moved quietly on in Paris, Texas, almost as though the battles were as far away as the moon. Over the next few days, the weather turned warm, windy, and very dry. The newspaper reported a man fell and died while painting a three-story building. A woman, a twin, gave birth to another set of twins. Some drunks broke a few windows in a house in town. Local columnists criticized the modern world. Various social groups announced meetings. There were reports of agriculture and pork belly futures. And, all local readers were ignorant of the pending, possible East vs. West confrontation about to happen in their little city. Not ignorant, Police Chief Drill and his officers were conspicuously absent from the streets, stores, and restaurants. So much so, it seemed, on purpose.

Late one afternoon, near sunset, Gunther left the Tree Top Hotel and started up his Chevy in the hotel's back stables and garage area. His plan was to drive the streets and run by Gustav's house and check on it. It took but ten minutes to find the house on the outskirts of town. As he approached, all looked the same as when he and Stinky were there last, just a few days earlier.

He pulled up the driveway. The interior of the house was still dark as before. Engine running, he stepped out of the car and looked the landscape over. He walked up the front porch steps and leaned in to look casually through a front window.

Without question, it was a man he saw inside that dove to the floor behind a couch. Gunther instinctively knew not to act surprised, but instead to act as though he did not see the motion. He slowly stood up and looked off to the right. Then slowly wandered that way. Who was that, he thought? Was that a member of the Asian gang? Hiding out in the house, waiting day by day for Gustav to return home? Were they all in there? Had they somehow learned where Gustav lived? Gunther walked back to the car, tipped his hat back and pulled out a map, as though lost, to appear less suspicious, or…at least not be hunting Asian gang members. He pulled the brim back down to eye level, raised up the map and faced the residence. In the slit between his brim and the map top, he squinted his eyes to study the house. Two dark, gray-headed silhouettes appeared peeking out of two front windows, left and right of the front door.

He folded the map, tossed it on the passenger-side seat, started the car, and got back behind the steering wheel. Then he turned the car and slowly drove off the property. He stopped at the road, looked both ways, and slowly entered the roadway. Not too fast. Not too slow.

He drove downtown and parked in front of the Ascot Hotel, and walked in. There he saw Stinky and Gustav at the usual table in the corner of the lobby. He walked up to them and said, "They're here."

Chapter 27
SIEGE OF CASTLE GUSTAV

"Ah Gawaine, Gawaine, ye have betrayed me; for never shall my court be amended by you, but ye will never be sorry for me as I am for you"

—Sir Thomas Malory, *Le Morte d'Arthur*

"How did they find out where I lived?"

"I don't know. They haven't been seen wandering around the town. Maybe those spies you talked about in the French police told them exactly where you lived?" Gunther said.

"Impossible. I told no one where I live."

"So, two of them?" Stinky said.

"All I could see. I am going back late tonight. I plan to crawl up and do some spying on my own. I have a feeling there are six others hiding out somewhere else, and the two at your house are just there in case you show up. You must tell your wife not to return to the house."

Gustav jumped up and ran to the lobby desk, got on the

phone, and cranked it to call the operator and place a call to his wife's family's house.

Gunther followed him over and when close, whispered, "Remember, the operator might be listening in. Word your message carefully."

Gustav nodded.

The warning call complete, Gustav returned to the table.

"I'm going with you tonight," he said.

"No! No, you can't. Their whole purpose is to catch and kill you at your own house. Kill you inside, then quietly leave Texas. The country. I'll go. Stinky and I will go, and Stink—you will lay back tonight. Back me up if there is any trouble. The first night, maybe…maybe two nights, I'll spy on your house, get a count of heads. See what's going on. Do you have an outhouse, or indoor plumbing?"

"Outhouse."

"Good. They gotta come out sometime!"

"Then what will you do?" Gustav asked.

"Catch two skunks," Gunther mumbled, in a concentrated gaze out the Ascot windows, thinking of a plan. "Kill one, catch one. Make him talk. Kill two." He looked back and over at Gustav. "They are all in your house, or not. I guess they might have a camp outside of town? Or near your house, but there are other houses nearby? I don't know. They might have even taken the residents of another house hostage, but…but…that would hamper their quiet escape…yeah…yeah. Or, the others are in a hotel in a nearby city."

"There is no nearby town with a hotel," Stinky said. "Right, Chief?"

"I think you are correct, Stinky."

"Okay. Anyway, we don't have a lot of time. I will make a plan after I watch the house tonight. But the rest of them will make a move soon. They can't stay skunking around here forever. You okay here alone?"

"I have to be, eh?"

"Tonight, Stink, tonight at about 3 a.m., we rent some horses, ride nearby, crawl out there. I'll crawl in deep, you stay back with your Winchester. You have a telescope?"

"The one he gave me," and he pointed a thumb to Gustav, "about twenty-five years ago."

"You have any dark clothes?"

"Dark enough."

"Night one...spy," Gunther said. "Night two, capture and kill. We need one alive."

Looking at Gunther's calculating military mind at work, Gustav's past admonishments slowly turned into admiration. He was watching West Point and much experience at work. Watching Cuba at work. Watching the Philippines and China at work. And all else he'd done.

"And if he won't talk?" Stinky asked.

"That won't be a problem. But will he speak English?" Gunther said.

"No," Gustav said, "but he will speak French." He grinned.

On this trip to the Gustav home, Gunther and Stinky leased horses as planned from Tree Top Hotel. Alone in the stable they saddled up at 3 a.m. for the ride out near Gustav's house.

The streets of Paris were deserted. The only sound was the eight horse hooves clopping on the asphalt in the main city limits. Then they made their way down the pounded flat old dirt roads. There were about fifteen city houses with acreage until the road led them out of town and became quite a bit more rutted, ragged, and rough. On Gustav's road, the wooden homes lined both sides of the road, and behind all of them were just wide-open fields, some of which were farmlands, some not. From the height of their horses they scanned for campfires or any signs of enemy outposts nearby the house. None seen. At a grove of trees behind the north side of houses they dismounted and left the horses on long lead ropes to eat grass and roam a bit. They studied the backs of all the dark residences they could see.

"If you hear gunshots? Come a runnin'," Gunther told Stinky.

Stinky handed Gunther a pair of handcuffs in case he needed them. Gunther slung his rifle over his back and pulled his dark maroon neckerchief over his face. He had a smaller brimmed, brown hat different than his usual wear, dark jacket and pants. He dropped to the ground and started crawling toward the Gustav house. He already missed Jefe and wished the Filipino was there with him, crawling through the fields as they did on missions from the Philippines and China and even their home turf of Fort Worth and on other North American cases and adventures. This time, he was alone, but for a distant Stinky. Good lawman, but unproven soldier. Unproven "crawler."

Gunther found a spot from which to watch the back and right side of the house with his binoculars. At dawn, he saw some smoke come from the chimney. In the early morning an Asian man, about forty years old, in an untucked shirt, pants, and barefoot, walked out the back door, across the yard and into the outhouse. Weaponless. He was in there just a few moments when another Asian man stepped out on the back porch, in the same type of clothes, and peed into the yard from the porch. He stretched and then went back inside. When the outhouse man came out and reentered the house, the second man jogged to the outhouse. Then quiet. No more smoke. Stillness for hours. Then the same two took turns in the outhouse again several hours later.

Gunther studied the outhouse construction. Typical. Narrow. Tall. Vertical, single boards. Shingle arched roof.

Gunther crawled slowly back to Stinky in the distant grove of trees.

"I think just two."

"Okay."

"I think we'll take them tomorrow morning."

"Okay. You have a plan?"

"I'm workin' on it."

They took to their horses, walked them off a ways, then rode back to the Tree Top Hotel. They changed to more suitable "city clothes." Then, they checked in with Gustav at the Ascot for a briefing.

Gustav listened intently, maddened that invaders had taken up a residence in his home.

"Well! These sons of scum!" he declared.

"Just asking, but has anyone seen the big new City Police Chief Drill, or any of his deputies anywhere, lately?" Gunther wondered.

Stinky and Gustav shook their heads, no.

"They are hiding," Gustav said. "Hiding from trouble. Cowards."

"I am going to get some gear," Gunther said.

"You got you a plan?" Stinky asked.

"No, not completely. I am going shopping for some inspiration."

Gunther took a walk to an old store, Flippin's Utilities, where he bought many things decades ago. The business sold ranch and farm supplies, and tools. A chat with Flippin's son had told him the bad news that the boy's dad, whom he'd known from years back, had died from consumption. Then Gunther wandered around the aisles, thinking. He bought a claw hammer, a length of thin, yet stout, brown rope, a thick towel, a canvas bag with a long strap, and some small nails.

After the shopping trip, it was another afternoon of street watching, but soon Gunther took to his hotel bed for some needed rest. Stinky did also. The three musketeers met for another dinner, late at the Ascot hotel.

"Where can we meet, a quiet, out of the way place, tomorrow morning," Gunther asked.

"Like a barn?" Gustav said.

"Yeah, that would be good. Like a barn."

"We could use the Loverland's barn. It's quite a ways back from their main house. It's old, and they use a new tin barn they built closer to the house. Gerald is a friend of mine. He won't bother us in his old barn. Why?"

"We will need a place to do some French translation. Draw us out a map to this barn and meet us there at 9 a.m.

Gustav looked at Stinky and Gunther with wide eyes.

"You have a plan?" he asked.

"Yeah," Gunther said, "and you don't want to know it. When you come? Bring some medical supplies."

"Medical supplies? For what? Stabbings, shootings? Beatings? What?"

"Yes."

"Yes? All? Okay, I will get one of the lobby boys to get some for me."

That night they started off a bit earlier. Two a.m., but they rented not two horses but three horses and tack. They rode the same path but settled into a different nearby grove of trees from the night before where they tied off the three horses. Gunther cut the rope he'd bought into several parts.

"Are you ready, big fella?" Gunther asked Stinky.

"Yes," Stinky said, checking his watch.

Both got low and started the crawl to Gustav's house, and Gunther was pleased that Stinky did well on all fours.

This time, Gunther had the new canvas bag with his towel, his hammer, his nails, and rope. By 4 a.m., he and Stinky slithered close enough. Then Gunther told Stink to stay put and he snaked up the rest of the way to the back of Gustav's outhouse. He stood up behind it studied its construction. As he'd hoped the structure of the outhouse was as poorly made as most he'd seen in the rural West.

He went to work on the back wall of the outhouse. He took out his hammer and stuck the claw end into the space between two boards and pried a board loose. He did it high and low and very slowly and quietly. Inch by inch he slowly removed the whole board. There before him was a wooden toilet seat, as expected. The back wall was behind the seat. He slowly pulled the other three boards loose. He pulled them off. The original nails were quite long. He put the first back in place with the very small new nails he'd bought. He covered the tapping of his hammer with the thick towel to dull the noise. He barely tacked the lower end of the board in place. He looped the brown rope

252

over the top, then barely tacked the top of the board in. He did the same with the other four boards. Now, he had the back wall boards barely held in place with a thin rope wrapped around the tops of the boards. He tied a knot on his side with the ends. He maneuvered straight back into the fields of tall grass and crawled back to Stinky. It was 4:35 a.m. He'd kept about three feet of that rope and stuffed it into his jacket pocket. They waited. It was another very dry night of mild air. The stars twinkled in the clear, abundant fresh air.

At 5:30 a.m. Gunther said, "Ready?"

"Ready." Stinky said.

They crawled close to the house. The home remained dark and quiet. Gunther stopped at the grass line right behind the outhouse. He couldn't see the residents and patiently listened for the back door. Stinky crawled near to the right, back porch corner of the house. And again, they waited and waited.

Dawn. Smoke from the chimney. The smell of bacon hit the air. Then coffee. They waited. Then the back door opened. The first Asian man from yesterday stepped out. Same clothes. Barefoot again. He stretched and yawned. He took a good look around and trotted over to the outhouse.

Gunther heard that back door open. He heard the groaning stretch. He heard the outhouse door open and close. He dashed the few feet to back wall, pulling out the rope from his pocket with his right hand. With his left hand he grabbed the rope loop in place on the back wall boards and yanked back ripping the wall from the structure. Then he looped the small rope piece around the Asian's head and onto his neck. He pulled the man back and ran backward, hauling the half-naked, skinny man off the seat and out into the yard. He was gagging, clutching at

253

the rope on his neck. As Gunther hoped, he had no idea what was happening to him. Gunther leaned over and beat his face and head, ready to remove the hammer from his bag and bash the man's head open, if necessary, but the Asian was out cold. Gunther tied the man's hands about as fast as a rodeo calf roper. All this was not without some sound, which concerned him and Stinky. Stinky heard the scuffle from his position closer to the house.

The second man stepped out of the back door, a rifle in hand, his head way up and searching like a groundhog for the odd sounds he'd heard.

"Hey!" Stinky stood and yelled, aiming a cut-off barreled, Winchester, pump-action shotgun at him.

The man foolishly, instinctively turned and raised his rifle, and Stinky cut his gun loose and almost blew the burglar into two pieces with a series of 12-gauge rounds. The man's guts disappeared, as chunks of him flew off onto the porch. The rifle went flying. He collapsed and slowly slid off the porch. Stinky spun, dropped to one knee, and aimed at the house, in case there were more men inside.

Gunther rounded the outhouse, pistol in one hand, the Asian's head hair in the other hand as he hauled the small, unconscious, man behind him halfway to the back porch. Both knew the house had to be searched, but they had this prisoner also to tend to.

"You got it?" Gunther asked.

"I got it," Stinky replied.

Stinky went in. Within a minute, he came out.

"Just them two," he said, and took a quick look at his pocket watch.

Gunther stood and looked the back porch over.

"This is quite a bloody mess you've made here."

"Yup."

"The Chief ain't gonna like this much."

"Nope," he said reloading his pump.

"Watch him and let me look around."

Stinky positioned himself by the prisoner, scanning the landscape. Gunther walked into the house. It was a mess. There were bags of gear and personal belongings. Clothes tossed everywhere. Weapons of foreign design laid about the rooms. Pistols and long guns. Boxes of ammo with Oriental writing. Gunther could now assume what the weapons of the remaining six enemies were. Where were these other six men? He planned to find out.

Gunther walked out and over to a kneeling Stinky and the captured man. He also knelt beside them.

"Okay, I got him," Gunther said. "Go get the horses."

Stinky ran through the field for the tree line. It was Gunther's turn to watch the surroundings.

Chapter 28
THE GREAT FIRE OF PARIS TEXAS, AND SUBSEQUENT SHOOT-OUT OF 1916

"We shall have made such a blaze that men will remember us on the other side or the dark."

—Rosemary Sutcliff, *The Sword and the Circle: King Arthur and the Knights of the Round Table*

Cold well water hit his face like an ocean wave. When the prisoner awoke, he realized he was tied by both arms and legs to a chair. He sat naked but for a shirt, as he was dressed in the last moment of memory, sitting on the toilet in the outhouse. He had no idea where he was and who was looking at him. But, after a moment he recognized Henri Gustav, the man in the photos he was shown many times, the man his cohort was supposed to kill. Then he eyed the other two men, a tall man with blond hair and a giant man with an odd face. He looked around. They were in a barn. The cracks in the walls and doors let sunlight in, so it was daytime.

The man started yelling in a foreign language. Gustav approached the captured man and asked him a series of questions in French. The man yelled angrily back at him also in French.

"What he say?" Gunther asked.

"He told me, in so many words, to run off into a dark cave and fuck myself."

Gunther walked up to him, pulled his bowie knife from his belt and slashed open the top of the man's left thigh.

The man screamed and rocked in the chair.

"Ask him again," Gunther said.

Gustav did, and he got the same answer. Gunther walked in again with the knife and the confined man moved so fast and hard away from him that the chair he was sitting in fell over. His feet were up and Gunther cut the bottom of his left foot open.

The man screamed again. He screamed one long cry for as long as he could, until his breath ran out. Then he gasped for air. Gustav stood the chair and man back up.

"You tell this piece of shit I will slowly carve him into pieces, while he's watching me do it, unless he tells us what we want to know." Gunther glared at his face.

The man yelled out in French. This time, not with much anger, but with animal desperation. And Gustav spoke to him again, with Gunther's threat included. This time there was a back and forth, in different tones. Calmer tones. Gustav got another chair and sat down in front of him. The Asian was scared, bleeding, and desperate. Gunther walked over to the medical bag Gustav brought and untied it.

After a full four minutes of talking, Gustav sat back in his chair, silent.

"What he say?" Stinky asked.

"You won't believe it. You won't believe it."

"What?" Gunther said.

"They arrived in the area, four days ago, but only one man came into town, the one who speaks English for them. His name is Tamoon. We did not see him because he is a half-breed. Half British, half Rangoon. He said that Tamoon walked around Paris to find me. To find out about me. Ask about me."

"Who told him where you live?"

"HA!" Gustav said with disgust. "Drill. Police Chief Garrison Drill."

"Drill? Why would he do that?" Gunther asked.

"Tamoon promised that they would not hurt the town or anyone in it. He promised that they would just kill me. Drill told Tamoon that I would eventually have to return to my home, away from the city, and they could kill me out there. Drill promised that he would let them all escape. He would wait days, to 'discover' my body. *He* told them where I lived." Gustav folded his arms high across his burly chest.

"Well!" Gunther said.

"Well!" Gustav said back.

"I told you he was no good," Stinky said.

"He said that they switch two men every few days at my house, waiting for me to show up. They are right. Of course, I would eventually go home, if even to check on my house."

"Where are the other six men?" Gunther asked.

Gustav asked him in French.

"Down the road. Down the road from here, way past my house. They are camping with a wagon. They got here pretending to be international horse trainers."

"We can't trust him, or believe that," Gunther said.

"I...I don't know," Gustav said.

"International horse trainers. When are they going to switch men again?" Gunther asked.

Gustav asked the man.

"He said tomorrow. Tomorrow morning."

"What's his name?"

"Shongie Shay."

Gunther brought the medical bag over and started cleaning out and treating the man's thigh wound. Gustav stood to get out of the way. He wandered the barn. Stinky followed him.

"A deal struck to save the town from a gunfight. Save innocent bystanders. A town's reputation."

"His reputation," Stinky added.

"Yes, yes, Stink. His reputation. It's a disgusting plan, but not *totally* crazy. It's a…a deal. And of course, it's all about killing me."

"That makes Drill an accomplice to murder," Stinky said.

"That it does."

Gunther lit a match under a stitching needle until it burned bright red and then started sewing up the thigh cut. The Asian gritted his teeth but did not look away. He did not make a sound.

"Can you get me some water?" Gunther asked. He bandaged the thigh.

Stinky picked up the bucket and left the barn. When he returned, he put the bucket on the ground by the medical operation.

"Can you tell this cretin I have a pair of pants for him from the house, but no shoes. I'm gonna fix his feet but we have no socks or shoes for him. This is gonna hurt and he could get his feet real dirty again, real fast. Which is a problem if he tries to run."

"Hmmm. This an Army trick?" Gustav asked.

"Philippines," Gunther said quietly.

"Hmmm. Loverland may have some shoes at his house. At least some undarned socks," Gustav said and then translated. The man nodded his head up and down in understanding.

"What are we gonna do with this Mister Shongie Shay," Gunther asked.

"I don't know," Gustav said. "What do you think?"

"I think we should put him in the city jail. For burglary. What do you say Mister Deputy Marshal?"

"I think so, too" Stinky said.

"That will be very confusing for Chief Garrison Drill, won't it?"

By mid-afternoon, Gustav's friend Loverlander did more than supply socks for the prisoner, he offered to cart the man in his open farm wagon for the fifteen-minute ride to downtown Paris. Shongie Shay was bandaged and dressed in a shirt, pants, and socks, with his hands shackled behind him.

The three lawmen rode beside the team. They each pondered what would happen next when they marched their suspect into the station, but as they approached the City of Paris Police Department, they spotted Chief Drill and several officers standing outside the front steps, the first time any of them had been spotted in days. Drill struck a quizzical face, and with an arrogant strut, he stomped down the steps to the sidewalk.

"We have a prisoner for your jail," Stinky said.

"Fer what?"

"Burglary."

"Of what?"

"My house," Gustav said.

The men dismounted. Drill walked to the wagon and looked over the sideboards into the back of the wagon.

"Who's he?"

"He's a friend of your friend," Gunther said.

And Drill's face went pale.

Gustav untied a rope that ran through the prisoner's arms, hitching him to the wagon. Then he grabbed the Asian's calves and pulled him to the open back edge of the bed. He grabbed an arm and helped him off the wagon.

"You can't…" Drill started to say.

"Yes, we can," Stinky said, aware of the law. Stinky and Gustav escorted their prisoner into the lobby of the station. Gunther smiled at Drill and followed.

The keys to the cells were still hanging on an inside wall, on the very hook Gustav hammered into that wall over twenty years before. He opened a cell door and they prodded Shongie Shay in.

"What…evidence…" Drill said.

"I caught him in the house, living there," Gunther interrupted. "But, you know that."

"I…"

"You know that," Gustav said.

Four Paris officers were now there in the lobby. Miss Maisy was behind the lobby desk, all staring at Gustav.

"Maybe some of you may know that too. That *you*," he pointed to Drill, "set me up to kill me." Gustav had been acting calm up to that point, but he lost all control now.

Gustav unleashed a few seconds of that "Cowboy Savate" all over Drill's body. Three rapid punches to his face, the solar plexus, a shin kick to the groin, and two more body blows, while chasing the thunderstruck, stumbling oaf backward. Drill half-crashed over a desk, expelling gasps and groans; then he hit the floor.

The four officers shook as though to take action. Gunther pulled his German Luger from his shoulder holster and Stinky pulled his revolver.

"No," Stinky said. "By the powers invested me, we are seizing the operation of this department until a federal judge can rule on this corruption. You men, and lady," he turned to the woman at the desk, "now work for me."

The men stood confused and still.

"Shiiieeeet!" Miss Maisy said.

"You will continue to work and uphold the law, until this is properly investigated."

Drill crawled backward, bleeding from the nose and mouth, coming to his senses.

"I will…I will put you…in jail," Drill tried to say.

"I BUILT THIS JAIL!" Gustav yelled.

Gustav leaned over and took Drill's pistol from his holster and flung it across the lobby. He grabbed the man's vest helped him up and shoved him onto a nearby chair.

"As a Federal Deputy of the United States," Stinky declared, "I hereby appoint Henri Gustav the temporary Police Chief of Paris, Texas, until such time as a federal judge conducts a hearing in this matter. I will begin to conduct the investigation, forthwith. You…" he pointed to a man on the left. "You will report this matter to the mayor and City Hall. Now go on."

The deputy was aghast.

"Go on!" Stinky demanded.

The officer stared at Stinky, then recognizing the logic, turned and left.

"You three will...will go on out and patrol the streets. As usual. Go on."

They left.

"You ma'am will continue to...to operate this front desk here, as usual," Stinky told Maisy. She lit up a cigarette, grimaced, grunted and nodded.

Gunther and Stinky walked away from the front lobby back to Gustav and Drill.

"You can...do all that?" Gunther asked Stink in a half-whisper.

Stinky opened his pocket watch and said," I don't rightly know, Gunth." He closed the watch. "But it did keep the peace."

Gustav sat atop a desk, hovering over Drill.

"We know what you did."

Drill wiped his mouth.

"This is a conspiracy to commit murder."

"No, it ain't."

"Oh. Yes, it is. You can't be as stupid a bastard as to not know that."

"All you have is the word of a bunch of Chinks," Drill said, spitting blood on the floor, "that don't even speak English. I didn't do nothin'. And when this is over, you'll ...either kill all of them, or they'll kill all of you."

Gustav smiled. "Johann, is Mister Loverland still outside? I think we need to take our prisoner out to the county jail," he said while staring and still smiling at Drill. "Our star witness is not safe here.

Gunther turned to look outside for Loverland, but just then, a wide-eyed, breathless man burst into the front doors of the station and yelled at the front desk, "*MAISY!* There's a fire! A fire! All of Lucas Street is on fire! Everything!"

Gunther thought that impossible. He stepped outside and spun around in place to see if Loverland was gone and what was on fire. Everyone and everything in view was in chaos. City alarm bells were ringing. Smoke was already swirling high in the air. People were running every which way. Screaming. Yelling. He dashed down to the intersection and looked down Lucas Street.

Indeed, every building on the west side of the street was aflame. People were running from the front and side doors, some with their hair, hats, and clothes on fire. Horses bolted and reared, escaping people in automobiles, and horses running riderless burst from the smoke running down the street. The strong wind shoved the roaring flames over the two-lane road and they licked the rooftops of the houses and buildings across the street, instantly igniting them. Before Gunther's eyes, one of the house roofs burst into flame like a tinderbox. Then the next one...and the next.

It was his turn to stand frozen in a state of shock. They had just ridden past this area, not ten minutes earlier! Now this? How? Distant sirens sounded off behind him. But how could a few city fire trucks deal with this tinderbox hell? Gunther immediately thought of bombs and war. He ran back to the police station. Gustav shoved Drill into a jail cell and locked the door.

"Lucas Street *is* on fire," Gunther said. "It's all exploding like bombs."

Maisy was on the phone, then hooked the earpiece on its

hook, disconnecting the call.

"Fire department has been called. Trinity Church rang the bell for the other volunteer fireman," she reported.

"Maisy, call Dolph. They'll need a lot of water," Drill shouted from his cell, grabbing the cell bars. He shook the cell bars like a frustrated monkey in a zoo.

"I did, Garrison," she said.

Stinky, Gunther, and Gustav looked at each other, then Gustav marched back to the cells. "You tell them where my wife was?"

"I did, you son of a bitch," Drill sneered.

Gustav grabbed the bars of the cell holding Shongie Shay.

"And you!" he said in French, "You were not going to be relieved tomorrow morning at my house, were you? It was *this* morning."

"Ah-haa. Yes." He said, grinning. "Today. They know. They know and they did this."

Gustav took off for the front doors.

"Let's go!" he said. "Lucy!"

Their horses, still tied off on the front hitching post, were nervous and side-stepping into each other from the excitement and smells of the street. In another moment they would have ripped the rail right out of the ground. The men mounted up and Gustav took off west. The other two followed. As they dashed past Lucas street, they saw the growing horror, as both sides of the street were now engulfed in flame and the blistering wind pushed the sparks and fire across the grass and the back-yards of the houses to the north and west. The sky was already worse than what Gunther saw a moment earlier. Two firetrucks were setting up and dangerously close. A car and its occupants caught fire and crashed into a telegraph and light pole.

Gustav led the way, as they passed people running to the fire to see what was happening and to assist. Down some streets, up some back roads to lines of single-story houses they went. In the yard of one, Gustav stopped and tied off his horse. He ran inside. Gunther and Stinky remained in their saddles, looking around. The sky had the dark swirling doomsday look like that of a pending tornado or a massive thunderstorm.

Gustav shuttled an older couple and Lucy, his wife, out the back door. The three were armed, the ladies with pistols, the man with a rifle.

"Stinky!" Lucy shouted with a half-smile when she spotted him. Gustav held her arm guiding her to a neighboring house.

"Helllllo, Lucy!" Stinky replied.

Once the three were next door, Gustav returned and said, "They are here. They know we have Shay and we killed their other guy. They weren't relieving them at my house tomorrow..."

"It was today?" Gunther said.

"Yes. This morning. They probably set this fire to flush us out and confuse the whole city and come in to kill us... me...and...and burn us alive. And, Drill *also* told them where Lucy was."

Gunther took a deep breath. Almost snorting. "Son of a bitch," he said.

"Yeeees. *Le salaud.*"

"What now," Stinky asked.

"We get every gun, and every bullet we can. We go back near the fire. We somehow...find them...and...and..."

"We kill them," Gunther finished.

"*Oui.* We kill them. I have only my pistol. All my guns are at the Ascot," Gustav said.

"Ascot's on the way, all the rest of our guns are at the Tree Top Hotel," Gunther said. "I've got my two .45s and a German Luger. My rifle. I've got a lot of bullets."

"I have my pistol and my pump shotgun," Stinky said. "I could do for some."

The three rode away bound for the Ascot and Tree Top hotels with Gustav in the lead, taking the newer backroads. The smoke got thicker, and blacker, and smelled of everything it already burned into cinders. The sky got darker, and the smoke above and ahead was tinged a dirty orange from the flames below. They didn't have to ride much farther to see the Ascot was nothing but a roaring fire, and two businesses next to it as well. The three stopped short of the horror.

"I hope everyone got out alive," Gunther said.

"Forget the Tree Top. There are guns at the police station," Gustav said. "Let's go."

And they galloped off, wondering if the station was even still there. The fire was glowing, blowing, and consuming everything in its jumping and rolling path.

The station was still there, thus far. It seemed the main fire swept west of it with the wind. The two front doors stood open. They charged in. Gunther pulled his rifle from off his shoulder and stood beside a window to look outside.

Maisy sat at her desk, on the phone, another cigarette dangling from her mouth. Then the shock came. Gustav saw that Shongie Shay lay half off his bunk, in his cell. Dead. Shot in the head. And Drill's cell door was open. He was gone.

"Where is he?" Gustav said, returning to the front desk.

"Who?"

Gustav swiped the phone off the desk and out of her hands.

"What happened to the Asian and where is Drill?"

Staring madly at him, Maisy opened her desk drawer, reached in deep, and Gustav saw her hand wrap around the handle of a pistol. He belted her across the face which knocked her and her rolling chair backward into the wall. Then he had to dive over the desk to get control of the pistol still in her hand. She fell out of her chair, and Gustav yanked the gun from her. Kneeling, he put the barrel of her gun to the cheek of her face.

"What happened to the Asian, and where is Drill?"

"Drill is gone!" she yelled. "I let him out. He is my friend and you are nothing to me. He is the police chief here, and you are nothing but a French pig." She spat in his face. He ignored it. "He has to help fight the fire."

"Who shot the Asian?"

"He did! Cleaning up your mess. You should thank him."

"He did himself a favor. He killed a witness against him, Maisy." He got up.

Stinky broke the door glass of the locked rifle cabinet with a powerful strike from the butt of his shotgun. He pulled out a lever action and grabbed a box of bullets from the bottom shelf. He handed Gustav the weapon.

"I'll keep this pistol," Gustav said to Maisy.

"I don't care what you keep," Maisy shouted, still on the floor and holding her injured face. "And you'll be dead by morning. All of you! Burned alive."

It was getting dark. Evening was falling. There was a dense, crackling roar outside, a low rolling thunder, from the many thick fires that were destroying so many buildings and homes.

"Get yourself out of here, Maisy. Go home if you still have one."

She got up, propping herself up on the fallen chair and then the desk. She limped to the front doors.

"Oh," Gustav said, "and by the way, you're fired."

"Drill and I will be back here in this office tomorrow, and you all will be dead."

Then, one of the back rooms seemed to explode! A blast of heat ripped through the office and flapped the men's clothes like a strong wind. The back room blazed. The three ran out into the street. Maisy stumbled out, fell and rolled in a lump on the sidewalk. Stinky helped her stand, and then she yanked her arm from him.

"I think we need to let these horses run free," Gunther said.

Gustav nodded. Gunther untied their reins and slapped their hindquarters. They naturally raced off in the only uncooked direction, northeast. Then the men had to jog away from the police station as the interior of the Paris Police Station suddenly fully ignited.

They stopped down the street.

"I guess Shay was lucky to be shot when he was," Stinky concluded. "He'd a been burned alive in that cell."

"Drill too," Gustav said.

A firetruck, in retreat, turned the corner to escape the flames and smoke. Some of the fireman, unable to jump on, ran as fast as they could behind it. The truck and crew sped by them. A fireman, filthy from soot and exhausted, waved at them to move on and said, "You fellers better get moving, it's a lost cause here. We're gonna set up by the 13th Street and try to save the houses there."

The three joined the men in their run.

"How'd it get started?" Gustav asked.

"We don't know," the fireman said.

Then they were all knocked down, deafened and blinded.

Gunther woke, numb. He sat up, not knowing where he was, or what happened. He looked around him to see Gustav sit up too and shaking his head, then Stinky sat up along with the knocked-over fireman. The firetruck, now driverless, started to slowly roll forward and one fireman got up, stumbled, and with great fortitude hauled himself up and into the cab. The truck stopped as he applied the brakes. Gunther laid back on his elbows. His hat was gone. He focused in on the fire ahead, about a block and a half away. It was Flippin's Utilities. Gone. Completely gone. And the stores next to it, gone. And the stores next to them on both sides, on fire or half-gone. Gunther realized that Flippin always had dynamite in stock for sale. He'd recognized and remembered the shock and awe of being close to enemy artillery. Too close to the big rounds. Too close to the explosions and what it did to you. He rolled over onto all fours, then got up in a stagger. He helped Gustav get up, then Stinky. Stinky stumbled backward and rested against the firetruck, almost falling over again.

"Wha..." he was breathless.

"Dynamite," Gunther said. "It blew up in Flippin's."

But Gunther's mind started to clear, recalling that dynamite usually needed a fuse and a blasting cap to ignite. He recalled from his Army days that dynamite could burn and not explode.

"Something is wrong here..." Gunther mumbled to the men around him.

A sizzling object flew in the air, over the firetruck from the other side, and rolled on the street.

"RUN!" Gunther yelled. "Run!"

It was dynamite. And this stick had a lit fuse. All the man scattered. Gunther pulled his Luger and when clearing the back of the firetruck started shooting at the other side of the street. He instantly knew the trap. Sure enough, smiling men with guns waited over there on the far sidewalk, crouched, but not at all prepared to receive such immediate incoming fire. They all ducked further or fell flat as an array of Gunther's cover fire zipped at them, shattering glass and spattering on and into the storefronts behind them.

The blast lifted the right side of the truck up several feet and dropped it back down in several bounces. Some of the more stunned men from the first blast were slow and got ripped apart. A fireman's boot, foot still inside, flew and hit Stinky in the back as he ran off, and Gustav was once again tossed off his feet in his getaway. Several firemen were also successfully afoot.

Gunther remained at a dead run, shooting until his Luger ran dry. He dropped to one knee as he pulled both his 1911 .45s and, with arms outstretched, he poured a slow and steady barrage at the enemy. One bullet at a time, right, then left guns, seconds apart, while Stinky, Gustav, and the surviving fireman could get up, moving and aware. It was military cover fire. Slow and steady.

They were the Asians. The enemy. The international killers. Dressed in black suits and black hats. And they rolled off and scattered under fire, smart enough to also fire randomly back, but this did not deter Gunther as he then went prone. Most ran behind the distant cover of the firetruck. Two ran to the west. Gunther followed them with the gun in his left hand and shot. He hit one in the hip and the runner fell. He hit the other in the shoulder and that runner stumbled. A blast sounded from behind Gunther, and it was from Stinky. Stinky shot the stumbling man in the chest with his shotgun. Then Stink racked the pump and shot the first downed man on the ground.

More gunfire sounded as Gustav shot past the firetruck. The firemen were all gone for safety, or presumed dead. Then, another stick of dynamite appeared in the air, and the three lawmen had no choice but to bolt off toward the inferno on Lucas Street.

When they turned the corner onto Lucas, the dynamite's sound and force ripped through the air on the street behind them. It was the Asian's form of their own cover fire to buy time, resettle, or escape. The three lawmen stopped. This corner brick building was not yet on fire. Stinky covered the streets as best he could while Gunther and Gustav reloaded. Then they watched as Stinky reloaded. Not far from them, an automobile was engulfed in flames and exploded, causing them to reflexively duck.

"Keep your heads," Gunther said. "There's four left."

"Huh?" Gustav said, as their ears were still dull and ringing from the blasts.

"Four!" Gunther repeated. "Four left. Keep your wits about you!"

Gustav nodded.

"They are either coming from this way," Gunther pointed to the way they came. "Or coming that way." He pointed south down Lucas, suggesting they would approach behind the gutted Flippin's and the police station onto Lucas. Part of Lucas was now just smoldering. The fire, seemingly a mile wide, and was now well across the street and moving fast, like a tornado.

"I guess they got the dynamite from Flippin's." Gustav said. "I guess…they robbed them and blew them up."

"I reckon so," Gunther said.

Stinky peered around the corner to the firetruck area and was met with a bullet ricocheting off the brick wall building near him.

"Somebody's still over here," Stinky said, blinking rapidly from the brick dust, his face angry.

Yet another stick of dynamite appeared, landing on the street corner, just some five feet away! But the fuse was long. Stinky was so mad he dropped his long gun, pulled his pistol, and ran out to it, firing down the sidewalk as he dove toward the stick. Surprised, Gunther had no choice but to move that way too. He got to the corner and with only his left hand exposed fired away. Stinky grabbed the explosive and lobbed it back up the street, back from where it came probably behind a burned-out car. He laid flat, as the bomb blew in the air, just before hitting the pavement on the far side of the car. Stinky looked at Gunther, and Gunther shook his head at this crazy move, this…bravery. Brilliant, but crazy.

Gunther, once an infantry commander and war vet from the streets and villages of Cuba, the Philippines, and survivor of the Boxer Rebellion in Peking, knew a right moment to charge when he felt one, the instant of an advantage, and he instinctively charged down the street, both 1911s out. He knew the gang would duck, run, or had been blown up from Stinky's surprise act of bravery. This was the magic moment to charge. So, he charged. Stinky stood. Gustav chucked Stink his dropped shotgun, and they followed.

Sure enough, a scorched, tattered body lay sprawled on the

pavement behind the nearby abandoned and now burned auto that must have coasted up and bumped into the slightly-raised sidewalk. To be safe, Gunther quick-shot him in the head, then ran to the next damaged car up the street. Burned and blasted, the four wheels were gone and the chassis lay flat on the ground.

He took a knee behind it to survey the street. Stinky and Gustav caught up with him and knelt too.

"Spread out a little," Gunther said, staring ahead. They did.

"Three left," he added. "They can't be far. Might be circling us round back."

Stinky by the rear of the wreck, turned to face the corner from whence they came, just in case. They reloaded.

Horrified people appeared on the street, scattering, fleeing the nightmare landscape, ignorant of any gun and dynamite battles.

And then, Gunther saw two of them, hunched over, running with rifles up the street toward them, unknown if they knew their quarry crouched behind the car.

Gunther rolled into a prone position, with both pistols already drawn and started firing at them. They broke left toward the charred ruins and alleyways of the businesses, but not before the one on the right lost part of his kneecap from a .45 round. He fell, and Gunther filled him full of rounds until his soon-limp body just shook from the concussions. The other man dashed into an alley. Gunther got up and took off after the escaping hoodlum with Stinky behind him. Gustav, a little slower with age, third in line, tried to keep up, as well as look around. Gunther and Stinky tore around the corner into the alleyway, with the Frenchman trying to catch up. Trying to keep up. Trying to…

Slam! Just before the corner of the alley, Gustav was struck hard from the right side. Tackled right down off his feet. He and the tackler rumbled and tumbled until the tackler got on top him. Gustav saw the face of the man, one of the gang, but he was not completely Asian. He must have been the "half-breed" Drill conspired with. Gustav squeezed his hand, realizing his pistol was gone from it, and his rifle gone too, strewn onto the sidewalk upon impact. He swiped aside several incoming punches to his face until he saw the big knife. The man grinned as Gustav grabbed the wrist of the weapon-bearing limb.

"I am here to kill you," he said. "for the insults and interferences you have wrought upon my family. My grandfather told us that if we could kill you slowly with a knife, we should, and he would be eternally grateful." He started to push the knife down toward Gustav's throat.

"And...here...I...am."

Gustav tried to shove the knife hand back. Then the killer leaned his upper body into him, pushing downward, and Gustav knew he could not fight this off. The tip neared his throat.

Explosion. Clang. Spark. Grunt. A bullet from the left hit the knife, knocking the tip way up and out of the man's hand. The round deflected off the knife and hit the killer's left arm. The next bullet hit the man in the head, slinging it off to the left and his body rolled lifelessly from atop Gustav.

Gustav, gasping, catching his breath, studied the dead man for a few seconds. Then, he looked to the side to see who shot. Ten feet away stood Paris Police Chief Garrison Drill, lowering his pistol. He walked up to Gustav and then looked over at the dead invader. Then he looked back at Gustav.

"I decided to take sides," Drill said.

"You decided to kill witnesses against you," Gustav said, gasping.

"That too."

He picked Gustav's pistol up off the ground and helped him to his feet. He handed him his gun.

"I tried to...to keep my city safe, Henri. I failed. Look at it. I...failed. I destroyed it instead. This is my fault," Drill said solemnly.

Gustav limped over to pick up his rifle.

"Maybe I can fix some of it. Some of...this. Are you with me?" Drill asked.

"I...I am with you."

"Where are your friends?"

"I don't know. We got...separated," Gustav said. "They ran off that way, when I got tackled."

"Let's go kill the last of them. End this for good," Drill said.

"Yeah. Let's."

The back alley was full of burned rubble. In some spots the collapsed burned buildings fell across it, causing Gunther and Stinky to stop, kneel, look, listen. Where had this gang man gone? They heard only the whimpering of men and women, searching for lost ones or pleas from the lost ones themselves. Trapped people, burned people, they screamed for help.

They saw an opening through two scarred brick buildings that led out to Lucas Street. They bolted down the passageway and stopped at the corner of the edifices. As they peered into the street, they saw more citizens turning over debris looking for friends and loved ones. Gunther decided to scramble across the street as fast as he could. Stinky remained still.

A firetruck from Hugo, Oklahoma, trolled slowly by. It stopped by some people helping remove a man from under some wood and fallen cement. Fireman jumped off and joined in the rescue. Gunther and Stinky ran down to the truck.

"There's a dangerous man with a gun around here," Stinky yelled to the group. "Try to get everyone out as fast you can and get out of here."

They looked the armed duo over, saw the badges, and nodded their acknowledgement. Gunther climbed up to the top of firetruck. He crawled on all fours toward the front to take a good look at the dark, charred street. The cab of the truck was roofless. The driver sat behind the wheel below him in the cab. The man heard the commotion and looked back at him.

"Deputy Johann Gunther, sir. There's a killer loose around here."

The driver's eyes widened. His black eyebrows shot up.

"A killer..."

Then suddenly, way, way down the street, a horse and rider bolted from beside some untouched buildings.

"There he is!" Gunther shouted.

Gunther dropped into the passenger seat. He still had his rifle slung over his back and it almost hung him over some rails.

"That man!"

"Huh?"

"That man down there is the killer, and he's getting away."

"I..."

Gunther pounded on the badge pinned to his shirt.

"Let's go! GO!"

The fireman hit the gas pedal and off they barreled down Lucas Street, as fast as the truck could run.

"WWhhhooooAAA!" They heard behind them.

Gunther looked back and up, and Stinky was now on the roof, hanging on some gear rails for dear life.

"I'm okay!" Stink shouted. "I am okay."

The truck drew closer and closer to the escaping felon, but it bounced radically with the ruts and lumps in the dirt road. The streetlights still worked in this unburned part of the town. Gunther, in cramped quarters, wrestled to get his rifle off his shoulder carry.

The Asian was an expert rider. Maybe they were part-time horse trainers? He glided with the horse and let the reins hook the saddle horn. With two hands free, he reached into his pocket and pulled out a stick of dynamite with his right hand and a cigarette lighter with his left. He lit the fuse and Gunther caught site of the flare-up burn.

"DAMN!" Gunther shouted. "Dynamite!"

The Asian chunked the sizzling stick over his shoulder and at the truck. The driver swerved violently. It hit the truck side, bounced, dropped, and the speed of truck left the explosion right behind them. The driver and Gunther crunched down in the cab, and Stinky regrouped his hold as the gangster could be seen lighting yet another. Sizzle! He tossed it high over his shoulder and this one was headed right for the cab of the truck! The driver was just getting his bearings from the last one and...

Stinky, on one knee, lifted his pump shotgun and shot the stick in mid-air like a clay pigeon. The dynamite rocketed off to the right and blew up on the roadside. Still disturbingly close, but they were still in the hunt. Gunther turned to his amazing friend as Stink dropped flat on the roof.

Meanwhile, the fireman had had enough of all this. Before

Gunther could look forward again, the driver pulled a revolver from somewhere inside his fire uniform, put the pistol in his left hand, leaned out and shot the criminal in the back. The Asian's arms went up and his head went back. In his right hand was yet another lit dynamite stick! He slowly slipped right off the horse. The steed continued running. The driver knew to keep racing away too. Stinky turned to see the last blast of the night, as the explosive blew the man to red hot bits.

"He's blowed up!" Stinky yelled out. "He's all blowed up!"

The truck stopped and the driver wiped his brow. He stuffed his pistol back in his jacket.

"What is your name sir?" Gunther asked.

"Rob Kloss. Hugo Volunteer Fire Department. We…we just got here."

Gunther held out his hand. Kloss shook it.

"This truck was bouncing bad enough to make a filling drop out of a tooth. You are one helluva shot, Rob Kloss, and cool under fire."

"Fire? You mean explosives."

"I mean explosives.

Then Gunther looked up at Stinky.

"And that was one helluva shot, Stink."

"Naaahh, just like duck huntin'."

"Shooting dynamite…" Rob Kloss said. "A little dangerous?"

"Naaah, You can…you can shoot it, burn it. It won't go off. It needs it's proper working to ignite," Stinky said.

"I guess it won't. What is going on here?" Rob Kloss asked.

"Mr. Kloss, it's a very long story. I'll tell ya on the drive back. I think we have quite a lot of people to help unbury back there."

Fireman Kloss got the truck turned around, and the three

made it back to the ruined part of the city. They passed the molten lava mound on the street that was once a deadly gang member. As they approached the scorched downtown, the truck's headlights lit up a very unlikely duo. Police Chief Garrison Drill and retired Police Chief Gustav Henri, side by side, holding rifles, awaiting their arrival.

The truck stopped, and the men jumped out. Kloss went to help the wounded. Stinky and Gunther walked up to the pair.

"You get him?" Drill asked.

Gunther looked at both of them, then at Gustav. Gustav nodded a yes.

"We got him. He tried to kill us with dynamite and that Hugo fireman over there saved our lives. For the record, his name is Rob Kloss."

Drill nodded to Kloss, "Thank you, sir."

"We got the sixth one. The chief here saved my life. I was about to be stabbed by their leader, the translator. With a huge knife. Drill shot him off of me."

"Oh," Gunther said.

"This is all my fault," Drill said.

Stinky checked his watch. Gunther grimaced.

"There's a lot of hurt people out here. If I can just get a drink of water somewhere, I think we should help these people."

"There are canteens on the truck," Stinky said, and he ran and grabbed one. "Here, Gunth."

Gunther screwed open the top and took a long swallow. His hand was shaking and some of the water fell out the sides of his mouth. Gustav noticed the shake. There were still some nerves left in Gunther's gun burned hands after all.

Chapter 29
THE SECRETS OF PARIS, TEXAS

"A blessing on those happy ages that did not know the dreadful fury of these devilish instruments of artillery, whose inventor is, I feel sure, being rewarded in hell for his diabolical creation, by which he made it possible for an infamous and cowardly hand to take away the life of a brave knight as, in the heat of the courage and resolution that fires and animates the gallant breast, a stray bullet appears, nobody knows how or from where—fired perhaps by some fellow who took fright at the flash of the fiendish contraption, and fled—and in an instant put an end to the life and loves of one who deserved to live for many a long age."

—Miguel de Cervantes, *Don Quixote*

The Dallas, Fort Worth, and Oklahoma City newspapers covered the fire in the next few days.

Paris, TX, Fires Destroy Most of the City

(It is estimated that the population of Paris, TX, is about 15,500. The city in northeast Texas, near the Oklahoma and Arkansas border, is a local trading center, with a larger business district than other cities of similar size and population.)

"A fire started about 5:30 p.m. on March 21, 1916, of mysterious origins in a southwestern portion of the city. The fire was lifted by the wind, which was estimated to be blowing at 35 miles per hour and set off further fires to buildings and houses many blocks away.

In the early minutes of the fire, occupants of buildings attempted to extinguish small roof fires with garden hoses and buckets of water to no avail. By 7:00 p.m. the fire had advanced, and aid from nearby Oklahoma and Texas towns and cities was requested. Multiple fire departments, such as from Hugo, Oklahoma drove in, and the Dallas Fire Department commandeered a train to get there as soon as possible. By 3:30 a.m. the following day, the fire was finally under control.

The devastation was remarkable with more than 264 acres burned. [There were] 1,440 buildings lost, resulting in the destruction of most of the business district, several churches, schools, and public buildings, and more than 700 homes.

The NFPA report on the conflagration was prepared by State Fire Marshal and NFPA Member S.W. Inglish. He described the fire and the devastation: "The firemen were not able to hold the blaze to the first building being burned, for the reason that the brands carried by the high gale had set on fire buildings four, five, six and even ten blocks away and, in practically every instance, the fire started on the roof of the building. These in turn, would send their burning brands on the wings of the wind to other buildings with shingle roofs until every dwelling on both the south and east sides of the business section was a seething, roaring, mass of flames; and notwithstanding the fact that the roofs of the business buildings had refused to take fire from the burning embers that had fallen upon them like a rain of hail for some time, when the half-circle of fire around the business district had closed in, the intense heat of the wind-driven flames and the flying brands and coals which were many inches deep in the streets, broke through the windows and doors. Once an entrance was affected, it doomed the business section."

There were reports of looting, rioting and various distur-bances during the fire, along with explosions of automobiles and buildings. Police Chief Garrison Drill said the entire event is under investigation but believes the city will quickly rebuild and return to its normal, tranquil self. Cities in the region are rushing food, water, and aid to the citizens of Paris. The mayor added that..."

Two days later

The Tree Top Hotel, made mostly of stone, cement, and brick and stood way east of the blazes, remained untouched, as did the stables and garages. Gunther had been happy to see that the three horses they released from the police station front rail the night of the fire, ran unscathed back home to the Tree Top Stables. And his favorite car, the Chevy Baby Grand, was pristine and parked in the shelter of the cement and stone-back buildings.

Gunther and Stinky loaded up the Chevy. Gustav watched

them. Then helped. When done, Gustav handed the federal badge to Stinky.

"I never thought I would need one, or wear one again," he said. "Nor did I want too."

"For a few minutes there," Stinky said, "you were the Police Chief of Paris again."

"Aghh! For a few minutes, yes. A horrible patch in my life."

"I guess, Garrison Drill will remain the Police Chief?" Gunther asked.

"Yes. He is still the Chief. He is a dolt. But Paris is quiet. Except for me, eh? I make the troubles. Drill and I have an… understanding now. A …secret. No one knows this gang started the fire. No one knows Drill tried to save his city by killing me quietly. In a way, a bad way, I understand him. And I wish to leave him alone, and he me, as I did before this mess."

Gustav reached into his pocket and pulled out a message. "Dutch, the other day I sent a cable to my friends in Scotland Yard." He waved the paper in his hand. "This came in last night. They told me that Dr. Milton Trafalgar died in 1912. Presumably of old age. He died in the Caribbean."

"They never caught him? He was probably there killing people and studying mosquitos."

"Never caught him. If you wish, here is the message. For your files."

"My files," Gunther said and chuckled, folding the paper and pocketing it.

"How long before the Indo gang knows you are still alive?" Stinky asked.

"This I do not know, Stink. Their gang will never return home. I will remain quiet. I won't even tell my old friends back in France. A secret!" His eyes opened wide! "Eh? I am still alive."

Gunther and Gustav faced each other.

"Goodbye, Dutch."

"Goodbye, Chief."

"You must stop calling me, Chief.

"Never," Gunther said.

"All for one," Gustav said.

"One for all." They shook hands.

"To the death of old enemies!" Gustav roared.

"To their death!" Gunther said. "Goodbye, Chief,"

He turned for the Chevy but stopped, "Oh, oh now, wait," Gunther stepped back to him again and reached deep into his pants' pocket. "Speaking of badges, here," he said. And he handed Gustav his old Paris, Texas, police badge. "I meant to get this to you through the Federales in the 90s. They wanted me to be 'official police' all the way to the front gates of West Point. But, when I got to West Point, I forget to hand it to my escort."

Gustav looked a bit astonished. He took the badge and looked it over for a second.

"You told me, warned me, that I would be fighting in a Medieval World. America's Medieval Time," Gunther said.

"I did."

"You did. You were right."

"It seems, *mon ami*, our Europe has once again become medieval. Your fatherland against my fatherland, and more joining in," Gustav said. "Soon there will be another big fucking war, eh?"

"Yes, it seems."

"It never seems to end, does it? Do you see yourself in a war over there? If the US joins in the war, will you volunteer to go?"

"I think I'll be about 45...47 years old when Wilson gets around to declaring war, if he does."

"War knows no age."

"Well, I know lots of people who will have ideas and plans for me to do things, other than sitting in a muddy trench like a young soldier. If it happens, I will, no doubt, be involved in some way. But I hope my days trapped on a battlefield are over."

Gustav nodded.

"Anyway, there's plenty of medieval left here in America to keep me busy," Gunther said.

"Plenty. Well then, goodbye, my good knights, who have indeed raced to my rescue. Pennants waving."

He handed Gunther the badge back. "You have officially returned the badge to me. The record book is now closed. Don't you have a special box at home where you keep your memories?"

Gunther thought for a second of the African Star jewel in his desk. He smiled.

"I do, but it's a desk drawer."

"Well, then, Dutch, you keep this badge in your desk drawer."

"I will," he said.

"And then you will remember me better, eh?"

"I will."

Gunther got behind the steering wheel. Stinky approached Gustav for an uncomfortable handshake but Gustav jumped in and gave Stink a mighty bear hug. One so stout, Stinky almost screamed. He did not return the hug, just let his arms dangle down and he suffered through it with a wincing face.

Stinky then checked his watch, then perfectly cranked the engine with a single swirl.

"Heading straight home to Fort Worth?" Gustav shouted

over the engine.

"No, sir, we have one more stop to make for a few hours, then on to Fort Worth."

They left the scarred, still smoldering, ruins of Paris, Texas, behind them. Stinky turned in his seat to study the damage.

"Do you think we will ever see him again?" Stinky asked.

"Oh, I don't know. Maybe. If we make a point to do so."

"Make a point to. Yup. Will I see you again, Gunth?"

"Well, sure, Stink. If we make a point to do so."

"Yup. Make it a point."

One hour later.

Lake Crenshaw, Paris, Texas. Birds chirped. Tree branches swayed. Ducks floated. A heron stalked the reeds by the waterline. Stretched out in rented canvas folding chairs from the bait shop, Gunther and Stinky Moses sat, quietly…fishing.

Rod in hands, Gunther dozed off a bit.

Stinky looked deep into the clear water. He could see to the bottom. This made him smile.

If You Like This, Take A Look At:
Be Bad Now by Hock Hochheim

HOW BAD IS BAD ENOUGH WHEN YOU MUST...BE BAD NOW?

In the 1980's a recession stampedes Texas. The oil industry dries up, laying high rollers low and sending the entire state of Texas into a tornado-like downspin. Northern mobsters invade these cracks in the Lone Star State. Their schemes: corruption, loan sharking, gambling, extortion, drug and human trafficking, and murder for hire -- all backed with strong arms swinging bats, psychos pointing guns, torture, violence and death.

The city of West Forge, a stone's throw from Houston, is Sgt. "Jumpin" Jack Kellog's town. When organized crime seeps in, Kellog's brand of justice knows no bounds. He tracks, fights, kicks and shoots his way through conspiracies, threats, ambushes and showdowns. Pushed to near-madness by angst with informants inside his agency and lurking everywhere, Jack tackles the thugs, bosses, lawyers, politicians and businessmen on the mob payroll, in a battle that takes him from the swamps of Louisiana, to the ghettos of Houston, to casinos in Vegas and even through the Halls of Congress in Washington D.C..

"If you like hard-core fast-moving police stories with a sense of justice, Be Bad Now is a definite read."

AVAILABLE NOW

About the Author

Hock Hochheim is a former U.S. Army investigator and 22 year veteran Texas police investigator, patrol officer, former private investigator and award winning author.

He currently owns and operates Force Necessary, an international combatives training company and teaches combat techniques and strategies in 11 allied countries around the world annually. He is the author of 10 non-fiction books and four fiction, and countless articles on policing, the military, street survival, close quarter combat and conflict psychology. He lives in Texas.

In 2013 Hock's book My Gun is My Passport won the Beverly Hills Book Award for Best Military Fiction. You may read more about him at http://www.forcenecessary.com or email him at hock@hockscqc.com